EARL LESSONS

LORDS IN DISGUISE
BOOK FIVE

VALERIE BOWMAN

JUNE THIRD ENTERPRISES, LLC

For my niece, Ell Pikor, who is finally old enough for me to
dedicate a book to.

He never wanted a title

Fresh off the battlefield, Captain David Ellsworth has returned home to discover the shocking and unwelcome news that he's the new Earl of Elmwood. Though David had no idea he was in line for a title, he and his sister must now navigate the snark-infested waters of the London *ton*. He knows how to be a soldier, an officer, and a brother, but he hasn't a clue how to be an *earl*. David will need all the help he can get. Even if it comes from the undeniably beautiful woman…who is the darling of the world he detests.

She never wanted a husband

The younger sister of a marquess, Lady Annabelle Bellham moves through elegant ballrooms with the ease of a lioness traversing the jungle. She's the most elusive belle at every ball, and gentlemen have long placed bets on which lucky man will finally win her hand. But Annabelle has no intention of falling prey to a man's charms. She's seen the destruction wrought by marriage and is dead set on avoiding a similar fate.

But here they are...

Thankfully, Annabelle's older brother hasn't pressured her to take a husband—yet. Which is why she feels obliged to agree when he asks her a favor: To teach the newly minted Earl of Elmwood how to act in Society. Still, the task shouldn't be too difficult. All Annabelle must do is spend countless hours in the company of a handsome, brooding ex-soldier—who's making her question every rule she's set for herself.

She and David have nothing in common except a fiery passion and some highly inconvenient feelings…could it be enough?

PROLOGUE

The Marquess of Bellingham's Town House, London, July 1797

The booming voice woke Annabelle from a sound sleep. Her heart beating rapidly, she clutched the covers to her chin. *Oh, no. Oh, no. Oh, no. Not again.*

It was dark in her bedchamber. She'd always been afraid of the dark, but the dark was nothing compared to what was happening down the corridor.

"By God, Angelina, I will not countenance your disobedience!" came his raised, terrifying voice.

Eyes wide, Annabelle hitched the bedclothes up to her nose, burying herself in their safety. Father was yelling at Mama again. It happened more and more often. It had been several weeks since last time, and Annabelle had been dreading the next time ever since.

"George, please. You'll wake the children," came her mother's thin, frightened voice.

Annabelle gulped. She was only five years old, but she knew how awful this was. It always started the same way, with yelling and then the thumps. It always ended the same way too, with Mama's screams and pleas.

Annabelle wanted to slide off the bed and hide beneath it. That was always her first instinct. To hide. But Beau might need her. Beau, her older brother. He was brave. Brave enough to try to fight off Father. Beau had suffered his fair share of bruises and even a broken arm trying to defend Mama from Father's drunken rages in the past. Annabelle shook with worry for Beau now. He would put himself in harm's way. He always did.

Annabelle had no doubt that Beau was already awake. At eleven years old, he considered himself the man of the house, ensuring that Mama and Annabelle were safe on nights like these, when Father became so unreasonable. But Beau was no match for their tall, brutish father.

Be brave. Be brave. Be brave.

Bracing herself for what was certain to be an awful encounter, Annabelle tossed off the covers and willed herself to slip from the bed. The darkness terrified her, but she forced herself to run across the wide expanse of the rug in her bedchamber to the door of her room. She cracked it open and peeked out into the empty corridor.

Silence.

Silence wasn't necessarily a good thing. Quiet was usually a prelude to the worst of it.

Be brave. Be brave. Be brave. She repeated the words again and again in her mind as she swallowed hard and forced herself to open the door wide enough to slip into the equally dark corridor. Her back against the finely papered wall, her breathing coming in bursts so heavy her lungs hurt, Annabelle slunk toward Mama's bedchamber.

Just as Annabelle suspected, when she passed her brother's room, his door was already open. A lit candle illuminated his empty bed. Beau had already gone to Mama's aid. Of course he had. Annabelle straightened her shoulders. *Be brave, be brave, be brave.* She continued her tentative journey toward Mama's bedchamber door.

The door was shut when she arrived. No doubt Beau had closed it behind him hoping she wouldn't wake due to the commotion. Annabelle took a deep breath and carefully reached out to grasp the door handle. A sharp slam made her wince and snatch her hand away.

A whimper came from inside the room. Willing away the tears that sprang to her eyes, Annabelle forced herself to grasp the handle with her small hand. Turning the knob, she pushed open the door a crack to see Mama cowering in the far corner of the room. Father loomed over her, a long silver candlestick in one hand, a glass filled with brown liquid in the other. He always had that glass on nights like this. Beau, brave Beau, stood in front of Mama, dodging Father's swings of the candlestick.

"Please, George," Mama cried again. "Don't hurt him. Beau, darling, go back to bed. Please."

The desperation and fear in her mother's voice made Annabelle shake. Her knees wobbled and her hand rattled the doorknob. She always felt as if she might retch on nights like these. But she couldn't drag her gaze away from the awful scene playing out in front of her. Tears dripped down her cheeks as she stared in horror.

Instead of retreating, Beau held up his fists, aiming them at his father. Even from far away, Annabelle could see that he was shaking too. She was terrified for him. But Beau was brave. He would fight until he couldn't fight any longer. There was nothing Mama could say to him to make him leave.

Annabelle briefly closed her eyes and said a prayer. She'd asked the vicar once what she should do if she needed God's help. The vicar had told her to pray. Pray and ask for what she needed, and God would see to it. Annabelle prayed every time this happened, but her prayers were never answered. Father never stopped yelling. He never stopped hitting until he'd drawn blood or broken a bone.

"Get out of my way, boy. I won't tell you again!" came Father's thunderous voice. Annabelle opened her eyes again in time to see Father swing the candlestick at Beau, but Beau was faster and more agile than Father when he was in his cups. Beau easily jumped aside, missing the heavy candlestick's blow, which only served to further enrage Father. Beau backed toward the door as the man advanced toward him and swung at him once more. He missed again and Beau continued to retreat. He was trying to draw Father away from Mama, trying to keep him from hurting her again. At his own peril.

Wiping away the tears with the backs of her hands, Annabelle opened the door wider. Hopefully, Beau would realize it was open and run through it if he needed to. But Beau wasn't one to run from a fight. Even an unfair one with a man three times his age and size. Once he'd drawn Father away from Mama, Beau squared his small shoulders and lifted his chin, raising his fists toward his father again and standing his ground.

"If you want to hit someone, hit me," came Beau's angry voice from between clenched teeth.

Mama reached out from the corner as if to try to save her boy, but the next swing of the candlestick caught Beau on the side of the jaw with a sharp crack, and flung him. He fell on his back, blood bursting from his mouth.

"No!" Mama cried.

Annabelle gasped, running to her brother's side. "Beau!" she cried, falling to her knees beside him, cradling his head in her night rail. A bright crimson stain was already making its way down the center of the garment.

Mama was there too, pushing Beau's blond hair away from his sweaty, bloody face to assess the damage. Her eyes were frantic with worry as she tended to her son.

Father stood over the three of them, eyeing Beau's limp body as if he didn't care whether he'd killed him. "Serves the blighter right," Father mumbled, before tossing the bloody candlestick onto the carpet and stumbling from the room. "He shouldn't have got in my way. Mind your own business, you brat," Father mumbled as he went.

Annabelle expelled her pent-up breath. Father was done…at least for the night. They all knew it. Once he'd seriously injured Mama or Beau, he always slunk away. It was a horrible way to guarantee his disappearance, but Beau had taken the hit on purpose for exactly that reason.

Silent tears slipped down Annabelle's cheeks as she waited, praying even harder now, that her brother would wake up.

"Annabelle, darling," Mama whispered, her own face wet from tears. "Go ask Mary for a hot cloth. Run."

Annabelle nodded obediently. Mama didn't want her to be here. Mama didn't want her to have seen any of this or even know about it. But Annabelle wasn't a baby any longer. She heard the screams in the night, and she had no intention of hiding in her bed while her mother and brother needed her. Only she hadn't yet worked up the courage to step in and incur Father's wrath herself. But she would. One day. She would. She promised herself. If she wasn't such a coward, she would have done it tonight.

Letting Mama slip into place to cradle Beau's head, Annabelle lifted the blood-stained skirt of her night rail and ran as fast as she could out of the room and down the dark corridor to the far end of the hall. *Be brave. Be brave. Be brave.* She opened the door to the servants' staircase and scrambled up the lightless staircase as fast as she could to Mary's bedchamber. Mary was her governess and the only servant Mama allowed to help them on nights like this. The bedchamber was the first one on the right on the fourth floor, and Annabelle slipped into the room without knocking, silently making her way through the terrifying darkness to the governess's side. She gently shook her.

"Mary, wake up," she said in a desperate whisper.

Mary's warm brown eyes flew open. "Oh, Annabelle, dear. It's you." Worry creased the servant's brow. Mary already knew why she'd come.

"Mama needs a hot cloth for Beau," Annabelle breathed.

Mary had already tossed back the covers and stood. She lit a candle and pulled on her dressing gown. "I'll go down to the kitchens and fetch it," she said in a calm, soothing voice. "I'll meet you in your mother's bedchamber."

Annabelle nodded. They'd had this conversation many times before. She didn't have to explain. Annabelle turned and rushed back out the door and down the staircase.

By the time Annabelle arrived at Beau's side again, her brother's ice-blue eyes were open, and his jaw was a hideous shade of purple, blue, and black. Mama had wiped up the blood as best she could with her own night rail. She cradled Beau's head in her lap, gently talking to him, and stroking his hair.

"Beau," Annabelle breathed, searching her brother's injured face. "Are you all right?" She laid a hand on her brother's cheek.

Beau nodded and winced, before lifting his gaze toward his mother. "Mama, are you all right? He didn't hurt you, did he?"

Tears fell from Mama's eyes. "Shh, my darling. I'm fine," Mama said to Beau. "You mustn't move."

"I'm almost big enough," Beau replied, his jaw clenched. "I'll be big enough soon to fight him."

"Shh, Beau. Just rest," Mama said, still stroking his hair.

A few minutes later, Mary came hurrying into the room with some cloths and a small basin of hot water. Without saying a word, she knelt next to Beau, dipped one of the cloths in the water, wrung it out, and applied it to his cheek. Mama and Mary exchanged a fraught glance before Mama's eyes filled with tears again and she nodded to Mary. Mama took over pressing the hot rag to Beau's cheek while Mary wrung out another cloth and began wiping the blood off Beau's face and neck.

After that was complete, Mary wrapped another one of the clean cloths around Beau's head to keep the rag in place against his injured jaw.

"I don't think his jaw is broken," Mama whispered as she helped Beau to his feet. "If it was, I doubt he'd be able to speak."

"This time," Mary said standing also. "Will you send for the doctor, my lady? To be certain it's not more serious than you think?"

Mama shook with fear. "You know I cannot do that, Mary. He'll make it worse next time." Mama bent her head, and Annabelle felt the shame and fear emanating from her.

"I'm sorry, my lady," Mary replied, her voice filled with resignation and sadness. She made her way toward the door with the wet, red rags and the bowl. Without looking back, she said, "I'll bring fresh night rails for you and Lady Annabelle, my lady. And I'll be back to fetch the others to wash."

"Thank you." Mama's voice was hollow.

Pressing the hot rag to his jaw, Beau limped away to his bedchamber. Annabelle stayed with her mother until Mary returned. Annabelle hurriedly tossed her blood-soaked night rail over her head and put on the fresh new one that Mary had given her. Mama went into her dressing room to do the same.

"I'll see to Lord Beaumont," Mary said, pausing again at the door on her way out. "I'll ensure his clothing is washed also."

"Thank you, Mary," Mama said again, before turning toward Annabelle.

"Annabelle, darling, do you want to sleep in my bed?" Mama asked after the servant had left.

"Yes, Mama," Annabelle replied, nodding. This was their ritual. Annabelle liked to stay with her mother on nights like this, so she could see that Mama remained safe. She wasn't being brave. Father had gone down to his study and would drink himself into a stupor, waking up halfway through the day tomorrow, gruff, and unapologetic. He always did.

Mama flung back the covers on the opposite side of her bed. Annabelle climbed up, then crawled over the mattress to snuggle at her mother's side. Mama pulled the covers over them both and hugged her close to her warm body. Mama always smelled like rosewater. Annabelle breathed in the familiar scent and let out her pent-up breath. At least it would be weeks before she would have to be this worried again.

They sat in silence for several moments before Annabelle worked up the courage to ask the question she'd always wanted to ask on nights like this. "Why does Father get so angry?"

Mama smoothed her hand over Annabelle's hair and hugged her closer. "Oh, darling. It's because he drinks. If only your father wouldn't *drink*."

"Did you ask him to stop, Mama?" Annabelle ventured next.

Mama's voice was resigned. "Many, many times, darling."

Annabelle frowned. "Why won't he stop, Mama?"

Mama rested her chin atop Annabelle's head and sighed. "I don't think he can, darling. I don't think he can."

"But why is he allowed to hit you, Mama?"

Annabelle felt the tiny pats atop her head as her mother's tears dripped onto her hair. "Because he owns me. I am his wife."

CHAPTER ONE

London, April 1815

David Ellsworth had been the Earl of Elmwood for a handful of months, and he was already doing a splendid job of making a fool of himself. In the span of the last hour at the Harrisons' dinner party, he'd already tried to serve himself from the soup tureen one of the footmen had been carrying around the gigantic table; he'd incorrectly addressed Lord Mayfeather's daughter, who apparently was a *Miss* and not a *Lady*; and he'd obviously taken up an inappropriate subject with Lady Cranberry, who looked at him aghast when he began recounting a story about his time fighting in the Army on the Continent. Apparently, the content was too graphic for her ears.

As a result, David had excused himself from the table and quickly made his way down the corridor in search of a place to hide…and to have a cigar. He hurried past a variety of doors and out onto the verandah behind the house. It was freezing outside, but he enjoyed the sharp air after being in the overly crowded dining room for the past two hours. He pulled a cigar from his inner coat pocket and lit it using the candle that flickered atop a table near the door. This was one of the last cigars he had left. They had been a gift from a Spanish officer on the Continent. He had every intention of savoring it.

David's younger sister, Marianne, had asked him to give up smoking cigars, and he would. But not tonight. Tonight, he sucked in the familiar smoke and closed his eyes, trying to forget all the foolish things he'd done in the dining room.

Marianne was right. He needed someone to teach him how to be an earl. After all, he, his sister and their brother, Frederick, who had died a hero in the war, had grown up in a small cottage in Brighton, none of them having any idea their father was the only son of the Earl of Elmwood. They thought Father was a woodworker, for Christ's sake. Not a bloody earl.

Marianne had served as a lady's maid until she'd met the Marquess of Bellingham, who'd asked her to marry him after two cases of mistaken identity and a trip to France. And now, here they were, two siblings who knew little about the infamous *ton*, both thrust into the roles of earl and soon-to-be marchioness. David would think it all ridiculous if it didn't happen to be true. Such was his life at the age of nine and twenty. Far, far different from the way he'd imagined it.

At first, David had assumed taking a seat in the House of Lords would be nothing but welcome. He'd use his newfound power to get bills passed that would help military men and their families. David still looked forward to that part of his new role. It was the other part he dreaded—the endless round of social calls and ridiculous amounts of etiquette that he continued to breach—that was driving him mad.

He sucked in and expelled a large puff of smoke as he leaned back against the cold brick wall behind him, closing his eyes. No. He wasn't about to give up his cigars quite yet. A good smoke was sometimes a soldier's only friend on a freezing, lonely battlefield that smelled like gunpowder and death.

Delicate feminine coughing met his ears and his eyes shot open to see a stunning blond woman step onto the verandah waving smoke away from her face.

"Pardon me," she said in a tight, unhappy voice as she continued to cough.

David pushed himself away from the wall and waved his arm in the air, trying to dispel the smoke. "I'm terribly sorry." *Excellent.* Knowing his luck, he probably just blew smoke into the face of one of the royal princesses.

The blond woman gave him a narrow-eyed stare. "You should be," she shot back, pulling an obviously expensive fur-lined pelisse more tightly around her shoulders.

"I didn't realize anyone else was out here." His gaze took in her lovely and equally expensive-looking pink evening gown that was partially covered by the pelisse. Diamonds wound around her throat and were entwined in her light hair. She had the most heavenly ice-blue eyes, illuminated by the candles on either side of the nearby doorway. He glanced around. She was young and lovely and appeared to be... alone. That was unusual.

"My apologies, my lady...*er*, you are a lady, aren't you?" Damn. He was a fool. He didn't know much about Society rules, but he was fairly certain asking a lady if she was a lady was a breach.

She arched a blond brow at him and laughed. "What do you think? Do I look like a lady?"

"Yes, well, *er, uh*, you look beautiful," he managed to choke out, wanting to kick himself for his inanity. What exactly was one supposed to say when one encountered a heavenly creature alone in a dark, cold garden? Nothing in his army career had prepared him for such an event. If she were a French solider, he would have shot her. Tried to, at least. If she were an English soldier, he would have offered her a cigar. Instead, he stood blinking at her like an idiot waiting for her to say something else.

"Allow me to save you trouble, Mr. …" She paused, waiting for him to supply his last name.

"Ellsworth," he spat out. Damn again. He wasn't supposed to tell anyone his name was Mr. Ellsworth. Not any longer. Not since he'd become the bloody Earl of Elmwood. But how could he correct himself to this vision of loveliness? He'd already proven himself to be an idiot, he didn't dare add more proof.

But wait. What had she said? Save him trouble? He frowned. What could she possibly mean? He was about to drop the cigar to the ground and crush it beneath his boot when she reached out and took the thing from him in her gloved fingers. He watched in awe as she brought it to her lips and took a drag, blowing the smoke up into the cold air above his head. Who was this young woman? Had he met her earlier when the company had been gathered in the sitting room? He doubted it very much. He would have remembered *her*. She wasn't someone you'd easily forget.

He narrowed his eyes on her. "Have you been here all evening?" he asked, uncommonly curious how he might have overlooked her presence.

She laughed and it was a harsh sound. "Not all evening, no. I'm afraid I'm often late to such gatherings. I slipped in halfway through dinner. On purpose. Makes the evening less of a chore."

"A chore?" he echoed, somewhat surprised that a woman who so obviously belonged here would be so clearly unhappy at a dinner party.

She eyed him up and down as if assessing every stitch of

his clothing. He was suddenly glad his soon-to-be brother-in-law, the Marquess of Bellingham, had helped him purchase a new wardrobe suitable for an earl. "You can save the pleasantries, Mr. Ellsworth. I know your game."

"Game?" He blinked at her. What the devil did she mean by that?

She sighed and rolled her eyes, taking another drag from the cigar. "Yes, I've seen it before, a hundred times. You saw me leave the table and you followed me out here. Only you're *pretending* you didn't follow me. You're *pretending* you didn't even know I was here. That's what I'm to believe, is it not?" She blinked at him aggressively.

David scrunched up his nose and crossed his arms over his chest, regarding her as thoroughly as she'd regarded him moments earlier. Did this young woman truly think he had come out here in search of *her*? "You may believe whatever you like, Miss..."

She rolled her eyes and laughed a haughty laugh. "Oh, and now you're going to pretend as if you don't know my name, either." She shook her head and pulled her fur more tightly over her shoulders. "Really, you men must begin coming up with more original schemes. I can't tell you how many times I've seen this one. It's grown quite stale, I assure you."

David made a noise that fell somewhere between a huff and a groan. Who did this young woman think she was? She couldn't possibly be one of the royal princesses. He highly doubted any of King George's many daughters would be traipsing about smoking cigars in a garden and being rude. "My apologies if my '*scheme*' is '*stale*', Miss. I'm afraid I didn't have much time to come up with something more original." He gave her a tight smile.

"I'd say you didn't," she scoffed. "Now, don't tell me. You're going to offer to escort me back to the dining room, and then you'll ask me if you may pay me a call tomorrow.

Allow me to save you time. You *may* escort me back to the dining room, but no, you may not pay me a call tomorrow, or any day." She finished her little speech with a prim nod.

David pulled the cigar from her fingers and took another drag on it himself. If she was going to be rude, he'd show her rude. "That's quite all right," he replied with a false smile pinned to his face. "Because the truth is that not only do I have no intention of escorting you back to the dining room, but I wouldn't pay you a call if you were the last lady left in London."

With that, he dropped the cigar, crushed it beneath his boot, turned on his heel, opened the door, and strode inside. He didn't so much as give her a backward glance. As he marched toward the dining room, alone, he had a self-satisfied grin on his face. He would not soon forget the look of pure shock and outrage that had appeared on the young woman's face at his words.

Priceless. Simply priceless.

That had been perhaps the most fun he'd had since stepping foot in London. Telling off one of the *ton*'s obviously pampered aristocrats. Really, these people needed to take themselves far less seriously. How in the world would he ever fit into this brash world full of self-important people and their tedious rules?

David shook his head. Whoever the chit was, she was clearly used to being the rude one, not having people return the favor. But he knew one thing for certain, it would be a day too soon if he ever had the misfortune of running into that arrogant miss again.

CHAPTER TWO

Mouth agape, Annabelle stared at the door the man had just disappeared through. Who in the world was *he*? In all her twenty-three years she'd never had a gentleman be so rude to her. Was he even a gentleman? The fact that he'd been invited to Lady Harrison's party made her guess that he must be, but she'd never seen him before, and she'd met *all* the gentlemen of the *ton*. Every one of their boring, predictable souls. She might have guessed he was foreign, but he'd spoken in perfect English without the trace of an accent. She didn't know many foreigners who spoke English so well. However, the funny cheroot she'd shared with him was wholly unfamiliar. Nothing like the ones she'd secretly smoked after pilfering them from the humidor in her brother's study. Perhaps the man *was* foreign, after all.

To make the entire situation worse, the man was handsome, blast him. He looked to be about thirty years of age, tall, with dark-brown hair and dark-blue eyes, a combination she'd always found intriguing. He had wide, square shoulders, a narrow waist, and a jawline you could strike a flint against. Half of his face had been covered in darkness when she'd first seen him, but when he'd stepped into the candlelight, the breath had nearly been knocked from her lungs. And *not* because he'd been smoking in front of her, of all impertinent things.

Normally, when men followed her outside and tried to compromise her, they did an awful job at pretending they didn't know she was there. This man had gone a step further and begun *smoking* in front of her. That was new. She'd admired his ingenuity. She'd taken a couple of puffs just to shock him. Sometimes behaving outlandishly worked to scare them off, causing them to decide immediately she wasn't wife material after all. Some of the prigs were downright horrified by her actions. Predictable. Boring. At times, funny. This man, however, appeared entirely nonplussed by her behavior. He seemed more affronted by the fact that she'd accused him of pretending to not know she was outside already. That was new, too. She did give him credit for being more original than the others. Plus, his rudeness at the end, saying he wouldn't pay a call on her if she were the last lady left in London… While slightly dramatic, it had been unexpected, to be certain. She narrowed her eyes and crossed her arms over her chest, drumming her fingers against the opposite elbows. Hmm. Perhaps she was mistaken. Perhaps this particular man *hadn't* known she was outside. Perhaps he truly *didn't* know who she was. Difficult to believe, but admittedly possible.

Annabelle sighed and opened the door to enter the house. Mama would have a conniption if she knew half of the things Annabelle had done to discourage suitors. But Mama didn't know. None of the men would tell her. They didn't dare risk drawing the ire of the dowager Marchioness of Bellingham, nor the ire of her brother, Beau, the Marquess, for that matter. Besides, no matter how outlandish her behavior,

Annabelle was trapped as one of the most eligible ladies on the marriage mart. And it wasn't just because she had an indecently large dowry and was from an impeccable family. No. The real reason she was a such a prize to the men of London's *Beau Monde* was because she'd had the grave misfortune to have been born beautiful. Uncommonly beautiful. According to nearly anyone she'd come in contact with for the last five years, she had a striking figure and an incomparable face. Blasted inconvenient, if you asked her. But apparently true.

Her beauty seemed to turn nearly every eligible male in the country into a raving lunatic when they were in her presence. She'd long ago stopped being flattered by the attention and now she was simply tired of it. She'd already turned down over a score of marriage proposals. Well, to be precise, Beau had turned them down on her behalf. But she hadn't been interested in any of them. Not a one. To her suitors, she was merely a prize to be won, and none of the men cared about her wit or her cleverness, not to mention her needs, wants, and dreams. Half the male population of the *ton* had attempted to court her and not one of them had ever asked her about her thoughts. She was sick of it. And even though Beau and her mother were despairing of her ever marrying, Annabelle refused to wed some puffed-up shirt who only wanted her on his arm because of her looks and her dowry. More importantly, she refused to *belong* to any man.

Thankfully, Beau hadn't pressed the matter and on the eve of her sixth Season, Annabelle had no more intention of picking a husband this time than she ever had. Though she didn't tell Beau as much. What her beloved older brother didn't know wouldn't hurt him. Besides, Beau had recently announced his own betrothal to lovely, red-haired Marianne. The wedding was soon, but it would surely keep everyone occupied for the first few weeks of the Season, at least.

Annabelle stepped into the house and shook off the chill from having been outside so long. She took a mint from a small tin in her reticule to hide the smell of smoke on her breath. Mustn't worry Mama.

Using a looking glass set above a table near the door, Annabelle poked at her coiffure. She turned her head from side to side. There was no help for it. She looked precisely as she always did. Perfectly put together on the outside, perfectly miserable inside. Though no looking glass could capture that. She would pray for looks to fade sooner than later, but she'd long ago given up the useless act of praying. It accomplished nothing.

Oh, what did it matter? Tonight's party was just like any of the other dozens of parties she'd been to over the years. With one exception. Tonight, she would go back to the dinner table and do her best to ignore that quite rude, albeit quite handsome, man. Whoever he was.

CHAPTER THREE

"I don't belong here," David said beneath his breath to his soon-to-be brother-in-law, the Marquess of Bellingham, as they strode through the door to White's the next day.

"Nonsense," Bell replied, turning and clapping David on the back. "You're the Earl of Elmwood now, and I am sponsoring your membership into the club. It's all but done."

David rubbed the back of his neck and winced. "It might be 'all but done,'" he allowed, "but I still don't belong here." He glanced around at the mahogany-lined walls, the plush carpets, the rich, leather chairs. He could nearly smell the money in the air in here. It was that obvious. After spending the last twelve years in His Majesty's army, living mostly in tents for the past five of them, such lavishness made David uncomfortable. He wanted to run from the building all the way back to the cottage in Brighton where he'd been raised. No. Regardless of what Bell said, David certainly didn't belong here.

"Come now," Bell said after he'd handed his coat to one of the footmen hovering near the door. Wherever they went, there was always a footman hovering near the door. David quickly handed over his coat, as well. He intended to mimic Bell's every move in here. How did one act at an exclusive gentlemen's club? David hadn't the first idea. The closest he'd come to such an establishment was the officer's tents in the Peninsular War. And they were a far cry from the marble, gold, and frescoed opulence they stood in now.

"Allow me to introduce you to some of the chaps," Bell continued, striding through the club as if it were his second home.

David took a deep breath and mentally prepared himself to meet 'some of the chaps.' Around here that could mean a duke or another marquess like Bell. Despite his wealth and obviously privileged upbringing, Bell was a good man. He was betrothed to David's sister, Marianne, but the two had met *before* David had any inkling that *he* was, in fact, the heir to the Earl of Elmwood, which made his sister a lady. David still couldn't believe it. After Bell, Marianne, and David had returned from France last autumn, he'd learned that his deceased father had been the only son of the Earl of Elmwood. But the last several months had done little to allow the reality to sink in.

Now, David was a nobleman, a toff, an aristocrat. It was all too much. In Brighton, they were raised if not in poverty, then certainly not in luxury. They lived in a simple cottage with three bedchambers. One for their parents, one for Marianne, and one for David and Frederick to share. They'd done chores and scrubbed floors and cut down trees for their father's work. They'd fished, and hunted, and gone to country dances, and when they'd come of age, David and Frederick had joined the army and Marianne had become Lady Courtney's companion.

But in their entire upbringing, nothing, nothing had given them the slightest hint that Father had been an earl's son. Apparently, he'd had a falling out with David's grandfather over the desire to marry David's mother, and instead of relenting, David's father had seen fit to renounce his future title and raise his family in Brighton, away from the crowds of London and his former life. But even on his deathbed, Father had not mentioned who he really was. It sometimes made David hope that the entire thing had been an enormous mistake. But General Grimaldi himself, Head of the Home Office, had been the one to track down the truth, and apparently there was no mistaking the fact that David's father had been the only son of the Earl of Elmwood. Which meant that David, as his surviving son, inherited the title upon Father's death.

"See, over there," Bell pointed to a group of men all hovered around a large book in the corner of the main sitting room. "That's the infamous betting book. All sort of things are wagered upon between the pages of that tome."

David didn't have the heart to tell Bell that he'd never heard of the betting book and furthermore, he didn't care about it. Wagers were placed by fools. Fools who were soon separated from their money. David had seen more than one poor sop in the army lose a month's pay or more by being far too ready to gamble it away on a silly chance.

"Come with me to the next room," Bell said. "Perhaps some of my friends are here."

Bell had barely taken two steps when another man materialized from the corridor and stopped him. "There you are, Bellingham. I've been looking for you. Might I have a word... in private?"

Bell glanced back at David, who gave him a quick nod before turning around, his hands clasped behind him to find something to occupy his time while Bell spoke with the gentleman.

David had learned that Bell had another life when he'd

come with Marianne to rescue him from a French prisoners-of-war camp. Bell, as it turned out, was a spy for the Home Office, and furthermore so was Marianne. Although David was sworn to secrecy on both counts, he was also accustomed to looking the other way when Bell was called away suddenly.

David turned back to look at the group of men near the betting book. It was the last thing he wanted to do, the very last, but he might as well be cordial to these men of his newfound class. He walked over to the small group and cleared his throat.

"Good afternoon, gentlemen. What are you betting on today?"

The men looked up at him, confused, as if a goat had wandered into the club and asked the question.

"I beg your pardon." David cleared his throat and wished he was anywhere else but here. "I suppose I should have begun by introducing myself. Terribly sorry. I'm... My name is..."

"You're Elmwood, aren't you?" one of the younger men asked, narrowing his eyes on David.

David tugged at his lapel. He still wasn't used to the bloody fine cut of cloth he was wearing these days. Bell had dragged him to one of the best tailors on Old Bond Street and now he was the proud owner of over a dozen shirts of the finest linen, two dozen pure white cravats, perfectly fitted breeches, and boots so shiny you could see your reflection in the toes. Not to mention the trousers, and socks, and waistcoats, and handkerchiefs. *Monogrammed* handkerchiefs. It all cost more than he might have made altogether in his previous life, David reckoned, but he'd soon learned that the title of Elmwood also came with a significant fortune. Apparently, his grandfather had been a very wealthy man.

"Yes, I am," David replied, admitting to his title, and

feeling like a complete fool. Of course they all knew who he was already. Bell had warned him that his name had been in the papers nonstop since the news of his arrival had spread through London like wildfire. Marianne had to hide in Lady Courtney's town house for weeks for fear of being plowed down by a gaggle of ladies eager to make the acquaintance of the sister of the new earl and the *fiancée* of one of the most elusive bachelors in the country.

The men shot each other uncomfortable looks, while David wished he was wearing brown so he could slink back against the wooden walls and hide. Had he said something wrong? Done something *gauche*? Apparently he had, because none of them were answering him, and some of them were shifting awkwardly in their seats.

"Can you keep a secret, Elmwood?" one of the men said, an unpleasant smile on his face.

"What sort of secret?" David replied, already wanting nothing to do with any sort of a secret this set might have.

"Don't tell him," the first man said. "He's tight with Bell."

"Yes," David replied nodding. "I'm quite tight with Bell." If these chaps had a secret to keep from Bell, David certainly didn't want to hear it. He began to slowly back away from the group.

"We're betting on a lady," the smug man continued.

David winced as if the act of shutting one eye, might cut off the access to his ears too.

"A lady?" he replied, already turning on his heel. He didn't want to hear another word. "Very well. Sounds good. I'll just go—"

"To be precise," the man continued, "we're betting on which of us a certain lady of the *ton* will marry."

For some reason, the lady outside at last night's dinner party sprang to mind. The woman was a handful, but she seemed like the type of lady one might place a bet upon.

Perhaps on how rude her next act would be. After he'd returned to the dining room last night, David had ended up making his excuses to his hostess and leaving for the night. He'd briefly considered not giving the rude blonde the satisfaction of thinking she'd chased him away, but the more likely scenario was that she wouldn't give him a second thought. She obviously had a great deal of experience being rude to men in private. She'd no doubt forgotten their encounter the moment he'd left her company. It seemed it would take longer for him to forget her. Was that what being an aristocrat would be like? Getting used to beautiful women being rude? He'd much rather go back to Brighton and find a nice, unassuming local girl to marry. He would need a countess eventually. Or so Bell had told him.

David shook his head, bringing his attention back to the company behind him. Certain he was about to regret it, he turned back to them and asked, "What does betting on a lady's marriage have anything to do with Bell?"

"Don't tell him!" the second man repeated.

A sinking feeling spread through David's gut. Damn. He shouldn't have asked that question. The bet did have something to do with Bell, after all.

"The lady in question," the smug man replied, still smiling in a way that made David uncomfortable, "is Lady Annabelle Bellingham."

David released his breath in a whoosh. Lady Annabelle was Bell's sister. He'd yet to meet her. She was not in London at present and hadn't been all winter. She and her mother were due back from the countryside for the Season any day now. All David knew about Annabelle was that she was several years younger than Bell and unmarried apparently. Marianne had been worried for weeks that Annabelle might not like her when they met. But Marianne had come back from her visit with Bell's mother and sister in the country, claiming they were both perfectly lovely and approving of her, which pleased David immensely.

David cleared his throat and tugged on his lapels again. He would certainly regret asking this next question, as well, but curiosity had got the better of him. "Why are you betting on who Lady Annabelle will marry?"

A crack of laughter came from one of the chaps in the group. David didn't like it. He didn't like it at all. These men were supposed to be the cream of Society? They were being crass and ungentlemanly as far as David was concerned.

"Have you ever *seen* Lady Annabelle?" the smug man asked, with a far-too-smug look on his face.

David shook his head. "I've not yet had the pleasure."

Another crack of laughter from the group made David narrow his eyes.

"Well," Lord Smug said. "Let's just say that Lady Annabelle has been out for five Seasons and has *yet* to pick a husband despite having at least a score of offers, according to the gossips."

David had to work to keep his face blank and not show his distaste for the subject matter. "So, you're betting on who the lucky *winner* will be?" He was being facetious calling Lady Annabelle's future husband a 'winner,' but his word choice only served to make the other men chuckle and elbow each other in the ribs. Vulgar, if you asked him.

"Who it will be, and when," Smug replied, steepling his fingers together over his chest.

"I see," David replied. Though he didn't see at all. It seemed to him that grown men with fine educations and fat pockets should have a score of better things to do than bet on such nonsense, but that wasn't for him to judge. He merely wanted to leave their company immediately. Being a nobleman wasn't for him. If this was the sort of foolishness he would be forced to participate in to be a suitable earl, he wanted to go back to Brighton and work in his father's woodshop, thank you very much. None of these men had spent a single day in battle. None of these men had watched their mates die in agony. None of these men knew anything beyond this privilege and rubbish wastes of time like placing bets.

Lord Smug narrowed his eyes on David again. "You don't happen to know if Bell has given her a deadline by which to choose a husband?"

David shook his head, his jaw tightening. "Lord Bellingham and I have never discussed his sister's marriage prospects, I can assure you." The nerve of these blowhards, thinking that he'd betray his friend's trust to a gaggle of loud-mouthed strangers.

The group laughed. "So formal? 'Lord Bellingham?' We call him Bell."

Of course David had messed up that bit. He was still trying to learn how precisely to call everyone by their formal titles. He was far from mastering nicknames. "Yes, well, *Bell* and I have never discussed Lady Annabelle. I'll just be getting back to—"

He turned to leave as Lord Smug said, "Don't tell Bell we're betting on his sister, Elmwood. We wouldn't want you to spoil the fun."

David pressed his lips together and nodded once before nearly running from the group to the far side of the room where he'd come from. He had no intention of telling Bell anything about his ridiculous encounter with those men. Not only would it be in the worst taste to repeat anything they'd said, he would not do his friend the disservice of repeating that nonsense in his presence. However…what if the proper thing for Bell to do would be to call them out? Perhaps he *should* tell him they were being disrespectful to his only sister. Wouldn't David want the same if someone was being so crass about Marianne?

Bell was back at his side moments later and David breathed a sigh of relief when they strode together into the next room away from the prying eyes of the group of men at the betting book. They entered a smaller room similarly outfitted as the first, with plush leather chairs and carpets, wood-lined walls, and expensive-looking paintings covering nearly every space on the dark-green walls.

"Made some new friends near the betting book, did you?" Bell asked, as they took seats across from each other.

David expelled his breath. "Not hardly." He bit his lip. Should he tell Bell what the men had said? Was now the time to say something? Or would it be in poor taste? *Damn. Damn. Damn.* "Who was the man in front of the book? The one sitting in the chair?" Lord Smug.

Bell cocked his head to the side and narrowed his eyes, obviously trying to recall. "Oh, that was Murdock. The Marquess of Murdock, that is."

Murdock? The name sounded vaguely familiar, but David had heard so many new names over the last several months. Names, rules of comportment, titles, politics. It was over-whelming. In fact, Bell had informed him that he had enlisted his sister, Annabelle, and his mother, Lady Angelina, to teach David how to go about in Society. The two women were unimpeachable members of the *Beau Monde* and if David needed anyone, it was a pair of experts. He wasn't precisely looking forward to his 'earl lessons,' as Marianne had dubbed them, but he was clever enough to know he was sorely in need of them. It was kind of Lady Annabelle and her mother to volunteer to tutor him. Which was another reason he didn't particularly care for Murdock and his group of smugs in the other room betting on Lady Annabelle. The young woman was about to do him a favor. The least David could do was keep those fools from besmirching her name.

A footman rushed forward to hand them each a drink they hadn't ordered. Bell's was tea, David's was port. He'd developed an affinity for the wine when he'd been stationed in Portugal. He blinked at the glass and frowned. How the hell did the footman know what he liked to drink? The servant scurried away again before he had a chance to ask him. David shook his head. *Privilege*.

"Make any bets?" Bell asked next, the side of his mouth quirking up in a half-grin.

David expelled his breath. Blast the *ton* and all its ridiculous rules of comportment. In this situation, he had no idea how to proceed. He hadn't had his earl lessons yet. But back in Brighton he would have bloody well told his mate and got it over with. Yes, fine. That's precisely what he would do. "No, and in fact. I'm not certain I should be the one to mention it, but…" He took a fortifying sip of wine.

"They were betting on Annabelle again, weren't they?" Bell asked, leaning back in his chair, and straightening his shoulders. He looked perfectly calm. Not at all like a man who was about to call someone out.

David choked on the port he'd just ingested. "What?" he managed to say. "You knew?"

Bell sighed and shrugged. "They do this every year, right as the Season begins."

David blinked at him, his eyes still watering from the choking. "You allow it?"

"Allow it? I'd bet on it myself if they'd let me. But they say I have an unfair advantage in knowing when to place my bet." Bell winked at him. "They may have a point."

David narrowed his eyes on the marquess. "It doesn't make you angry?"

"You'll learn everything is a bet here, Elmwood," Bell

replied with a wry grin. "And as for Annabelle, well, you'll see for yourself soon. She and Mother just returned from the countryside yesterday afternoon. In fact," he pulled his timepiece from inside his coat pocket and glanced at it, "we're meeting them at my town house at four o'clock. Mother and Annabelle are both greatly looking forward to your earl lessons, Elmwood. I cannot wait for you to meet them."

CHAPTER FOUR

Annabelle sailed across her bedchamber in her brother's town house with a wide smile on her face. Today was a good day. Not only was she back from the confoundingly dull countryside, she would finally see Beau again. There were few people in the world whose company she enjoyed more than her brother's. Not only was he a hero as far as she was concerned, he was gone far too often on business for the Crown. She didn't get to see him nearly as often as she'd like.

Besides, Beau had written her to ask if she would do him a favor, and she would do anything for her wise, brave, older brother. His favor had nothing to do with her own courting or trying to find a husband. To be precise, the favor was more for her soon-to-be sister-in-law, Marianne. Marianne had met Beau at a house party last summer. There were quite a lot of secrets involved in *precisely* how they'd met, but the outcome had been that not only had Beau asked Marianne to marry him, but he'd volunteered both Annabelle and their mother to help Marianne acclimate to Society. Marianne and her brother had recently discovered that they were the grandchildren of the former Earl of Elmwood. The earl had died, and their father was dead as well, leaving Marianne's older brother, David, to take up the title.

Apparently, David had been a captain in the army, and had been taken prisoner in France. Annabelle shuddered. The man must be quite brave to have survived such an ordeal. But according to Beau, David had no clue how to behave in Society, which could prove to be quite awkward if something wasn't done about it. Beau and Marianne had agreed that Annabelle and her mother would be the perfect pair to go about teaching Lord Elmwood how to be a proper earl. She had so little occasion to do anything worthwhile such as teaching a former army hero how to navigate the waters of London Society. She was greatly looking forward to it.

She glanced at the clock on the mantel across the room. Nearly four. Beau and Lord Elmwood would be here any moment. Marianne would be arriving, too. Annabelle quickly surveyed herself in the looking glass. Perfectly presentable. Of course, it didn't matter much. Spending the afternoon teaching the son of a woodworker from Brighton how to be an earl didn't require her to look her best, but Annabelle was committed to doing what she could for the poor man to ease his transition into Society. According to Marianne, Lord Elmwood was in dire need of help with everything from his comportment, to his speech, to his manners. It sounded like quite a challenge. Annabelle wasn't a magician, but she would do what she could to help keep the newly minted earl from bringing shame on her brother and new sister-in-law.

Besides, Annabelle could think of no better use of the ridiculous knowledge of all things to do with Society that was floating around in her head than to help poor Marianne and her clueless brother to fit into the *Beau Monde*.

After all, Annabelle detested the endless round of social outings and silly parties like the one last night at the Harrisons'. At least today she'd be doing something worthwhile, helping two people who needed her.

Waving off her maid's help in assisting her with freshening her hair, Annabelle marched down the stairs to the foyer, eager to see Marianne again and meet her new charge.

Annabelle had barely got to the first floor when the door knocker sounded. She hurried into the white salon near the front of the house to await her visitors. A few moments later, Stockton, the butler, escorted Marianne and her chaperone, Lady Courtney, into the room.

"There you are, Annabelle," Marianne said. "Stockton tells me that my brother and Beau have not yet arrived."

Annabelle stood and greeted both women with warm hugs and kisses to their cheeks. "I expect them any moment," she informed her future sister-in-law.

The two took their seats near Annabelle.

"Beau told me he was taking David to White's," Marianne said, a look of apprehension on her face.

Annabelle frowned. "Does that concern you?"

Marianne winced and nodded. "I'm afraid it does. Even though the Season has already begun, I've asked Beau not to take David out in Society much. Not until he's had a chance to…benefit…from your tutelage."

Annabelle laughed. She reached over and pressed her warm hand atop Marianne's cold one. "I'm certain your brother is at least capable enough to handle a few men in their cups at the gentlemen's club."

Marianne bit her lip. "I don't know." She shared an uneasy look with Lady Courtney. "David is not quite used to going about in such circles. Neither am I, of course, but at least I've had Julianna's and Frances's help, in addition to Lady Courtney here."

"Lady Julianna Montgomery and Lady Frances Wharton?" Annabelle clarified. The two ladies were the betrothed of Beau's closest friends. Julianna was betrothed to Rhys Sheffield, the Duke of Worthington, and Frances was betrothed to Lucas Drake, the Earl of Kendall.

Marianne nodded.

It stood to reason that Julianna and Frances would take Marianne under their wings. Frances's father had been arrested last autumn in a large scandal, but Lord Kendall had stood by her, and along with their other friends, they'd managed to keep Frances's reputation intact. In fact, the three couples were all getting married together in only a few weeks' time at the Duke of Worthington's large country estate.

"I've told you countless times, Marianne, dear. I wouldn't worry about your brother," Lady Courtney interjected. "He's a capable man, and I daresay once the ladies of the *ton* get a look at him, they'll hardly be concerned about his manners."

Annabelle arched a brow. What exactly did *that* mean? She wasn't entirely certain, but it sounded intriguing. Was Lord Elmwood particularly handsome? His sister was certainly lovely, with long red hair and bright blue eyes. Annabelle had never been particularly attracted to men with red hair, but no doubt some of the ladies of the *ton* would be. Besides, with an earldom to offer, his looks would hardly matter to several of them. They were hunters, and a man with an eligible title and a large fortune were their prey. According to Beau, Lord Elmwood had both.

"Yes," Marianne replied, nodding toward Lady Courtney "I know, but David and I... Well, you know how we were raised, Lady Courtney. Mama did her best to ensure we weren't completely unaware of certain things, but we were hardly part of Society."

Annabelle's heart wrenched. Her poor lovely sister-in-law

had no business being worried about the blowhards and backstabbers in London Society. She patted Marianne's hand once more. "The truth is, I've never met anyone as dear as you are, Marianne, in all my years of living in Society. If your brother is half as kind and caring as you are, I'm certain he'll be better than the lot of them as well."

As if on cue, Stockton knocked at the door again. "Lord Bellingham and Lord Elmwood," he announced with a bow before stepping aside and retreating.

Beau stepped into the room first as the three ladies rose to greet the men. Her brother's form blocked Annabelle's view of Lord Elmwood at first and she didn't dare be impatient enough to lift up on tiptoes and crane her neck to try to see the man. That would be uncouth. She waited while Beau stepped forward to give her a hug. She squeezed him tightly. "It's so good to see you, Beau," she whispered.

"I've missed you, Annabelle," he replied warmly.

"Annabelle," Marianne said as soon as Beau had stepped away from her side. "Allow me to introduce you to my brother, David Ellsworth, the Earl of Elmwood."

Annabelle lifted her chin to take in the dark-haired man who stepped forward.

Her jaw dropped. She quickly snapped it shut.

Standing in front of her in impeccably tailored clothing, wearing an ironic smile on his too-handsome face, was the self-same man she'd been unbearably rude to the night before in the Harrisons' garden. The man who hadn't been back at the dinner table when she'd returned, causing her no small amount of frustration. She'd nearly asked her hostess about him when she took her leave. Only stubborn pride had kept her from it.

"Ah, Lady Annabelle, is that your name, then?" Lord Elmwood said, his smile not wavering.

If Annabelle had been a different person, the kind of

person who hadn't spent years perfecting the art of showing no reaction when she chose, her face would have been up in flames by now. Instead, she was perfectly calm and collected when she allowed the smallest hint of a smile to lift one side of her mouth and replied, "Yes, my lord. A pleasure to make your acquaintance."

"Ah, but we've already met, haven't we?" he replied, his dark brow quirking into a frown. "Unless I'm mistaken. Wasn't that you in the Harrisons' garden last night?"

Annabelle inhaled sharply. Her face still blank. Very well. The man wasn't going to do the honorable thing and pretend as if this was their first meeting. Marianne was right. He wasn't trained in the subtle art of social niceties. Fine. "Yes." She straightened her shoulders. "It was."

"Ah, then surely you remember me." He pointed at himself. "Don't you recall? I am the only man in the country who *isn't* trying to court you."

CHAPTER FIVE

If he were being honest with himself, David could admit that he enjoyed seeing the look on Lady Presumptuous's face when he introduced himself as the only man in the country who wasn't trying to court her. It was a mixture of pure shock, a healthy dose of discomfort, and a hint of anger. Good. She should feel aghast after having treated him so rudely last night.

His sister's elbow promptly met his ribcage, however, and he jerked forward, coughing slightly. "Don't be *rude*, David," Marianne said through a fake smile. "This is Beau's *sister*."

At the moment, David didn't care who Lady Presumptuous was to Beau, but he promptly replaced the smug smile on his face with a more suitably bland one. "A pleasure," he said, bowing to her the way he'd been instructed to by Lady Courtney.

Lady Annabelle cleared her throat and tossed back her head. "Lord Elmwood is correct. We've met," she announced to Marianne with her own painfully tight smile. "At least… well, I didn't realize who you were at the time, Lord Elmwood," she finished quietly. "I believe you introduced yourself as *Mr. Ellsworth*." The hint of irritation sounded in those last two words.

"Would it have made a difference in how you treated me, my lady?" he replied, still smiling. He didn't care if he got Marianne's elbow again, *that* comment had been worth it.

Marianne glanced back and forth between the two of them, her brow furrowed. "I don't understand. You've met? When?"

"Yes," Lady Annabelle hastened to answer, clearing her throat again uncomfortably. "At Lady Harrison's dinner party last night. We ran into each other…in the garden."

A thunderous look came over Marianne's face. She turned to glare up at her brother. "David, please tell me you weren't smoking again."

David glanced at Lady Annabelle. He lifted a brow. Would she expose him? Given how rude she was, he wouldn't put it past her.

"Oh, no. No. No," Lady Annabelle hastened to say. "At least, I didn't see him smoking." Her voice was sweet, lovely, and entirely convincing. He might have even believed it himself, if he didn't already know it was a lie.

David narrowed his eyes on her. So, she wanted to play nice now that she knew who he was? Lady Annabelle's eyes met his with a clearly pleading expression in them. She was silently requesting that he play along. Fine. It was decent of her to not mention the smoking. He wouldn't mention it, either.

"I don't see why a grown man cannot enjoy a cheroot from time to time," Bell interjected.

"David doesn't smoke cheroots," Marianne replied. "He smokes hideous cigars from Portugal."

"The cigars are from Spain," he clarified. "I only *received* them while I was in Portugal."

"Regardless," Bell replied. "I say you should be able to smoke whatever you like."

Marianne quickly took up that argument with her affianced while David eyed the young lady who stood in front of him today wearing a simple but obviously expensive white gown and matching white kid slippers. A wide pink sash was tied behind her back in a bow. Her blond hair was pulled up effortlessly in a bun on the back of her head and her cheeks were bright and full of life. She had a distinctive twinkle in her eye that he'd noticed last night, but today it was even more pronounced. He had not been wrong about her looks, either. The woman was gorgeous. There were no two ways about it. Too bad her beauty had obviously gone to her head and made her vain. She was clearly only attempting to be cordial to him now because she hadn't realized before that he was the brother of her soon-to-be sister-in-law.

After he'd left the party last night, David had reflected upon their interaction all night. It had bothered him. If Society was full of a bunch of simpering prissy geese who thought they were the center of the universe, he truly was not going to like it here. For God's sake, he would eventually be expected to find a wife among this type of young ladies. No, thank you. He much preferred the guileless girls in Brighton who smiled and laughed and danced and didn't go around trying to accuse you of following them out into a garden where you went to have a cigar in peace and quiet.

And somehow this particular young lady, who clearly believed herself to be the princess of the *debutantes*, was not only going to be related to his sister through marriage, but she was supposed to be the one to teach *him* how to behave politely in Society? It was like having Atilla the Hun teach you subtlety. How could *she* teach him anything about being polite? She'd been beyond ill-mannered last night. Why in the world had Marianne and Bell thought she was the correct person for the task? Was it possible they had no idea how discourteous she was to bachelors?

Marianne finally turned back to David and Annabelle. "At any rate, I hope you'll both be eager to start your lessons. I know David has been looking forward to it."

Had been looking forward to it. David mentally corrected his sister. Or at least had been resigned to it. Now he didn't trust the tutor. Or her knowledge.

"Oh, yes, ever so much," Lady Annabelle replied in that same sweet voice that was clearly fake. Where had that voice been last night in the Harrisons' gardens?

David gave both women a skeptical look. They were merely exchanging pleasantries and being polite, but his years in the army had taught him not to equivocate. "May I speak to Lady Annabelle alone for a moment, please?"

The room instantly fell silent.

"What?" David asked, glancing about from person to person. "Is that…unacceptable?" Excellent. He'd already blundered and he'd ostensibly just met the woman.

"It's not entirely proper, my lord," Lady Annabelle replied quickly. "But I don't see what harm it would do if we were to go into the next room for a few moments with the door open."

She glanced around the group as if to dare anyone to question her logic.

"That's fine, dear," Lady Courtney said with a regal nod, granting her approval.

Marianne looked as if she might chew off her bottom lip, but Beau merely laughed. "I swear the rules of Society can be stifling at times. Go. Go." He waved them both off.

Lady Annabelle led the way to the next room while David followed closely behind her. As expected, the next room in Bell's town house was as finely appointed as the first had been. David had found that wealthy people in London had several rooms for doing nothing more than entertaining callers. In Brighton, they'd had a big room for sitting and laughing and dancing and entertaining and sometimes even eating. They'd never stood on formality there. Sometimes he wondered if his father had left his formal life to get away from these stifling clothes and these stifling rules. He wouldn't doubt it. Father had been a fun-loving man who welcomed anyone into his home, regardless of their social standing in life. David still missed him every day.

As soon as they were alone in the next room, with the door properly wide open, Lady Annabelle turned to face him with a pleasant smile on her lips. But David didn't miss the trace of apprehension in her ice-blue eyes. "What did you wish to speak to me about, my lord?" There was that fake-sweet voice again.

David scrubbed a hand through his hair. He already knew what he was about to say would probably be far too forthright for the Society-bred miss he was talking to, but he didn't give a toss. He did, however, lower his voice, just in case the others were listening from the adjoining room.

"Look, I'm certain we both know why *you* trying to teach *me* how to go about in Society is a bad idea. Let's simply tell them all so." He jerked a thumb back in the direction of the other salon. "They may be temporarily disappointed, but I'm certain you don't want to teach me any more than I want to be taught by you."

If he hadn't known better, he would have thought a look of disappointment flashed briefly across her pretty face. Disappointment and perhaps…embarrassment? Hmm. That was interesting. He hadn't thought the disdainful lady he'd met last night would be capable of embarrassment.

"Oh, no, no. I'd like very much to teach you," she replied with a smile that at least *looked* sincere.

David narrowed his eyes on her. "Really?"

She nodded convincingly too.

"But I don't see how we can work together if you believe I'm attempting to court you."

She snort-laughed at that, surprising him.

"I don't believe that any longer, my lord," she announced.

He eyed her skeptically. "You don't?"

"No." She shook her head. "Now that I know who you are, I—"

"But that's the thing, Lady Annabelle," he replied. "You didn't know who I was last night in the Harrisons' gardens. Had no clue, in fact, yet you treated me as if I were the lowest form of life. How am I to trust you?"

She took a deep breath and clasped her hands together, biting her lip and looking terribly guilty. "I understand, my lord, and I'd like to apologize."

He cupped a hand behind his ear. "What was that?" Did she actually look contrite?

"I'd like to apologize," she repeated. This time the look on her face told him she also sort of wanted to grind her heel into his foot for making her repeat herself.

"You'd like to or you're going to?" he asked with as much smugness as he could muster.

"I am sorry, my lord," she said, through slightly clenched teeth.

"Sorry for what, precisely?"

"Sorry for the way I behaved last night. I was…out of sorts and I…took it out on you. I apologize."

His face softened. "That's gracious of you, and I do appreciate it," he allowed. Hmm. Perhaps he'd been wrong about her. She was mature enough to apologize, and he wasn't so petty that he'd reject a sincere apology. Hers felt sincere.

"May we simply begin again?" she asked in small, hopeful voice. "I *am* sorry for my behavior last night. We clearly got off to the wrong start."

Begin again? David rubbed his chin and considered it all for a moment. He didn't entirely trust her, but she would be in his life regardless, given that his sister was planning to marry her brother. And he still needed lessons. They may as well make the best of it. He truly had little choice. He made his decision quickly. "Very well. I'm willing to start again if you are."

A look of relief washed over her face. "You'll allow me to teach you how to go about in Society?"

"Yes." He nodded. "The truth is, I could use the help."

She smiled and her face lit up, reminding him once again how pretty she was. "Just promise me you won't fancy yourself in love with me and we'll do fine." She winked at him.

"Don't worry, Lady Annabelle," David replied, shaking his head. "I assure you. You're the last lady in London I would attempt to court. The very last."

CHAPTER SIX

That night Annabelle tossed and turned in her bed. Her bedchamber was completely black. She'd long ago conquered her fear of the dark. Her father had been dead for years, and she no longer allowed darkness to frighten her.

Memories of her earlier episode with Lord Elmwood rolled slowly through her head like a broken carriage. Especially that last bit. He didn't have to be quite so rude about it when he'd told her she was the last lady in London he'd attempt to court, did he?

But she clearly had deserved his distrust. She had behaved abominably toward him the night before. She was used to having men toss themselves at her, make bets upon her marriage prospects, and generally hound her. She hadn't expected a man who wasn't even aware of her existence. Now that she had time to think about it, it *was* haughty of her. But it seemed that everywhere she went in Society, she had a bull's-eye pinned to her back. She'd become so accustomed to it, she'd forgotten what it was like to meet a man who had no idea about any of it. It was a singularly novel experience. Lord Elmwood must think she was completely self-absorbed. She couldn't blame him.

At least she'd been able to convince him to reconsider allowing her to teach him. It would have been beyond embarrassing to have had to explain to Beau and Mama why Lord Elmwood wanted nothing to do with her. He'd made her feel like a complete ass. And she *had* been an ass. But she would make it up to him. She would be the very best tutor in London. She would ensure he knew precisely how to behave in every social situation. Why, by the time she was through with him, Lord Elmwood would be the catch of the Season. A few whispered remarks behind her hand to the right debutantes and he would have the *ton*'s most beautiful and accomplished girls clamoring for his attention. That's what Annabelle could do for him. And she would. To make up for her earlier rudeness.

Besides, Lady Courtney was right. The man was sinfully good-looking. It wouldn't take much to turn him into the Season's catch. His clothing already appeared on-point. Everything she'd seen him wearing to date looked positively smashing on him. Beau had obviously already helped him in that department. It didn't hurt that Lord Elmwood's stomach was flat, his waist was trim, his shoulders were broad and— *ahem*. That sort of thinking was not helpful. She'd do well to think of Lord Elmwood as the brother of her future sister-in-law, who merely needed her help, and nothing more.

As to that. Lord Elmwood clearly did need help. He was too blunt. Announcing to the room at large that they'd already met and asking to speak to her privately hadn't been the proper thing to do, but something about his brashness had sent a rush up her spine. She wasn't used to men saying exactly how they felt and behaving how they wished. She was used to the art of subtlety and the game-playing inherent in the *ton*, where strict rules governed everyone's every thought and deed.

It seemed a shame to cure him of such a novel habit, but Lord Elmwood couldn't go around saying whatever he wished to everyone he met at parties. That wouldn't do. Though the thought did make her smile. Heaven knew it would be refreshing to hear him take down a few of the most obnoxious blowhards with his brashness.

No. No. She'd explain to Lord Elmwood precisely how he must say things in such a manner that they might be construed in more than one way. After all, if one could deny one's misconstrued intent, one never had to answer for one's insults. The *ton* loved nothing more than the least obvious way to say a thing. It was dreadfully complicated and took far longer than it should, but, well, it was simply the way things were done. And if she were to be a helpful tutor, she would teach Lord Elmwood the precise way things were done in their world.

Propping a second pillow under her head and staring at the darkened ceiling, she spent more time than she cared to admit wondering why the man wasn't already wed. According to Marianne, Lord Elmwood had left Brighton for the army at a young age. He'd been the eldest son, but the eldest son of a woodworker would do well to join His Majesty's army.

Apparently, he'd joined the enlisted ranks as a lad and worked his way up to a commission. He'd been a captain when he'd learned of his deceased father's title and ordered to come back to London. The Crown, it seemed, wanted its noblemen safe and sound on good, solid English soil, which was the same reason Beau had to work for the Home Office instead of fighting in the wars. Beau had claimed to be married to his work until he'd met Marianne. Perhaps that was also why Lord Elmwood had yet to take a bride.

But according to Marianne, her brother *was* interested in finding a wife. He had the title to secure, after all. Part of what Annabelle and her mother had been asked to teach him was how to go about properly courting a young lady of the *ton*. And there were quite a lot of them to choose from. The formal debut at the queen's court had taken place last week—Marianne had made her debut and her beauty had been commented on by the queen herself—and the first ball of the Season was to be held in a matter of days.

Annabelle had briefly flirted with the notion of asking Lord Elmwood if he would pretend to court *her*. An outrageous notion, yet one that might fool Mama for the remainder of the Season. But that would be selfish of her, Annabelle ultimately concluded. She still had no intention whatsoever of taking a husband, though Lord Elmwood, however, would no doubt prove to be a prime catch. She mustn't deprive those poor, ignorant debutantes, who actually looked forward to marriage, of an excellent prospect.

Annabelle turned onto her side and hugged the pillow to her chest. Even though Lord Elmwood had made it clear that she was the last lady in London he'd ever want to court, they'd left things on a high note. He would be coming by in the late morning tomorrow to begin their lessons.

The thought filled Annabelle's middle with butterflies. She tamped them down. After all, it was merely the challenge that excited her. She hadn't had anything this interesting and worthwhile to spend her time on in years. She was about to make the newly minted Earl of Elmwood the most eligible gentleman of the Season.

CHAPTER SEVEN

When David arrived at Bell's town house the next morning, it was as if he'd stepped into a conservatory instead of a foyer. Large vases of flowers lined every conceivable space in the entryway and stood side-to-side upon the table and along the wall near the salon. There were roses, lilies, daffodils, and a variety of other flowers he couldn't even name, in all shapes, sizes and colors. The sweet smell was nearly overpowering.

An older blond lady stuck her head around one of the vases on the corner of the longest table. "Oh, Lord Elmwood, is that you?"

David straightened his back as if called to attention. "Madame?"

The older woman emerged from behind the vases and presented her hand. She was wearing a dark-blue gown. "I'm Lady Angelina, the Dowager Marchioness of Bellingham. I'm so pleased to meet you. Pardon me for the informality, but I was away yesterday when you came to visit."

Not at all certain he was paying proper respect to a marchioness, David bowed over her hand, while she fell into a curtsy. Bell's mother was lovely. Lady Angelina was around fifty years old and had a trim figure and a beautiful face. She looked like an older version of her daughter. There was some graying hair at Lady Angelina's temples, but he certainly could see the family resemblance. She had the same arresting ice-blue eyes as both of her children.

David decided to say the thing that lingered on the tip of his tongue. "I can only guess you had as many suitors when you were Lady Annabelle's age," he said, glancing about at the flowers.

Lady Angelina flushed and David immediately regretted his remark. Damn. That was probably a forward thing to say, especially given that he didn't know her well.

"I had several offers my first Season," the older woman replied, smoothing a hand over the top of her head. "But Lord Bellingham quite swept me off my feet and we married quickly."

"I see," David said, not wanting to make her any more uncomfortable. He should limit his speech until he'd been properly tutored. He pivoted on his heel and cleared his throat. He'd already bungled the proper thing to say to a dowager marchioness. What was next? Er, what, precisely, was the proper thing to say when faced with so many *flowers*? "I've never seen so many flowers," he finally uttered, feeling like an idiot.

Lady Angelina shook her head and lifted a large vase of daisies into her arms. "They're for Annabelle," she said with a sigh. "Word has clearly got out that she's back in London."

David frowned. "Lady Annabelle must have many suitors," came the next sentence from his mouth. Excellent. He was clearly committed to saying obvious things today. Bad form.

Lady Angelina lifted her gaze skyward. "You've no idea. It's become quite tiresome…particularly because Annabelle has shown no interest in any of them." The older woman set the daisies on another table on the opposite side of the hall.

David nodded. "Is that so?"

"Yes, she's had a score of offers the last five Seasons and has turned them all down with hardly a moment's thought." Lady Angelina's voice was filled with frustration. "Oh, but I must tell you I wouldn't mention such a thing to you if you weren't nearly family already. It's considered ill-mannered to brag about one's daughter's marriage prospects, but truly, Annabelle is the most trying young lady. Beau and I have nearly given up on her ever choosing a husband."

David kept his mouth shut. The way he understood it, Bell was the one turning down the offers, not Annabelle. The marquess obviously took his sister's wishes into account, however. That was good of him. David would have done the same for Marianne had she received other marriage offers before becoming betrothed to Bell.

But a score of offers? David's mind flashed back to the men at the club. What was it Lord Murdock had said? *"Let's just say that Lady Annabelle has been out for five Seasons and has yet to pick a husband, despite having at least a score of offers, according to the gossips."* Apparently, the gossips were right. Perhaps *that* was why Lady Annabelle had behaved the way she had that night in the Harrisons' gardens. If she were pursued to the extent that the men at White's made it seem, if she were hounded by men the way these flowers implied, no wonder she'd been rude. But why didn't she simply pick some chap and marry? *That* was certainly curious.

"Pardon my distraction, Lord Elmwood," Lady Angelina said, turning back to face him. "I sent Stockton for more water. I'll show you to the salon. Annabelle is already there. We're eager to begin your lessons."

David highly doubted that. Clearly the two ladies were only helping him as a favor to Bell, but regardless, he would take their assistance. "Thank you, my lady," he said as he followed Lady Angelina toward the salon.

When they reached the salon door, Lady Angelina opened it. Lady Annabelle was standing at the windows, sunlight streaming in and making her hair look almost silver. She was wearing a dark-pink gown and had a white rosebud in her hair. She looked stunning. David immediately wondered how he'd ever fit into this world with these beautiful, wealthy people. Apparently, it was in his blood, but it certainly didn't feel that way at the moment. He'd much rather be back in a camp a thousand yards from a battlefield. Dirty and so tired he couldn't sleep. *That* made sense to him. That was something he could handle. This was…nerve-racking.

Lady Annabelle turned at the sound of the door opening and quickly crossed the deep rug to greet David. "Good morning, my lord. I trust you slept well."

"I did." He nodded and cleared his throat. "And you?" Was it ill-bred of him to ask a young woman if she'd slept well?

"Yes, indeed," Lady Annabelle replied, with a smile. Apparently not. Unless she was only humoring him for the moment. He supposed he'd find out soon enough.

Lady Angelina smiled and nodded at them both. "If we hadn't had so many deliveries this morning, I would join you, but as it is, I'll just leave the door open and you two can begin. I'll be in the foyer if you need me."

"Yes, Mama," Lady Annabelle said. She turned to take a seat on the settee near the windows and gestured to David to take a seat across from her.

"Would you care for tea or coffee, my lord?" Lady Annabelle asked when they were both seated.

David eyed her warily. "Let me ask you this…if I were calling upon a young woman I fancied, would I accept an offer of tea or coffee?"

Lady Annabelle smiled and it lit up her eyes. She was even prettier when she smiled. "Well, first, you wouldn't be calling on a young woman until afternoon," she explained. "Social calls are made then. That reminds me, do you have your cards made up?"

David nodded and fished inside his coat pocket. He pulled out a card and handed it to her.

She read aloud his name, title, and address.

Lady Annabelle studied it carefully. "Lovely engraving. Lovely vellum. Simple. Clean. This is an excellent calling card, my lord."

"Thank you. Your brother helped me to procure them." At least he'd got the calling cards right.

"And I notice it doesn't say 'Mr. Ellsworth.'" Her mouth quirked up in grin.

He took the card back from her and stuck it into his pocket again. "That was an honest mistake. I'm not used to calling myself 'Elmwood.'"

"Understandable," Lady Annabelle allowed. "As for the coffee or tea, yes, it would only be polite to accept if your hostess offered you either. Unless you were eager to leave."

David frowned. "Why would I pay a call on someone if I wished to leave immediately?"

Lady Annabelle's eyebrow arched, and she smiled again. "I see we have much to discuss, my lord. I can think of a half dozen reasons why one would pay a call on another person and desire to leave as soon as possible."

David frowned. "It wasn't that way in Brighton. We paid calls on our friends, people we actually liked and wanted to spend time with."

She nodded. "Yes, that happens here too."

"But?" He drew out the word and cocked his head to the side, waiting for her explanation.

"But there are also reasons why we pay calls we don't

want to prolong." She finished by primly folding her hands in her lap.

David sighed and scrubbed a hand across the back of his neck. "Confusing, if you ask me."

She gave him a knowing smile. "I never said it wasn't confusing, my lord. But I will teach you the intricacies."

David leaned forward in his seat. "Why must it be so intricate? And as for calling me 'my lord,' I truly wish you wouldn't."

Lady Annabelle crossed her arms over her chest and stared at him, blinking at him prettily. "It would be entirely inappropriate for me to call you anything else."

"My name is David," he replied.

"Be that as it may, we do not know each other well enough for me to call you by your Christian name, and you don't know me well enough yet to call me by mine. Only close friends use each other's Christian names."

He grinned at her. "Does that mean there's hope once we get to know each other better?"

Her mouth quirked up again in the smile he was quickly coming to realize was uniquely hers. "Yes, there's hope." She shook her head. "Now. Allow me to ring for tea, and then I suppose we may start with the proper usage of the cards."

"Coffee," David said.

"Pardon?"

"I prefer coffee."

"Oh, of course. That's fine." Lady Annabelle rang for the butler, who appeared moments later and promised to return with the refreshments forthwith.

As soon as the servant left the room, Lady Annabelle cleared her throat. "So, again, today you're here early because I'm tutoring you, but normally one wouldn't pay a call until early afternoon. If one is told by the butler that the lady of the house is not home or is indisposed, you would leave one of your cards with the butler and he would see to it that the lady received the card upon her return, or when she next came downstairs. Or perhaps he might send them up on a salver for her perusal."

David frowned. "Why would she refuse to see me if she were home?"

Lady Annabelle smiled at him. "Perhaps she's abed with a megrim. Perhaps she drank too much champagne the night before and isn't feeling quite well, or perhaps she..." Her words drifted off awkwardly and she glanced away.

"Perhaps she what?" David prompted. What did Lady Annabelle not want to say?

She bit her lip. "Perhaps she doesn't care to speak with you. Though I'm certain that wouldn't happen to *you*...often."

David's laughter filled the room. These lessons were already taking a turn for the ridiculous. "I see. But how am I supposed to know if she's got a megrim or if she's avoiding me?"

Lady Annabelle tapped her cheek, clearly considering the question for a moment. "Well, when I'm avoiding someone, I don't return the call. Even though that's considered to be awfully rude. Just ask Mama, she's constantly listing the calls I should be paying."

"I see," David replied, giving her another smile. "I appreciate your honesty, Lady Annabelle. I would hate to pay a call on a young woman who wanted nothing to do with me."

"As I said," she hastened to add, "I doubt that will happen to you."

"Really? Well, I'm completely out of my element and no doubt will say blunt and crass things to every lady I meet, so I'm not entirely certain how many of them will welcome my calls the night after a party. But I suppose I'll find out, won't I?"

"Oh, but with your looks—" Lady Annabelle froze, and

her cheeks turned bright pink. "I mean…" She tugged at the cap sleeves of her gown and glanced away conspicuously.

David arched a brow. "My looks?"

"Yes, *erm*. I mean that…"

"Why, Lady Annabelle, do you find me to be—dare I say? —handsome?" He couldn't help the grin that spread across his face.

He could see her swallow a lump in her throat. It even made a cute little noise.

"We shouldn't be talking about such things," she offered lamely.

"On the contrary, I'd like to hear more," he said, still grinning like a fool from ear-to-ear.

Lady Annabelle plunked her hands on her hips and stared at him sternly for a moment, but she couldn't keep from laughing. "I bet you would."

"No, seriously, please tell me. Am I handsome?" he prodded.

She eyed him warily, narrowing her eyes on him. "Oh, come now. Don't play dumb. Is it possible that you don't know you're handsome?"

"I'm not certain, my lady. I don't have half the occupants of London sending me flowers the way *you* do. So I doubt I'm as good-looking as you are."

Her blush deepened before she answered primly, "Gentlemen don't receive flowers."

"What do they receive then?"

She shrugged one shoulder. "Compliments, I suppose. If they're fortunate. Though one hopes they would receive them with more…grace." The stern stare was back on her face.

He nodded. "Point taken. And I must say I consider it a great fortune that someone as coveted as you clearly are thinks I'm handsome, my lady. Thank you for the compliment."

Lady Annabelle nodded, but her cheeks remained slightly pink. "Yes, well, as I was saying—"

"May I ask you a question, my lady?"

"Very well."

"It seems you have your pick of suitors, why haven't you chosen one?"

A slight gasp emitted from her throat and David winced. "My apologies. Was that rude of me?"

She nodded slowly. "Yes, well. To be honest, it's *not* a question one should ask an unwed young lady."

David winced again. *Damn.* He'd already made more than one mistake this morning. "I take it back then. With apologies."

"No, no. We are going to be in the same family eventually. We needn't stand on ceremony. I don't mind answering your question."

CHAPTER EIGHT

Lady Annabelle took a deep breath and clasped her hands together. She seemed to be thinking about her answer for several moments before she replied. David decided it was best to give her all the time she needed. He was too blunt. Too blunt and far too used to spending most of his time with other blunt men. Army men didn't have the luxury of mincing words.

"The truth is I'm not interested in marriage," Lady Annabelle finally said with a resolute nod, as if that explained everything.

David stared at her. Then he tilted his head to the side, regarding her at an angle. "Any particular *reason* you're not interested?"

"No." Her voice sounded slightly strained, and she glanced away as she said it.

He tilted his head up again. "And here I thought perhaps you'd fallen in love with someone you couldn't marry. A tradesman perhaps. That's not it, eh?" he asked, watching her carefully.

Lady Annabelle's eyes widened. "Lord Elmwood, you are far too direct in your speech."

David scrunched up his nose. Damn. He'd done it again. "I know. I'm trying. Believe me. But it's much more efficient to get straight to the point. You should try it sometime."

He'd been jesting, of course, trying to lighten the mood after his obvious *faux pas*, so he was nothing but pleased when the next thing she said was, "Very well. Are *you* interested in marriage?"

He settled back in his chair and regarded her before shrugging. "'Interested' may be too strong a word," he replied with a chuckle. "But I understand it will *eventually* be my duty to marry and produce an heir."

"You'll marry *only* out of duty?" she prodded, leaning toward him slightly as if she'd found a subject she was heartily interested in.

He crossed his booted feet at the ankles. "Duty, yes. But I'd like to find a woman who likes me and *wants* to be my wife too. Someone whom I love, and who loves me back."

Lady Annabelle's back stiffened and a look of pure amazement came over her face.

David chuckled again. "Did that answer surprise you, my lady?"

"Yes, actually," Lady Annabelle allowed.

The butler returned with the tray of drinks just then and sat it on the table between them. David watched as Lady Annabelle went about pouring him a cup. She even did that elegantly, no doubt carefully trained in the fine art of pouring drinks.

"Sugar?" she asked.

"Never."

"Cream?"

He pulled a face. "An army man doesn't use cream. No cows following us around on the battlefield and all that."

She blinked at him as if his words had confused her. "Yes, but you're in London now."

"Don't want to get soft." He cracked a grin at her.

She shook her head "That's just silly, if you ask me. If you prefer cream, have some."

"I don't. But I'm much more interested in why my answer surprised you than whether I should take up requesting cream in my coffee."

Lady Annabelle handed him the cup and saucer prettily. He took the pair and set it in front of him. Did he do that properly? No doubt these people had rules for precisely where to set coffee cups and saucers.

Lady Annabelle switched to pouring herself a cup of tea. With cream. "I've never heard a man say that he wants to marry for love."

David considered her words for a moment. His parents had been in love. It was obvious in the way they treated each other. They talked, they laughed, they even held hands. They enjoyed dancing together in the great room of the cottage, too. "I suppose there are other reasons to marry. But love is the most important, as far as I'm concerned. It's certainly what I'm after...*eventually*."

Lady Annabelle finished stirring her tea and took a dainty sip. "You keep saying that word, 'eventually.' Does that mean you won't be looking for a countess this Season?"

"I'm not arrogant enough to believe that love comes when you call, my lady. I may not be looking for it, but if the right match appears, I don't want to miss it, either."

"Oh, good. Then you won't mind if I introduce you to some of the more accomplished ladies of the *ton*?" She eyed him over the rim of her teacup.

"'*Accomplished*?'" David frowned, pronouncing the word in an overly dramatic voice. "I'd prefer the *kind* ladies, or the *witty* ladies, or the *clever* ladies. *Accomplished* is not my first criterion."

Lady Annabelle froze again for a moment, then nodded, before bringing the teacup back to her lips and taking another sip. "I only meant some of the ladies are more… desirable than others."

David lifted his cup and took a sip of coffee. Smooth, refined. Not at all the harsh stuff he'd been served at camp. Would probably taste even better with cream. "Like you?" he asked.

Their eyes met over the rim of their respective cups and their gazes held for a moment. Finally, Lady Annabelle glanced away. "Yes, like me. Only younger," she replied with a laugh. "I'm nearly considered on-the-shelf at my age."

"Oh, how old are you?"

She glared at him. "Lord Elmwood, *that* is a wholly inappropriate question."

David chuckled. "I knew it the moment it left my mouth. But let me just say that if you're on the shelf, apparently no one told those chaps who sent all the flowers." He nodded toward the foyer.

She glanced at him sideways, rolling her eyes. "Those chaps who sent the flowers don't care how old I am. They only want to win the unattainable."

"I see." David nodded. "It's true that most men enjoy winning."

"Horse races and marriage proposals should not be considered equal."

"I agree with you."

"You do?" She blinked at him as if she hadn't understood what he'd said.

"Yes, and in addition to that…" David cleared his throat. "You apologized to me yesterday, but it seems I owe you an apology as well."

Lady Annabelle cocked her head to the side, her brow was furrowed. "Apology for what?"

"I judged you too harshly the other night. I assumed you were incredibly vain, but it's true that every man in London *is* after you, if those flowers out there are any indication." David wasn't about to mention the betting pool at White's. He didn't need her to tell him that *that* would be in bad taste, indeed.

She sighed and set down her cup. "You didn't judge me too harshly at all, my lord. I can only imagine how truly vain I seemed." Sincere regret sounded in her voice.

"If you've been dealing with scores of suitors chasing you about for years, I can well understand why you believed I was just another one in a long line of men trying to get your attention."

Lady Annabelle gave him a patient smile. "It was still exceedingly ill-mannered of me, my lord. I'm sorry to have given you the wrong impression. Unfortunately, I've been considered the most elusive catch of the last several Seasons."

He narrowed his eyes on her again, studying her. "At the risk of asking another impertinent question, why exactly do you consider that unfortunate? I would have thought it would be a young woman's dream."

"For most young women, perhaps." She took another sip. "It's simply that..." Lady Annabelle shrugged again. She glanced away. "I suppose I've always had this funny notion that people should marry because they *like* each other, because they intend to treat each other with respect and kindness, *not* because one is trying to win the other like a prize hog at a fair."

"And you're the prize hog?" he said with a grin.

"Precisely," she replied, meeting his eyes once again and returning his smile. She lifted her cup to her lips once more.

"Well, that I can certainly understand. I'm glad we started again, Lady Annabelle."

"So am I," she said, giving him a smile that made his insides light up. "And I'm three and twenty. I trust you will not repeat that to another living soul."

CHAPTER NINE

That afternoon, Annabelle arrived at Lady Courtney's town house at precisely one o'clock. Her maid, who was acting as chaperone, waited in the carriage as she marched up the steps and used the brass knocker against the tall black door. Annabelle had something specific she wanted to ask Marianne.

Annabelle had spent the entire ride here being completely preoccupied with two things, both of which Lord Elmwood had said to her this morning. First, he'd said he wanted to marry someone for *love*. Love! She honestly thought she hadn't heard him correctly at first. She'd had more discussions with men about marriage than she cared to think about. And in all those discussions—every single one—the word 'love' had never been uttered. Oh, no. Beauty had been mentioned. Dowries, family lineage, titles, children, and duty had been mentioned. Even the word 'affection' had been bandied about from time to time. But love? Never.

Lord Elmwood was unlike any of the other men of the *ton*. They'd all grown up with the rules drilled into their proper little heads. Love wasn't part of the rules. Love might as well be a giraffe, as rare as it was in London. No doubt about it. Lord Elmwood had thoroughly surprised her when he'd admitted he was looking for love.

The second thing Annabelle couldn't stop thinking about was the casual way in which Lord Elmwood had mentioned the things Annabelle had always wished a man would care about when it came to looking for a match. When she'd said she would introduce him to some of the more accomplished ladies, he'd told her he preferred kind or witty or clever ladies instead. Imagine that! He'd surprised her so much with that statement she'd nearly dumped her tea in her lap. What sort of strange fellow was he? A gentleman who cared about more than beauty and dowries? In fact, he'd never even mentioned a dowry. He had to know they existed, didn't he? Marianne would be bringing one to her marriage with Beau. How could an earl want a wife for her wit? A love match? The concept was so foreign she could barely believe it.

She might be preoccupied by Lord Elmwood's unconventional speech and declarations, but neither of those things were why she'd come to visit Marianne today. No. Annabelle's purpose in today's call was much more practical. If one wanted to learn about a man, one should speak to his younger sister. If only all those silly women who'd thrown themselves at Beau for years had bothered to ask *her* advice, one of them might have caught his interest. As it was, she was glad for Marianne. Annabelle couldn't have wished for a better sister-in-law. Unpretentious, caring, obviously adoring of Beau. Marianne would make a fine addition to their family. And Annabelle was determined that Marianne's brother, Lord Elmwood, would make a fine match for some fortunate debutante as well. Hence, the reason for her visit.

After being ushered inside by the staunch butler, Annabelle waited patiently in Lady Courtney's front salon until Marianne came breezing in, her bright red hair piled atop her head and a lovely mint green gown gracing her lithe frame.

Annabelle immediately stood and exchanged cheek kisses with her soon-to-be sister-in-law.

"It's good to see you, Annabelle. What are you doing here?" Marianne asked before the smile dropped away from her face. "Wait. Is this about David? Has he done something awful? I do hope he hasn't embarrassed you."

Annabelle laughed and shook her head. "No. No. Nothing like that. Although I did want to discuss David, if that is all right with you," she ventured.

The wary look remained on Marianne's face. "Are you certain he hasn't done something? Said something?"

Annabelle followed Marianne to the dark-blue settee near the front window, where they both took a seat.

"We had a pleasant chat this morning," Annabelle continued as she settled into her seat. "We discussed calling cards and his marriage prospects."

"Really?" Marianne arched a brow, a wary look in her face.

"Why do you sound surprised to hear it?" Annabelle asked next.

Marianne glanced down at her skirts and smoothed them. "It's just that, well, David's never been one to discuss his marriage prospects. Our dear Mama was beside herself trying to pry the slightest bit of information out of him."

Annabelle narrowed her eyes. "Is that right?"

"Yes, he's been completely mum on the subject for years."

"I understand how he feels," Annabelle mumbled under her breath.

"What was that?" Marianne asked.

"Nothing, it's just that I was hoping you could tell me some things about Lord Elmwood. Uh, erm, perhaps what type of woman would be a good match for him? It will help me narrow the list of ladies I intend to introduce him to this Season."

A bright smile spread across Marianne's face. "Oh, that's too good of you, Annabelle. I knew you'd be the perfect person to help David navigate Society. You're far too kind."

Annabelle returned her friend's smile. "Honestly, it's the least I could do after the atrocious start Lord Elmwood and I got off to the other night."

Marianne winced much like her brother often did. "Yes, I was afraid to ask you about that yesterday. You said David wasn't smoking, but—"

Annabelle reached out and patted Marianne's hand. "Don't worry one bit. I assure you I was the rude one, not your brother."

Marianne gave her a look that clearly indicated she didn't believe a word Annabelle had just said. "I find that difficult to believe, but I do appreciate your assistance in helping him. I'm certain Lady Courtney, Julianna, and Frances have been at their wits' end teaching me."

"Nonsense," Annabelle squeezed her hand. "You've been perfectly behaved in every situation I've seen you in."

Marianne gave her a wry smile. "That's good of you to say, but the Season has barely begun. I'm as nervous as tailor with no thread."

Annabelle laughed. "There's absolutely nothing to be nervous about. You and Lord Elmwood will both do fine."

Marianne nodded. "It certainly helps that I'm already betrothed. I cannot imagine the nerves I'd have if I had to brave the events of the Season in hopes of finding a husband. That's why I'm surprised David spoke to you about it."

Annabelle tilted her head from side to side. "Well, to be precise, he said he realized that he'd need to find a wife... eventually. And that's why I've come. I could ask him myself, of course, but I happen to know that if you want to know the truth about a man, you ask his younger sister."

Marianne laughed. "I suppose you did share with me quite a few delicious secrets about Beau."

Annabelle nodded. "Tell me, what sort of a lady would make a good match for your brother?"

Marianne straightened her shoulders and smoothed her skirts again. Clearly warming to the topic, she turned to face Annabelle directly. "Well, she must be kind, patient, and quick to laugh." Marianne ticked off the qualities on her fingers. "Clever, honest, and understanding."

"Those sound reasonable to me," Annabelle replied, mentally cataloging the lot of them. "But is there something else you can tell me, something that will really make me understand how your brother sees the world?"

Marianne thoughtfully tapped her cheek for a few moments before snapping her fingers. "Oh, yes, here's something. It's been ages since I've thought of this."

Annabelle nodded and eagerly leaned in to hear more.

"When we were children," Marianne began, "David felt responsible for Frederick and me. He was the eldest, after all."

"Yes," Annabelle replied, swallowing the lump that suddenly formed in her throat as she thought of how Beau had felt responsible for both her and their mother.

"Being older, David was always better at everything than Frederick," Marianne continued. "He ran faster, swam farther, and jumped higher. It made poor Frederick terribly frustrated."

"Go on," Annabelle said. She and Beau had been the only children in their family, but she could well imagine how difficult it would be for a younger brother to always find himself falling short.

"Well, David knew that Frederick was unhappy because

he never won in any physical competition between the two of them. One day, our town hosted a race for the boys. It was meant to be fun, but the winner would win a prize pie from the baker's shop."

Annabelle nodded.

"David was the strongest, fastest boy in town and he could have easily won the competition, but he knew that Frederick wanted to impress a young girl he fancied. The girl was watching from the finish line of the race."

Annabelle held her breath. "Oh, dear. What happened?"

"David made certain he and Frederick were far ahead of the pack of boys in the final race to the finish line. They'd both turned the corner around Mr. Hodges' house and were headed to the tree behind the church."

"And?" Annabelle prompted. She was nearly on the edge of her seat.

"David slowed enough to allow Frederick to pull ahead of him and win, right in front of the girl he fancied." Tears pooled in Marianne's eyes. "Frederick proudly picked out the pie and shared it with the girl…and with David and me, of course, later."

Annabelle sighed. "David let him win?" she breathed. "In front of the whole town."

"He didn't just let him win." Marianne smiled through the tears. "After the race, the girl who *David* fancied at the time asked him if he'd purposely lost."

"What did he say?" Annabelle asked, holding her breath again.

Marianne's face was full of pride. "David said no, and the girl told him she didn't want to spend another moment in the company of a loser."

Annabelle gasped. Outrage shot through her. "She didn't!"

"Yes." Marianne nodded. "She did. David came home, and

I asked him what happened. He said he didn't care to keep company with a girl like that."

Annabelle shook her head. "I don't blame him. She sounds awful."

"Oh, she was," Marianne replied, rolling her eyes. "Mama never liked her, either."

Annabelle laughed at that. "Well, Lord Elmwood certainly sounds as if he is right-minded when it comes to ladies. No wonder he told me he wasn't interested in accomplishments."

"'Accomplishments'?" Marianne frowned at the word in much the same way her brother had hours earlier. "No. I can't see David being particularly impressed by accomplishments. I must say I'm glad Beau isn't either, as I'm not particularly accomplished myself," she finished with a laugh.

"You are lovely, Marianne. And accomplishments are silly things the *ton* invented to make debutantes feel as if being no more than a prize at the market is actually worth something."

"I suppose you're right," Marianne replied. "Tell me. Which young ladies will you introduce to David?"

Annabelle gave her a sly smile. "I'm still deciding but I do have a few prospects. Young women who have just made their debut, mostly."

"There were some lovely young ladies at the Queen's court," Marianne replied.

Annabelle decided to ask the question that was on the tip of her tongue. "Did you know your brother intends to marry for love?"

A bright smile covered Marianne's face. "I'd expect nothing less." She stared at the wall and after a few moments, a more somber countenance replaced her smile. "Our Mama always told us *marry for love and you'll never regret it.*"

Annabelle swallowed and glanced away. Well, that sentiment wasn't true. Her own mama had married for love and had certainly come to regret it, but Annabelle wasn't about to tell that to a woman whose wedding was in a matter of days. "What else should I know about your brother?" she asked instead to change the subject.

The smile returned to Marianne's face. "David is kind, generous, funny, caring, and handsome, of course. Do you know he led a charge against the French in Portugal knowing it was tantamount to suicide? The enemy took him prisoner because he refused to stop running back again and again to save as many of his men as he could."

Annabelle sucked in her breath. "Oh, my goodness. He sounds ever so brave."

"He is," Marianne said, pride obvious on her face. "He risked his life repeatedly, facing almost certain death."

"That is something I've never been," Annabelle breathed.

Marianne frowned. "What's that?"

"Brave," Annabelle whispered. "I've never been brave."

"Well, I should hope you would rarely have cause to be," Marianne replied, this time reaching over and patting Annabelle's hand.

Annabelle smiled and shook her head. "Of course. Now, what else?" She pasted a bright smile on her face.

Marianne launched into another tale of her brother's valor, this time a story of how he saved a young hare from a trap, bandaged its paw, and nursed it back to health before releasing it into the forest. How could one not think the man was a saint?

Annabelle listened to story after story, peppering questions about Lord Elmwood's likes and dislikes in between. Two hours later, when she stood to leave, she felt as if the air had been sucked from the room. She must have asked Marianne two dozen questions about David's tastes, dreams, hopes, and preferences, and in the end, she certainly had one lady in mind. A lady who met all the criteria and then some. A lady who was eligible, accomplished, witty, clever, and possessed of both a fine family and a small fortune of a dowry. A lady who never would have blamed him for purposely losing a competition to make his younger brother feel special, and would have gladly helped him nurse the hare back to health. In fact, a young lady who just might fall in love with him a little for doing both.

Herself.

CHAPTER TEN

The next morning, David arrived strictly on time for his lesson with Lady Annabelle. He'd said and done some unfortunate things yesterday. Asking her age had been particularly wrong of him. But he hadn't been able to stop himself. Besides, she'd proven herself to be game enough when she'd cheekily answered him later.

Lady Annabelle had proven his assumptions wrong on a handful of scores yesterday as well. It appeared she was not the vain, pampered debutante he'd thought she was after their initial meeting. She'd been witty and wise and kind to him yesterday, not scolding or prim or haughty in the least. She even made fun of herself, referring to herself as 'on-the-shelf.' Nothing could be further from the truth. He had absolutely no trouble seeing why flowers were streaming through the door, or why the betting book at White's was filled with bets on her marriage prospects. Though David could also understand why it all seemed ridiculous to her, especially since she clearly had no intention of taking a husband. She still hadn't exactly explained *why* she was so set against it, but he supposed that was none of his business. Lady Annabelle had been kind enough to offer to help him learn the rules of Society, and he intended to do so expediently. He would be a model pupil.

To that end, he was recommitted to being a complete gentleman in her presence today. How difficult could it be? He only needed to stifle the urge to say nearly anything he'd normally say and pretend to be interested in things he would never be interested in. Like titles and parties and calling cards. He smiled to himself as he jogged up the stairs to Bell's front door.

Within moments of knocking, David was escorted past even more flowers in the foyer and into the salon. Were some of the new arrangements from the same men who had sent flowers yesterday? That seemed overdone. Or did ladies like that sort of thing? He frowned. Lady Annabelle hadn't seemed to give a toss about the flowers, but did other young ladies desire daily bouquets? How would he ever learn all these things?

He was still contemplating the perils of sending too many flowers when Lady Annabelle came floating into the room. She was wearing an ice-blue gown that made her eyes seem brighter. She wore white gloves and slippers and had a small daisy in her hair. No doubt pilfered from one of the many arrangements in the foyer. She looked fresh and rested and as lovely as ever.

"Good morning, Lord Elmwood. How are you today?" she asked as soon as she saw him standing near the window. "I'm sorry to report that Mama has taken ill this morning and sends her regrets that she cannot attend the lesson."

David bowed to her. "Good morning, my lady. Best wishes for your mother's recovery." There was an awkward pause that he felt obligated to fill so he added, "I see you have more flowers." He immediately wanted to kick himself for the comment. Not only was it obvious, it was clumsy.

Couldn't he find something better to say? He should have told her how beautiful she looked. How she made the rest of the space fade into a blur when she stepped into the room. How the scent of her perfume put the fragrance of the flowers to shame. Damn. What was becoming of him? Was he in danger of waxing poetic? He sincerely hoped not. Army men were not poetic.

"Yes, well, gentlemen can be so predictable," she replied with a sigh, waving her hand toward the foyer filled with flowers.

He arched a brow. "I take it you don't prefer flowers?"

"Flowers are lovely," she replied, with another noncommittal wave of her hand. "They're just…predictable. Mama said that Father practically bought a conservatory for her every day the first sennight they were courting."

"Yes, your mother mentioned they married quickly. I suppose she was impressed with the flowers."

"She was," Annabelle replied in a monotone voice. "Little substance though they held."

"It sounds as if it will take more than some flowers to impress you," he prodded.

Annabelle shook her head. She was staring unseeing at the far wall. She swallowed hard. "Much more. Flowers and gifts are merely distractions. A man's character is what's truly important."

Well, *that* was interesting. "Tell me." He stepped closer to her, intent on finding out what a lady like her would prefer to a vase full of predictable flowers. "What would you rather receive?"

She stepped in a small circle contemplating the question before turning to him and saying, "A book perhaps. One the gentleman picked out because he had asked me what sort of books I prefer to read. One he saw in a bookshop while browsing and it made him think of me."

"You like to read?" Reading was one of David's favorite things to do. So much more enjoyable than talking or exchanging pleasantries with strangers.

"Yes, do you?" she asked, a hopeful look on her face.

"Indeed, I do." He rubbed his chin. "I regretted that I could only fit one book in my rucksack on the Continent."

She clasped her hands together. "Oh, do tell me, what was it?"

"In English you would call it *The Ingenious Gentleman Don Quixote of La Mancha*, but I had the Spanish version."

"Oh, I've heard of it. *Don Quixote*. A comedy, is it not?"

The hint of a smile touched his lips. "Marianne gave it to me. She said I would need something silly to cheer me on the battlefield. But I read it so many times, I must say my opinion of the book changed, more than once."

"How so?" she asked, a truly interested look on her face.

"At first I thought it was a comedy, then I came to regard it as a tragic novel, because Quixote was considered mad and treated like a lunatic. But in the end, I found it to be life-changing."

She continued to study his face. "How so?"

David took a deep breath. "The book saved my life, in more ways than one. Reading it kept me sane all those long, sleepless nights in the cold. I was fortunate enough to be in an officer's tent, of course, where I could read by candlelight. The average soldier did not have such luxuries."

"How else did it save your life?" Lady Annabelle asked, her brow furrowed.

A humorless smile on his lips, David said, "It quite literally saved me from death. When the French captured me and a small group of my men, they began executing the officers. Only when they got to me, they rifled through my rucksack and when they saw the book, they realized I could speak

Spanish. That was of use to them, so they kept me alive as an interpreter."

Lady Annabelle gasped and cupped a hand over her mouth. "Oh, dear, now that you mention it, I remember Marianne telling me you were spared because of your ability to speak Spanish."

He nodded. "By giving me that book, my sister helped save my life," he breathed. "I'll be grateful to her forever."

"My brother saved me too," Lady Annabelle whispered, a faraway look in her eyes.

David was not certain he'd heard her correctly. "Pardon me?"

"Never mind." Lady Annabelle shook her head and replaced the stark look on her face with a bright smile. "I didn't mean to bring up such a sad subject. We have lessons to attend to. Shall we begin?"

"By all means," David replied, his smile equally as bright. He clasped his hands behind his back. He shouldn't have said so much. Lady Annabelle didn't want to hear poignant tales of battlefields and being a prisoner of war. No one wanted to hear those things. He turned to her. "What will you teach me today?"

She nodded. "I thought we'd begin with some rules of decorum. Would you like a pen and some paper to take notes?" She folded her hands together primly.

David nearly snorted. "Notes? Why would I take notes?"

She blinked at him. "How do you intend to remember it all?"

He pointed to his temple. "With my mind."

She gave him a skeptical look. "Very well, but there are a great many rules."

"How many?" He was beginning to feel as if he'd been shut in small space and couldn't breathe.

She ran a fingertip across one fine brow. "There's no defined number, but I do recommend taking notes."

He pursed his lips. "Try me."

"If you insist." She took a deep breath and settled her hands into her lap again. "Let's begin with general manners."

"Sounds delightful," he said, fluttering his eyelashes at her.

She lifted her chin, barely smiling at his playfulness. "Now then. First, a man never smokes in the presence of ladies. He may smoke with the other gentlemen after a dinner party when the ladies have left the room."

David cracked a smile. "What is the rule for a lady smoking in front of a gentleman?"

Lady Annabelle widened her eyes at him. "Well, for one thing, if a gentleman happens to be privy to such an event, he should never, ever, be ill-mannered enough to mention it, either to the lady herself or any of her relations."

David laughed. "I see. Very well. Duly noted."

Lady Annabelle nodded and continued. "You must stand sedately. You must not fidget, scratch, or otherwise act impatiently."

David pursed his lips. "What if I am impatient?"

"Pretend you are not," Lady Annabelle said, straightening her shoulders and sitting up even more erect in the chair.

David drew his brows together. "I don't like pretending."

Lady Annabelle lifted her nose in the air ever so slightly. "That's unfortunate. A great deal of the correct behavior in the *ton* involves pretending."

David rolled his eyes. "Why am I not surprised? Very well, no fidgeting. Go on."

She took another breath. "On the street, a gentleman always rides or walks on the outside of a lady so that she is protected."

David nodded. "That's easy enough. I've been doing that for years with my mother and sister."

Lady Annabelle nodded approvingly. "A gentleman should always bow to a lady before leaving, rather than simply walking away."

"Yes, Lady Courtney already taught me that one," David admitted, clearing his throat. "What else?"

"Let's see. Handshakes are permitted between men, but only if they are of equal class."

"That's ridiculous."

"I didn't make the rules. I am merely imparting them."

Another eyeroll. "Very well. What else?"

"A gentleman always waits for a lady to acknowledge him first with a curtsy and then he may tip his hat. But he must use the hand furthest from her."

David frowned. "What sense does that make?"

Her only answer was to arch a brow at him.

"Fine. Go on."

"It's considered ill-mannered to introduce yourself to someone. You must wait to be formally introduced by someone else. Especially if the person is of higher rank."

"How am I supposed to know who is of higher rank?"

"That will come in due time when we study *Debrett's*."

"Oh, God. What does that mean?"

She looked at him as if he'd taken leave of his senses. "*Debrett's Peerage of England, Scotland, and Ireland*? It's a book."

"And?" he prompted.

"It's a famous book. It lists all the peers, their titles, their marriages, their offspring. It's essential reading for anyone who aspires to be a part of London Society."

He crinkled his nose. "*Aspires* is far too strong a word. Perhaps I can skim it."

"Nonsense. Mama shall read it aloud. And we'll drill the names into your head."

David sighed. "I suppose that will help me not make a fool of myself the next time your brother takes me to the club."

"Oh, yes. All of the members of White's will be listed in *Debrett's*, you may count on it."

"Good, then I'll get to know all about Lord Murdock and his cronies."

"Murdock?" Apprehension skittered across her features. "You met Lord Murdock?"

"Yes, and I can't say it was a particular pleasure."

"He's currently considered the most eligible bachelor in London at the moment, you know?"

"Really? Is he?" The most eligible bachelor placing bets on the most unattainable debutante. David didn't like what he was hearing. "What makes him so 'eligible'?"

"Well, Lord Worthington and Beau *were* the two most eligible," Lady Annabelle replied with a smile. "But now that they are both betrothed, Lord Murdock is the most eligible."

"Eligibility having everything to do with loftiest title, I suppose?" David drawled.

Lady Annabelle nodded. "Yes, of course, but it's not just a title. It's also his family, his fortune, his wardrobe, and the fact that he's handsome."

"Is he handsome?" David nearly sneered. "I hadn't noticed." Murdock was detestable, and if he wasn't currently doing his best to be such a gentleman, David could tell Lady Annabelle precisely why he thought so.

"Don't worry," Lady Annabelle replied with a bright smile. "I have it on the best authority that there is another gentleman who just might rival Lord Murdock for most eligible this year."

"Who?" David asked, tugging nonchalantly at his cuff. It was all a lot of nonsense, at any rate. He wished for the hundredth time that he wasn't required to give a damn about any of this.

"You!" Lady Annabelle replied with a laugh.

David froze. "Me?" He pointed to himself. "Rival Murdock?"

"You're an earl, aren't you? Single, possessed of a hefty fortune, well-dressed," —she eyed him up and down—"and we've already established that you're handsome, though I hate to repeat it, as I'm certain it'll go to your head."

"Too late," David replied with a grin. "Though I had no idea I was considered a rival to Lord Murdock."

"You aren't," she clarified, "yet. But by the time Mama and I have completed your lessons, you will be."

Was it David's imagination or did she wink at him? The truth was, he wasn't at all certain he *wanted* to be a contender for most eligible bachelor in London. Though he supposed it was better than being the opposite. A sort of male wallflower. Was there a name for that? He was about to ask Lady Annabelle when she cleared her throat.

"As to that, we should resume our lessons. We don't have many more days before the Talbots' ball."

"Yes." David nodded. No doubt asking about male wallflowers would only result in him making yet another *faux pas*. "Now, where were we? I believe you were reciting an extremely long list of things that a gentleman must remember. Tell me, what are ladies supposed to be doing?"

Lady Annabelle smiled and fluttered her lashes at him. "Oh, there are even more rules for ladies, I assure you."

"Such as?" He lifted his brows.

"Such as, we cannot cross our legs. We cannot lift our skirts above the ankles. We cannot fail to acknowledge someone, unless we are purposely giving them the cut direct."

"It all sounds extremely tiring. And boring, if I'm honest."

Lady Annabelle gave him a conspiratorial smile. "Can I tell you a secret, Lord Elmwood?"

He leaned toward her. "Of course."

"I find it boring and tiring, too."

"What's this?" he asked with a smile. "The most popular debutante and the most novice earl have something in common? How can that be?"

She laughed and slapped playfully at his sleeve. "It's not such an outlandish turn of events, my lord. After all, I do hope that eventually you'll consider me a friend."

"A friend?" He arched his brows again. "If we're to be friends, I do believe we should call each other by our Christian names."

She narrowed her eyes on him and pressed her fists to her hips. "Are you purposely using my own words against me?"

His smile grew even wider. "Why, yes, I am. Friends use each other's Christian names, you said so yourself."

She pursed her lips. "Very well. I suppose we're soon to be related by marriage, also."

"Yes. Good point. Excellent. Now that we are established friends, I feel it's appropriate to point out that you never answered my question yesterday. Not directly at least," he said.

She arched a brow. "Which question was that?"

"Is the reason why you've not chosen a husband because you're in love with someone your brother won't approve of?"

She laughed and shook her head. "Is that the only reason you can think of why I wouldn't want to marry?"

"No. Not at all. In fact, I can think of a half a score of reasons. Would you like me to ask you each individually?"

"No!" She nearly jumped toward him.

He laughed. "Then tell me, why don't you plan to marry?"

She shrugged. "Marriage has more benefits for men than women."

He nodded slowly. "I cannot argue with that. But you are preoccupied with the rules of your social set, and it seems to me that getting married is highly valued in London Society. That is what the Season is for after all, is it not?"

"It's precisely what it's for," Annabelle replied. "Which is why we must get you prepared. Now, your sister gave me a list of the types of things you want in a wife."

David's brows drew together sharply. "My sister?"

"Yes, I paid her a visit yesterday," Annabelle informed him.

"You asked my sister and not me?" He pointed to himself.

She shrugged. "I am asking you now. I'm curious to see if the two sets of answers align, actually."

He grinned and shook his head. "Heaven help me. I don't understand females."

"Yes, Marianne mentioned that. A pity. We're quite easy to understand, you know. We simply want to be treated as human beings."

"Rather than prize hogs?" he asked, grinning at her.

"Exactly. Now, shall we begin? The first question is—"

"If Marianne told you my answers, I dare say I don't need to repeat them. She knows me as well as anyone, I suppose. But I'd be quite curious to hear *your* answers to the questions."

Annabelle stopped and blinked. "Wha…what?"

"What's the first question?" he asked.

"What is your favorite meal?" she breathed.

"Yes, well, go on, then. Answer it." He nodded toward her.

She frowned. "You want to know what *I* think about food?"

"Very much so. Food, politics, religion, the best color of drapes for a sitting room? Anything and everything."

She stared at the wall, a disoriented look on her face.

David winced. "Oh, no. Have I been rude again? Is it improper to ask you such things?"

Annabelle's ice-blue gaze met his and the look in her eyes was a mixture of confusion and…delight?

"You don't have to answer any of those questions if you don't want to, of course," he assured her.

"No, no. I'm happy to," she said, the adorable quirky smile popping to her lips. "It's just that…no gentleman has ever asked me any of those things before."

DAVID TOUCHED her hand and a spark shot up her arm, making her feel warm all over. She glanced up and his gaze captured hers. It was as if he were looking deeply into her soul. "What sort of books do you like to read, Annabelle?"

CHAPTER ELEVEN

"When exactly is the Talbots' ball?" Lord Elmwood—no, *David*—asked the next morning as soon as Annabelle had entered the salon. Mama was still abed with a megrim, so Annabelle had come down to meet him alone.

He was wearing a fitted dark-blue coat, white shirt, white waistcoat, expertly tied cravat, and buff-colored breeches with perfectly polished black boots. He looked as handsome as ever, and smelled heavenly too. Some mixture of soap and cologne that was making Annabelle's head spin. She'd told him he needed to take notes. Now she needed to, to keep to the subject at hand. Every time she glanced up at his dark-blue eyes, she inwardly swooned a little.

They'd spent the remainder of the morning yesterday talking. He asked her a variety of questions about herself, her life, her favorite things, and most special memories. To her own surprise, she'd told him. All of it. In fact, she'd been embarrassed when Mama had to come into the salon at noon to tell them it was time for luncheon. Lord Elmwood had refused the invitation Mama had extended for him to join them, clearly thinking he'd overstayed his welcome. Meanwhile, Annabelle had traipsed into the morning room for lunch in a somewhat hazy fog. She'd just had the most unique experience in all her social life. A gentleman had asked her about *herself*, beyond the usual pleasantries such as how she found the weather and if she was enjoying the opera. He'd asked real questions, and even more amazingly, had *listened* as she'd answered every single one. And David hadn't just listened, he'd listened *intently*, as if he was truly interested in the answers, as if he was hanging on her every word. It had been the most profound feeling, being paid attention to for more than her beauty. Speaking to David yesterday, she'd got the distinct impression that the man cared about her mind.

By the time it was over, she did think of him as a friend. Calling him David only seemed natural. Though she wasn't about to announce their agreement to Mama and Beau. Not yet. She'd wait till after Beau's wedding. Then perhaps it would seem less forward.

David had asked her a question just now. What was it? Oh, yes… "The Talbots' ball?" she replied, purposely glancing away from him, and placing a hand at her throat. "Saturday next."

"That means we only have a few days?" David clarified, his countenance draining of color.

"That's right."

David scrubbed a hand across his face. "Is there any hope I'll be ready in time?"

Annabelle cocked her head to the side and smiled at him. "There's every hope. Besides, if you do or say anything too egregious, we'll simply tell everyone it's the new rage."

He chuckled, the color slowing returning to his features. "Is that all there is to it? Why, if I'd known that, I wouldn't have been so worried."

Her brows shot up. "You're worried?"

He grinned at her. "You can't tell?"

"Not at all." She shook her head.

David expelled his breath while rocking back and forth on his feet. "I suppose after seeing war, nothing is as daunting, but make no mistake, I'd much rather be on a battlefield than meeting ladies at balls. I'm certain to make a complete cake of myself."

Annabelle frowned. "I cannot believe a man as handsome as you are would be worried about attracting ladies."

David cracked a grin. "Perhaps it's because a very attractive lady once read me the riot act in a garden."

Annabelle couldn't help but smile at the fact that he'd called her 'very attractive.' "But seriously, why would you be worried about meeting ladies?"

"I don't know," David replied, pacing in front of the fireplace. "I wasn't worried about meeting ladies in Brighton. But I won't be meeting ladies from Brighton at the Talbots' ball. I'll be meeting ladies from London."

"Ladies from London cannot possibly be much different from ladies from Brighton," Annabelle assured him, having absolutely no idea if she were speaking the truth. But regardless, the man was anxious, and she wanted to do whatever she could to make him feel more comfortable. Besides, how different could the ladies in Brighton possibly be? Marianne was lovely, and she was from Brighton.

"I knew the ladies in Brighton. I grew up with the ladies in Brighton," David continued, scrubbing a hand across the back of his neck. He was quite cute when he was nervous. "I'm certain to say something rude to a lady from London that will mark me a clod immediately. I'm likely to ask to borrow her finger bowl at the dinner table or something equally ill-mannered."

Annabelle eyed him carefully. He'd said it as if it were a

jest, but she sensed something deeper behind his words. Could it be that he was truly worried about the silly *ton* and all its nonsense? Why, this man had nearly given his life for his country. He spoke Spanish. He saved a baby hare. He was a better man than most of the fops and blowhards strutting around the *ton*'s ballrooms in their peacock-like ensembles, dandies who'd never performed an honest day's work in their lives.

"You'll do fine," she assured him. "Besides, I'll be there, and Mama and Marianne will be too. We'll make certain you don't make a cake of yourself."

David stopped and braced a hand against the mantel. "I appreciate your confidence in me, but I'm afraid my cakelike status is nearly inevitable."

"Please give me more credit, my lord. I am your tutor after all."

David dropped his arm and turned to look at her. "Quite right. I'm terribly sorry. Of course." The tension seemed to drain from him. He straightened his shoulders. "I do have the best tutor in Society. If you cannot help me, I cannot be helped."

Annabelle shook her head. "Nonsense. You can and you shall be a model of societal propriety. Today I plan to teach you how to ask me to dance, how to bow while I curtsy, how to take my hand and lead me to the dance floor at a ball. Tomorrow we'll move on to the actual dancing."

"Most of our dances in Brighton were public. Is there another way to go about asking at a private ball?"

Annabelle contemplated the question for a few moments. "First, you should know that you cannot ask a lady to dance without a proper introduction. But that shall not be a problem as Mama will be there to perform the introductions. And if Mama cannot, we shall employ the skills of Lady Talbot, as she is the hostess."

"Very well. That sounds reasonable." David smoothed his hand down his shirtfront once again.

Annabelle brought her hands together and folded them primly in front of her. "Now. Let's begin by you showing me how you would currently ask a lady to dance at a ball."

Nodding, David stepped toward her.

Annabelle sucked in her breath. He was only a pace away from her, towering over her and smelling so good, she wanted to bury her face in his neckcloth. She stared directly at it so she wouldn't be so distracted by his penetrating eyes. "Tell me. Did your valet tie your cravat for you this morning?"

David chuckled. "I don't have a valet. Can't quite wrap my head around the notion of someone dressing me each day."

Annabelle let out a small gasp.

David scrunched up his nose. "I suppose if I don't have a valet, it'll make me the most unconventional earl in town, won't it?"

Annabelle considered it for a moment. "I don't see why you *must* have a valet. But perhaps Beau can enumerate their merits."

David sighed. "Believe me. He's already tried. Instead, I tipped his man to show me how to tie several of these ridiculous knots in my cravat."

"You must be a quick learner. It looks perfect." She gulped.

"I was an army man, not a navy man, but I suppose tying a knot or two isn't terribly difficult. And if I'm doing it correctly, perhaps I don't need a valet after all." He winked at her.

He most certainly was doing it correctly. He looked like a dream, and smelled like one, too.

She swallowed and stared at his cravat again. "Go on,

then. Pretend I am a lady on the sidelines of a ballroom. Ask me to dance."

Clearly quite willing to play the game, he walked away, nearly to the door of the salon, turned, and came striding back toward her, staring at her intently as he made his way to her side. For a split second, Annabelle wished they truly were at a ball, and he truly was about to ask her to dance. The fops who usually asked her to dance never looked that focused on her, and so intent to win her over. But he was *pretending*, she had to remind herself. This was merely a lesson.

"I'm assuming we've already been introduced?" he asked.

At her nod, he nodded too, and said, "Very well then. Lady Annabelle, you look lovely this evening. Would you do me the honor of dancing with me?"

He bowed, and she quickly sniffed his hair before saying, "Yes, my lord. I should enjoy that greatly." She lifted her skirts and curtsied to him.

He held out his arm, straight and firm, bent at the elbow. An excellent offering. Annabelle nearly forgot to tell him he must ensure she remained on his right.

Once her hand was firmly atop his sleeve, he led her to the center of the room, where he turned to her and pulled her into his arms as if a waltz were about to begin.

"We, ah, we'll practice the dancing tomorrow," she said in voice that sounded shaky even to her own ears.

"Yes, you said as much," he breathed.

All Annabelle could think of was his nearness, his scent, the feel of his muscles beneath his coat. His hand held hers tight, sending a tingling sensation all the way up to her throat. The other hand was on the small of her back, sending unfamiliar sensations zinging around back there, as well.

"Perhaps we should…try it again?" she finally managed, swallowing the lump in her throat his nearness had caused.

"Try what?"

"You, er, you asking me to d…dance?" When in heaven's name had she become tongue-tied?

When he'd touched her. That's when.

"Oh, yes, of course." He dropped her hand and pulled his other from her back, stepping away, and leaving her feeling bereft. She watched as he made the short journey back toward the door and then she returned to the place she'd previously been standing.

He came walking toward her again, the hint of a smile on his face this time, and Annabelle's heart fluttered. He was going to touch her again, and she was greatly looking forward to it. She smiled to herself as the most delicious thought entered her mind. She could tell him they needed to try this no less than a half dozen times if she chose. He needed practice, after all, didn't he?

Oh, this would be a fun morning. A fun morning, indeed.

CHAPTER TWELVE

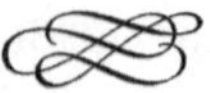

The next morning, while Lady Angelina read aloud from *Debrett's* book of the peerage, David danced with Annabelle. He didn't need much in the way of dance lessons. If there was one thing his mother had taught him, in addition to languages, arithmetic, maths, literature, and science, it was dancing. His parents had loved to dance. They danced all over the house to songs they hummed. Sometimes Mama would play the small pianoforte in the corner of their cottage. Sometimes Marianne would play it, but no matter what, there had been dancing in the Ellsworth home. David hadn't told Annabelle that he was already proficient in dancing. First, that would seem like bragging, and second, he wanted her to be the judge of his dancing skill. For all he knew, dances in London weren't done the same way.

"You're quite good at this already, you know?" Annabelle said as he spun her around to a waltz she was humming.

David breathed a sigh of relief. "Thank goodness. That makes one thing I'm proficient at," he said as they continued their three-step count.

"Not just proficient, Lord Elmwood," Mama interjected. "Good. Quite good, indeed. I've seen few gentlemen who are as graceful as you are at the waltz."

David smiled at that news. It was the first time he'd felt as if he were worth a damn as an earl. He'd been listening to Lady Angelina recite titles all morning until his head was spinning. There was little hope he'd remember all that nonsense. The layout of battlefields, the planned attack, the coordinates of the enemy, those were things that stuck in his memory as if he could see them written upon a page. But all of these lessons on manners and titles and the proper fork to use when there were five sitting on the table, such things flew from his mind like bits of gossip Marianne repeated from his Aunt Emily's letters.

He glanced down at Annabelle. Did she regret volunteering to teach him how to be an earl? Yesterday, they must have practiced his asking her to dance over half a dozen times. He clearly hadn't got it right, because each time he led her to the pretend dance floor in the middle of the salon, she asked him to try again.

Poor girl. He'd been in danger of wearing a hole in the floor yesterday. Today, Lady Angelina had ordered the butler to bring in a special round rug, which they were using as their makeshift dance floor.

Annabelle was kind. She didn't have to take time out of her no doubt busy schedule to teach him to go about in Society. He owed her a favor. Actually, more like he owed her a half a score of favors, but he would start with one.

A knock sounded at the door and the butler stepped in.

"Keep dancing," came Lady Angelina's directive as the butler cleared his throat.

"My lady," the butler said, "it seems there's a slight problem at the door with the flower deliveries."

"A problem, Stockton?" Lady Angelina asked, her brow furrowed.

"Yes," the servant replied, looking sheepish. "The line to deliver flowers is so long two of the delivery boys have got into a tussle in the street. They are demanding to see the owner of the house."

"Are you quite serious, Stockton?" Lady Angelina replied, shaking her head. "Well, Beau is gone on business, so I'll go out and see to it."

"Would you like me to take care of it?" David called, pausing in the dance. A lady of Bell's mother's age and station shouldn't have to break up a street scuffle.

"No. No," Lady Angelina said, waving a hand in the air as she stood and made her way toward the door. "Dance. Dance and make conversation as you would if you were at a real ball. I'll be back shortly."

The door closed behind Lady Angelina and David resettled his hand on the small of Annabelle's back. Annabelle glanced up at him. Was it his imagination or did she look… shy? No, that couldn't be. Annabelle wasn't the shy sort. But why did she glance down again nearly as quickly? And why did she seem to be staring at his cravat so much? After yesterday's lessons he'd begun to feel…warm when she'd placed her hand on his sleeve. Her nearness had caused him to breathe in the light scent of her perfume (orchids, perhaps?) and the soap she used on her hair. By the time he'd escorted her to the dance floor for the seventh time, it had been so hot in the room he'd been about to pull off his blasted cravat.

It was ridiculous to be thinking such thoughts about Annabelle. Annabelle was…his friend. A gorgeous friend, perhaps, but it wasn't as if he had never seen a beautiful woman before. She was helping him learn how to properly court a woman, and meanwhile he was having a host of inappropriate thoughts about her that involved glancing far too often at her *decolletage* and clenching his jaw. He'd gone home last night and taken a very cold bath.

Today, it was worse, actually, because she was in his arms, and he'd been spinning her around and around while she prettily hummed the melody of a popular waltz. He had a perfect view of her *decolletage*. It took all he had in him to stare instead at a fixed point on the wall and when he did that, Lady Angelina kept telling him he should look into the eyes of his partner and make polite conversation.

"Don't worry about Mama," Annabelle said, pulling him from his thoughts. They continued their one, two, three steps even though Annabelle had stopped humming.

"I do hope she's all right. Should I go check?" He would love to have a reason to leave the room. Perhaps go in search of a block of ice to sit on.

"No. Don't worry. Mama won't brook any foolishness from the delivery boys. You may count on it."

David shook his head. "I suppose it was bound to happen at some point. A scuffle between the delivery boys. I mean, with that number of bouquets arriving."

Annabelle rolled her eyes. "It's a waste of perfectly good gardens, if you ask me. Besides, I'm certain the one causing the trouble is Lord Murdock's boy."

David's ears perked up. "Murdock? Has he been sending you flowers?"

"Every day," she replied with a sigh. "The largest bouquets are always from him. That's why his boy gets into fights. Whenever there is a larger arrangement, he tries to trip the boy who is carrying it. Quite silly, if you ask me."

David frowned. "How do you know about that?"

"Cara, my maid, told me. She talks to the footmen who've been out there watching the proceedings each day. A lot of foolishness."

"Indeed," David said, focusing on the innocuous spot on the wall once again.

"Well, I'd say you're so good at the waltz you could teach *me*," Annabelle announced, coming to a stop.

David pulled his arms away awkwardly and their gazes met before he turned away from her and quickly moved over to the mantelpiece to put some much-needed space between them. What was happening to him? It had been quite some time since he'd bedded a woman, but he didn't usually react this way to merely dancing with one.

"What's our next lesson?" he asked from the safety of the space about fifteen paces away from Annabelle. He was facing the opposite direction so she couldn't see him.

Annabelle cleared her throat. "I believe Mama intends for us to dance more tomorrow. The quadrille, the country dance, the scotch reel."

David closed his eyes. Lord, have mercy. He couldn't spend a third morning cooped up in this house with Annabelle, touching her. He'd go mad.

"I'm quite proficient at all of those dances," he announced. At least that was true. He said a quick prayer that his mother had trained him properly on the dances Annabelle had just mentioned. Devil take London if they danced them differently than he knew how. The waltz hadn't been different. It stood to reason the others would be the same, as well.

"I must say, I'm becoming restless being confined to this house. I'm used to being outside more than the lessons allow."

Annabelle's regretful voice met his ears. "Unfortunately, nearly everything I have to teach you is best done in a ballroom or salon."

He turned to face her, a grin on his lips. "Oh, come now. There must be *something* we can do that involves leaving the house. For a day, at least."

Annabelle appeared to be contemplating the matter for a few moments before her face lit up. "Very well. Tomorrow we'll go for a ride in the park. I'll teach you how to behave on a carriage ride while courting a lady."

David expelled his breath in a rush. Freedom. Sweet freedom. "That sounds perfect."

CHAPTER THIRTEEN

Annabelle was already wearing her traveling boots and pelisse when David arrived the next morning. She tied her bonnet beneath her chin, noting with a smile that he seemed positively relieved to see that she was still planning on leaving the house for once.

"We'll take Cara with us," Annabelle explained as David opened the front door for her. "After all, a young lady must be chaperoned at all times."

"Yes," he replied, nodding. "I know that from Marianne's adventures. But why isn't Lady Angelina coming?"

Annabelle sighed. "Poor Mama is out at the flower shops this morning, asking them not to deliver any more. She says the household cannot take it."

David glanced around the foyer still filled with loads of flowers in various states of decay. "I wondered why the delivery line wasn't as long this morning," he replied with a laugh. "And I cannot say I blame your mother for wanting it to stop." He helped Annabelle down the stairs, past a smattering of delivery boys holding flower vases, and out into the waiting coach. Annabelle's maid followed them.

Not half an hour later, Annabelle and David were in Hyde Park riding atop his curricle, while Cara sat properly in the back, tending to her sewing. The vehicle was clearly new, and the lovely horses pulling the thing were spirited yet well-trained. Annabelle couldn't remember the last time she'd ridden in such a fine vehicle. She directed David up a busy dirt road near the Serpentine until they came to a more private lane that led down to the water's edge.

David expertly maneuvered the horses along the narrow path. "Stop here," she called when they came to a spot where she knew they would have privacy to talk.

David brought the horses to a standstill, let the reins go slack, and turned to face her. "So, if I meet a lady I fancy at the ball, I should plan to ask her to go riding in the park the next day?"

Annabelle folded her gloved hands together in her lap. "Yes, well. First, you must ensure you've made her acquaintance outside of the ballroom. An introduction in the ballroom is fine for a dance, but to greet her on the street, you must pay her a call first and receive a proper introduction."

He frowned. "You must be jesting."

She gave him a sweet smile. "Do I look as if I'm jesting?"

"No." He sighed. "Very well, so I pay her a call, get a formal introduction, and then I may ask if she'd like to go for a ride in the park?"

"Yes," Annabelle replied. "A ride in the park, or to get an ice at Gunter's, or perhaps you could invite her and her mother to the opera or the theater."

David groaned. "I detest the opera."

Annabelle laughed. "So do I. But it's a highly approved outing. That is, of course, after you've received her parents' approval. Then, she must be chaperoned at all times—and you must know, the papers will report upon it immediately."

David's brows shot up "What? Why would the *papers* possibly care?"

"The papers are quite attuned to the Season in London. There are entire pages set aside for gossip and innuendo. You've already been reported on extensively this Season. You and Marianne. Don't you read the *Times*?"

David groaned again. "I read it. But Bell already warned me to steer clear of the gossip pages, lest I become tempted to find the authors of such pages and sock them in the jaw."

Annabelle laughed. "Yes, well, perhaps that's for the best, then. But let me assure you, yours and Marianne's arrival in London has been nearly the biggest story this year, next to Lady Frances's father, Baron Winfield, being arrested for treason."

"Yes, I was there for that," David replied. "Sad scene to see a traitor to his country."

Annabelle leaned toward him. She'd forgotten that part of David's rescue from the French prison camp involved Beau and Marianne capturing Baron Winfield. "Tell me, is it true that he and his mistress turned on each other at the end?"

David shook his head. "I seem to recall something like that, but honestly, I was so pleased to see Marianne and Bell, I don't recall many of the details. I hadn't eaten or slept in weeks."

Annabelle gasped, clapping a gloved hand over her mouth. "Weeks?" She'd had no idea his experience had been *that* awful. She slowly lowered her hand back to her lap. "I'm sorry you had to go through such an ordeal."

"Are you jesting?" David cracked a smile. "It was nothing compared to being forced to fit into London Society."

Annabelle shook her head and promptly changed the subject. "Come. Help me down. We'll go for a walk by the water."

David glanced about. "Is that usually how it's done…when riding in the park?"

"No," Annabelle replied, with a sly smile. "But you said you wanted to get out of the drawing room, didn't you? Besides, it's only you and me. No one will be the wiser. Cara won't say a word."

David didn't say another word, either. He hopped down from the bench and made his way over to her side of the curricle. He raised both arms to help her down.

Annabelle braced her hands on David's shoulders as he lifted her off the seat and placed her gently on the grass. When it was done, she was awkwardly staring up at him, her hands still atop his broad shoulders. Even through her gloves, she could feel his coat was not padded. More than she could say for a variety of gentlemen whom she'd danced with through the years. She gulped and snatched her hands away as if they'd been burned.

Placing both hands firmly behind her back, she turned toward the small dirt path that led to the water's edge. "This way," she offered, taking off at a decent pace. David gamely followed.

They made their way down to the water and both silently walked along the bank for a few moments. Reeds and trees blocked their view across the entire expanse. They were in their own private spot, where spring daffodils had begun to bloom, and bright green grass was shooting up all over.

David stopped. Bracing his legs apart, his arms folded behind him, he stared off across the expanse, clearly lost in thought. Annabelle tentatively watched him from several paces away. He looked so confident and certain of himself. Like an army captain, about to give orders to a group of men. His jaw was rock hard, and his eyes had narrowed on the horizon. The fact that he was anxious about attending a silly ball remained unbelievable to her. David had been involved in the things that *truly* mattered. He'd stared death in the face. There was no way the *ton* would break him. He was too strong. She could sense it. He would do fine.

She gave him a few moments of privacy before walking over to stand next to him. "A penny for your thoughts, my lord," she said softly.

He moved his hands on his hips, still staring out at the green water. "Honestly, I was thinking how much I'd like a cigar right now."

Annabelle laughed. "You know I don't normally smoke, don't you? I've been meaning to tell you the truth on that score for days now."

He arched a brow and smiled at her. "You could have fooled me after your performance in the Harrisons' gardens. You seemed to know precisely what you were doing."

She readjusted her bonnet, pulling tight at the bow. "I admit, I sneaked a cheroot from Beau's study a time or two, mostly because I cannot countenance the fact that women aren't allowed to do certain things based solely on their gender."

David pulled open his coat and retrieved a cigar from a pocket. "Would you like to share one now? I won't judge you for it."

She glanced around, feeling positively scandalized and a bit excited. "Should we dare?"

David shrugged. "I don't see why not. We seem to be quite alone here." He pulled a flint from his coat pocket and struck it against a rock near his feet to light the cigar.

"Ladies first," he said, offering Annabelle the cigar.

"No. No, you go ahead." She waved it away.

He shrugged again and took a long, deep pull from the cigar, closing his eyes and blowing out the smoke in the opposite direction from Annabelle. Then he offered it to her.

She took it apprehensively, feeling nowhere near as

confident as she had that night in the Harrisons' garden. It was quite different when one didn't feel as if one had the moral authority. Now she was simply a young woman standing near a lake in the light of day with a handsome young man, doing something illicit. A thrill shot through her. She loved that David wasn't appalled by the fact that she would smoke a cigar if given the chance. Holding the thick middle of the thing, she put it between her lips and sucked in. The heady smoke stung her mouth, and she blew it out with a long sigh.

"I'm trying to quit, for Marianne's sake," David said, as Annabelle handed the cigar back to him. "She thinks it's a nasty habit. She's probably right." He took another long pull and returned the cigar to her.

"Younger sisters can be pests, can't they?" she replied with a laugh, taking another pull herself.

David's voice was soft. "I'd do anything for Marianne."

Annabelle's mind flashed back to a vision of young Beau lying unconscious on the floor of Mama's bedchamber, bloody and bruised. "I know what you mean. Beau would do anything for me, too," she breathed, handing David the cigar again.

"I know I don't need these things," he said, lifting the cigar. "But…it's…comfortable. Familiar, I suppose. Makes me feel as if I'm back in the army. Where I belong."

Annabelle furrowed her brow. "Why do you say that? You belong here now, of course."

"Do I?" He looked at the ground, kicking at the grass with one boot. "I don't even know what 'here' is. It feels as if I'm playing dress-up, inhabiting someone else's life. I know how to be an army captain. I know how to be a woodworker's son. I have little idea how to be an earl."

Annabelle frowned. Sadness tugged at her heart. She'd never stopped to think about how different everything must be for David in London. He'd been an army captain, used to risking his life and sleeping in tents with only one book to read. Meanwhile, she and her set were sleeping in perfect peace, in luxurious beds with fine linens, with five-course meals and plenty of cream for coffee. David had been called away from everything he knew, everything he was familiar with, to come to London and be the Earl of Elmwood.

"I suppose it won't help to tell you it's much safer here," she offered with a small smile.

A humorless smile touched his lips. "It's safe here because of the men fighting out there." He looked off into the distance, taking another long pull from the cigar.

"Of course," she whispered. "Of course."

"Listen to me today," he said, turning toward her and shaking his head. "This is no doubt an inappropriate conversation for a supposed courting."

Annabelle nodded. "Yes, well. I would say it's probably not fodder for a *real* courtship, David. But I do understand. I've never had to leave everything I know and am familiar with, but I have spent my life feeling as if I don't completely belong here either."

Nodding, David offered her the cigar again. When she shook her head, he tossed it to the ground, rubbing it out with his boot. "Well, before we get back to the lesson, I'm hoping you'll allow me to show *you* how to do something for once, my lady."

She watched as he went off into a nearby copse of trees for a few minutes and came back with a thick stick.

"We have a retriever at our country house who can do that, too," she announced with a laugh.

He gave her an ironic stare. "I'm not done yet. In fact, I haven't even begun."

Annabelle watched him with a mixture of confusion and

curiosity. What in the world did he intend to do with a stick, of all things?

He fished in his inside coat pocket and pulled out a rather formidable-looking knife.

Annabelle's eyes widened. "What is *that* for?"

David grinned at her. "It's for whittling."

"Whittling?" Her eyes went wide.

"Yes, and woodworking. My father taught me. I can make all sorts of furniture and things. In fact, he and I once refitted the entire interior of a ship."

"Really?" she asked, cocking her head to the side.

He gave her a skeptical look. "You're thinking it's not a terribly useful skill for an earl, aren't you?"

"No, not at all," she replied. "I was thinking you never fail to surprise me."

He grinned at that, but kept his concentration on the stick and knife in his hand, where he'd begun carving.

"What other unexpected things do you know how to do, my lord?" she asked as she carefully picked up her skirts to climb over a fallen tree.

He glanced up from his work. "Shall we?" he asked, motioning toward the fallen log.

Her brow furrowed. "Shall we what?"

"Shall we sit? Here?"

"On this log?" she asked, pursing her lips.

He chuckled. "Never mind. I suppose a lady as fine as yourself would never do something as primitive as sit upon a fallen log."

"Now, wait a moment," Annabelle replied, suddenly quite offended that he'd think so little of her. "I was merely surprised because I didn't realize we were going to sit. I'm perfectly capable of sitting upon a log." As if to prove the point, she promptly lowered herself onto the log, allowing her skirts to fan out around her.

While he watched with a grin on his face, she pushed her legs out in front of herself and crossed her booted ankles.

"I thought a lady wasn't supposed to cross her legs," David pointed out.

Annabelle winked at him. "I won't tell if you won't."

He threw back his head and laughed at that before taking a seat beside her. His knees stuck out due to his height, but he continued diligently working on the stick with the knife.

"You never answered. What other things can you do?" Annabelle prodded.

He rubbed his chin with the back of his wrist and appeared to contemplate the question for a moment. "Let's see. I can cut down a tree with an ax to make lumber. I can raise chickens and pigs. I can make a fire with only a stick and a rock, though I do prefer a flint. I can shoot the button off a French officer's coat at fifty paces, and I can dance a waltz. But you already knew that last one." He winked at her this time.

Warmth shot through Annabelle's middle at his wink. The man was too handsome by half. And the things he'd said nearly took her breath away. How terribly unexpected of him. Everything he'd listed were all much more interesting than the things the gentlemen of the *ton* could do. Race a horse. Gamble. Drink heavily. Who cared?

"Those are quite impressive feats." She concentrated on her feet so she wouldn't swoon if he winked at her again. She'd never swooned before. She'd always thought it was silly. But then again, she'd never been winked at by David. The man's hooded eyes and chiseled jaw might make a non-silly lady swoon. Or at least *want* to swoon, and that wasn't good, either.

"In the army, I was known for being able to climb the highest tree and run the fastest," David continued.

"Yes, Marianne mentioned you were a fast runner." Hmm.

She had a scuff on her boot. She'd have to inform Cara when they returned home. What else could she distract herself with?

"Marianne told you that?" His brow was furrowed. He shook his head. "Regardless, something tells me none of those things will be particularly useful to me as an earl."

"You never know. As the Earl of Elmwood, you may be called upon to whittle something." She smiled at him.

He shrugged. "If I'm lucky." But there was a look in his eye that told her he meant it.

She leaned forward to catch his eye again. "You're serious, aren't you? You don't feel as if you have the skills to be an earl."

"I don't. You're teaching me everything I need to know. And everything I already know is useless."

"That's not true, at all." She studied his face. How could this man possibly think he was unworthy of his title?

"Isn't it? Aside from the waltzing, has there been one thing I already knew how to do? I know how to be an army captain. I don't know how to be an earl. I was never meant to be one."

She nearly gasped. "Of course you were meant to be one. You were born the eldest son of the former earl's only son."

David shook his head. "I may be an earl by rights, but that's not what I meant. I mean I'm not cut out for it. I don't think my father ever intended to tell me the truth. If I hadn't been a prisoner of war and found by the Home Office, I would still be in the army right now. That's where I truly belong."

Annabelle bit her lip. She wasn't certain what to say. She'd never been in such a situation, sitting next to a man with a title who wanted no part of it. In her world all the men with titles were like peacocks, strutting around with them, proud of them. Well, perhaps Beau and his friends weren't overbearing about *their* titles, but they certainly understood their duty, and didn't want to renounce their positions.

"Perhaps it was meant to be," she finally said softly. "Perhaps everything that happened has led you back to who you were meant to be."

He gave her a wan smile. "Thank you. For trying to make me feel better." He cleared his throat. "That's quite enough about me. What are *you* good at, my lady?" he asked, his knife flying over the stick, while bits of bark and thin pieces of wood flew off it.

She laughed. "Oh, I'm ever so accomplished," she batted her eyelashes at him so he'd know for certain she was jesting. "I can do all the things a young lady of good breeding can do."

"Such as?"

"I can play the pianoforte with reasonable skill. I can dance all the dances necessary at a ball. I can read and write. I can paint with watercolors. I can even do needlework both plain and fancy."

"Fancy, eh?" The smile he gave her made her knees wobble.

"Oh, yes, and on top of all of that, I daresay I'm an expert at the art of flirtation."

"Really?" His brows shot up.

"Oh, yes. I've been known to flirt with the best of them."

"Very well. If you were flirting with me, what would you say?"

She felt her cheeks heat. She couldn't flirt with *him*. Not with *him*. She was actually attracted to him. The whole reason flirting worked was because it meant nothing, one was only engaging in meaningless talk. Flirting with someone she actually wanted to kiss—oh, dear, she wanted to kiss him—was an entirely different proposition altogether. If it were possible to kick herself while sitting atop a fallen log, she would have done it. Why, oh why, had she mentioned flirting? In *his* presence?

"Oh, no, no, no, no, no," she breathed, feeling like a complete fool. "I...I couldn't possibly flirt with you."

"Why not?" He looked hurt. "Am I not the sort of chap you'd flirt with?"

Yes, actually. She plucked at the ribbon beneath her chin. "It's only that...flirting is best done at ball and parties, when I have a fan in my hand." Dear lord. That was perhaps the silliest thing she'd ever said.

"A fan?" He frowned. "What does a fan have to do with it?"

"Everything," she rushed to assure him. "I suppose that's yet another lesson for you. Fans have many subtle meanings."

Still whittling, David cocked his head to the side. "Fans?" The look on his face was beyond skeptical. He sighed. "I know I'm going to regret this, but go ahead and tell me. I'll do my best to try and remember."

Annabelle cleared her throat, and folded her hands in her lap, beyond pleased with herself for turning the conversation away from a demonstration of verbal flirting. "If a lady is carrying her fan open in her left hand, it means, come and talk to me."

His brows drew together in a thunderous expression. "Seriously?"

"Yes.

His eyes were narrowed. "How is one supposed to know the message is meant for him?"

"She will catch your eye," Annabelle insisted, plucking at the collar of her pelisse.

David frowned again. "Very well. What else?"

"If a lady carries her fan in her right hand in front of her face, it means follow me."

His brows shot up. "Really? What else?"

"If she carries it in the left hand in front of her face, it means she is desirous of an acquaintance."

"Left hand in front of face. I hope to remember that one, at least." He chuckled.

"If she draws it across her eyes, she is saying she is sorry."

He nodded at that, still focused on the stick in his hand.

"If she twirls the fan in her right hand, it means she loves another."

He winced. "Another good one to remember."

"If she drops it, she means to say that you shall only be friends."

His lips formed an O and he scowled. "Too bad."

Annabelle waved her hand in the air. "Fanning slowly means she's married, fanning quickly means she's engaged. And finally, if she touches the tip of the fan with her finger, she is saying…kiss me."

David's head snapped up. "Does *that* happen often?"

"I couldn't say—these are all more theoretical in nature. I, for one, rarely use my fan for anything more than cooling myself at the opera."

David laughed. "But you could be telling some poor chap across the way that you're engaged."

Annabelle laughed too. "No doubt I've done that more than once."

"It sounds like a lot of nonsense to me, but at least I'm done with my whittling project." David held up his creation and Annabelle realized that in the short span of time they'd been talking, David had fashioned a rudimentary flute out of the stick. He put the knife back in his pocket and lifted the flute to his lips and blew through the opening he'd made in the end. A high-pitched whistle came out and he played a little song for her using his fingers on the small holes he'd carved into the stick.

When he finished, she clapped and laughed. "Now, *that* is impressive. Any earl should be proud to have such a skill."

He stood, offered her his hand, and helped her to her feet before handing her the flute. Then he bowed. "For you, my lady. Thank you for teaching me all the things I need to learn. I can only hope I don't embarrass you and your mother."

"Nonsense," Annabelle replied. "You'll be a smashing success at the Talbots' ball."

CHAPTER FOURTEEN

David smoothed his hand down the front of his fine black evening attire for what had to be the hundredth time already this evening. He and Marianne were standing in Lady Courtney's foyer, where they'd come to escort Lady Annabelle and her mother to the Talbots' ball.

David had even allowed Bell to send over his valet to help him dress, on the chance the servant might know something David wasn't privy to about evening attire worn by gentlemen of the *ton*. Now he was outfitted in all black with a white cravat, shirt, and waistcoat, and according to Bell's valet, David was the image of a well-to-do gentleman on his way to a ball.

Bell was not with them tonight. He'd been called away on business for the Crown, which meant David was escorting all three ladies to the ball alone. Nausea had hit him earlier when he'd contemplated walking into a ballroom full of London's finest. They would all be staring at him, no doubt wondering how the clod from Brighton would behave in London Society.

He had no problem commanding a hectic battlefield full of soldiers with ease, but the thought of walking into a crowded ballroom filled him with dread. He smoothed his hand down his shirt for the one hundred and first time.

A sound at the top of the staircase caught his attention and he looked up to see Annabelle come floating down the steps toward him, several steps behind her mother. David had to do a double take. A lump formed in his throat. Annabelle was a vision. Tall and lithe like a swan, she was wearing a glowing golden gown that only served to make her blond hair shimmer in the candlelight. Her hair was pulled back in an elegant chignon, and gold and diamonds covered her throat, with diamond ear bobs and a diamond bracelet on her wrist. She shimmered like a goddess coming down from Olympus. When she reached the bottom of the staircase, she stopped directly in front of him.

"Close your mouth, then," Marianne whispered in his ear.

He immediately snapped his mouth shut while Marianne and Lady Angelina traded greetings. David greeted Lady Angelina as well before turning to face Annabelle.

"You look lovely," David finally said to her, knowing the word was inadequate.

"Well," she said, returning his smile, "seems I've taught you how to flatter a lady properly."

"No flattery involved," he replied. "You truly are a vision."

"You look quite handsome yourself," Annabelle replied, eyeing him up and down.

"Thank you, my lady. I hope I'm somewhat worthy to escort such a beauty to a ball."

Marianne and Lady Angelina exchanged a look, while David took Annabelle's arm and escorted her outside. At least his carriage was on point. His grandfather had been rich, there were no two ways about it. And since David had taken over the title, Bell had helped him by giving him the name of London's finest coach outfitters. In addition to purchasing the new curricle, he'd had the entire interior of his grandfather's finest coach redone with deep sapphire velvet upholstery. He'd installed the shining mahogany woodwork himself, but only because he wanted it to be perfect, not to save money. If he wasn't confident in his actions, manners, and speech while making his debut to the *ton*, at least he could be confident in the quality of his clothing and his belongings.

With the help of the two footmen who'd accompanied the coach, David helped the three ladies to alight before pulling himself up into the conveyance and taking a seat next to Annabelle. Marianne and Lady Angelina had sat together across from them.

"I must say, you two make a gorgeous couple," Marianne said as the vehicle took off down the street. "All of London will be jealous of the two of you."

"Yes," Lady Angelina agreed. "Our little party may start some gossip tonight."

"What gossip?" David asked, suddenly apprehensive. He knew enough to know that gossip was bad. He wasn't looking for himself or any of his companions to be the subject of gossip tonight.

"Oh, I'm only teasing," Lady Angelina assured him with a soft smile. "I meant that since Annabelle is unengaged and so are you, some people may wonder if you're…together."

David settled back into the seat a little easier. "I would be flattered to start such gossip," he replied with a chuckle.

"Oh, no, no, no," Annabelle said, "that wouldn't do at all. Why, I've spent all afternoon planning which ladies to introduce you to this evening. We don't want them to think you fancy *me*, of all people."

"Ladies? Do tell? Who have you decided upon?" Marianne asked, clasping her hands together with obvious glee.

Annabelle gave all three other occupants of the coach a conspiratorial smile. "I've decided on Lady Elspeth Morgan, Lady Titiana Homer, and Lady Heloise Maitland."

One of Lady Angelina's golden brows shot up. "Lady Elspeth, really? That's a surprising choice."

Annabelle frowned. "Not really. Not when you consider she's already rumored to be the Season's best catch. I expect Lord Elmwood here to be the most sought-after bachelor, and there's no better way to make that happen than to pair him with the most sought-after debutante."

"I thought *you* were the most sought-after debutante," David said, grinning at Annabelle.

"He has you there, Annabelle," Lady Angelina replied with a knowing smile.

"I may be sought after," Annabelle replied with a sigh, directing her reply to her mother, "but I've been out for five Seasons. Lady Elspeth is the best chance Lord Elmwood has at catching the *ton*'s attention immediately." She gave David a self-assured smile. "Leave everything to me."

Two hours later, Annabelle had introduced David to all three of the young ladies she'd mentioned in the coach. Then she'd been forced to watch while he danced with each of them in turn. Of course, Annabelle had been asked to dance by a half-dozen of her regular suitors, including Lord Murdock, who was particularly officious this evening. But she'd turned them all down to stand with Marianne, drink lukewarm champagne, and watch as her charge, David, made a smashing success of himself at the Talbots' ball.

He truly was handsome. That was simply fact. Why, he'd nearly taken her breath away tonight when she'd seen him at the bottom of the stairs. He'd been standing there wearing all black and white, his sapphire eyes glowing in the shadows of the foyer. Tall and muscled, his jawline bold, his shoulders square, he'd never looked more alluring. If he was apprehensive, it didn't show. The man knew precisely how to hide emotion. A skill that would do him well as a member of the *ton*.

Adding to her dismay, Annabelle had hardly been able to take her eyes off him all evening. In addition to his good looks, he was so unlike the other stuffed shirts in the ballroom. Half of them were wearing bright peacock blues or royal-looking purples, for heaven's sake. They came buzzing around, smirking, preening, and trying to impress her with their golden snuff boxes and jeweled rings. David didn't wear any rings, and she seriously doubted he owned a snuff box, golden or otherwise.

He stood out not only due to his height and sophisticated fashion, but he was also *debonair*. The man had a mild manner yet a commanding presence that made you want to speak to him. Made you want to stand next to him and be in his company. He didn't have to be the center of attention in every conversation. She soon learned he made his mark by being affable and steadfast, offering a clever remark or a witty response that was never at the expense of another in the group. He was kind, she realized. Kind and classic. A perfect partner.

Annabelle forced herself to take her eyes off David's dance with Lady Heloise to scan the ballroom. Lord Murdock was staring at her like she was a prize mare at Tattersall's. She should have remembered this Season she had Lord Murdock to deal with. The flowers he'd sent were just the start of it. The Marquess of Murdock had been the purported catch of the last few Seasons. He'd finally offered for Lady Julianna Montgomery, who had eventually tossed him over for the Duke of Worthington. Now that Murdock was back on the market, the marquess had apparently taken Annabelle in his sights. He'd been after her during her first Season, but she'd managed to stave him off. The man was handsome with dark-blond hair and dark brown eyes, and he was certainly well-dressed, but every time she spoke to him, he seemed…petulant, self-obsessed. No. She was definitely not interested in the marquess. But he wasn't one to quietly go away. She would have to fend him off at every turn.

Quickly averting her gaze from Murdock, Annabelle glanced over to see David escort Lady Heloise back to her mother's side. Lady Heloise was smiling up at him as if David was a Greek god and she, a mere mortal. Good heavens. Annabelle had picked Heloise because she was supposedly demure and well-mannered, but at the moment the lady was making a cake of herself. Annabelle seriously doubted David would be impressed with such a girl. After all, he'd said himself he was interested in true love. Lady Heloise seemed the type who'd declare her undying love after a ten-minute dance. Far too clinging.

Perhaps Lady Titiana would prove to be the best choice. She'd clearly been interested in David. Annabelle noticed the sparkle in the young woman's eye when she'd been introduced to him by her mother, though she had played it much cooler than Heloise. Lady Titiana nodded and smiled and declared how pleased she was to make David's acquaintance, but she hadn't nearly tackled him the way Lady Heloise had. Annabelle hadn't mistaken the look of obvious interest on Lady Titiana's face when David had turned away after meeting her. She might well be a viable choice.

Lady Elspeth, however, was already annoying Annabelle. She'd been the first one to be introduced to David, mainly because she and her mother had made straight for the earl and his party the moment they'd entered the ballroom. Lady Elspeth and her mother had swooped upon them, demanding an introduction and staying overly long, as far as Annabelle was concerned. Then Lady Elspeth had proceeded to laugh far too much for far too long at every clever thing David said, and she'd had the unmitigated audacity to reach out and *touch his sleeve*. His sleeve, for heaven's sake! What sort of hoyden was the girl?

As Annabelle had mentioned to David earlier, Lady Elspeth had unofficially been named the Season's best catch. When she'd made her debut in front of the queen, that esteemed lady had declared her 'ravishing.' And she was... with golden brown hair and pretty hazel eyes, Lady Elspeth was indeed a fine-looking young woman, and she certainly came from a good family. But Annabelle didn't like how Elspeth kept staring at David over the top of her champagne flute while he danced with the other two ladies. She eyed him with a sort of feral gleam in her eyes, like he was a fox and she the hound. There was nothing subtle about her.

Adding to the complexity, it wasn't only Lady Elspeth and Lady Titiana who Annabelle had to consider. There were all the other ladies who seemed to descend on David in droves, vying for an introduction. Why, she, Mama, and Marianne had nearly been knocked over by the hordes, for the first hour after their arrival. Thank heavens David had already met most of the young ladies at this party or they might still be fighting them off.

Annabelle had turned to look for David again when Lady Elspeth stepped in front of her. Annabelle instinctively stepped back. "Lady Elspeth, ah, good to see you again. What brings you over?" She did her best to paste a smile on her face as she pressed a glove to her diamond necklace.

Lady Elspeth gave her a narrow-eyed once over.

"Lady Annabelle," the younger girl began in an overly confident voice. "I was hoping you'd take a turn around the room with me."

Annabelle gave her mother and Marianne a look that clearly said, 'save me,' but there was little they could do. Mama shrugged while Marianne mouthed, "I'm sorry."

"Very well," Annabelle finally said to Elspeth. What could the debutante possibly want to say to her? Perhaps she'd ask for some advice about how to handle the bevy of suitors the girl obviously was already acquiring. A group of gentlemen had formed near Lady Elspeth's mother and were staring over at them pensively as if disappointed that the lady had chosen to leave them.

Smiling obsequiously, Lady Elspeth hooked her arm through Annabelle's, and they began to walk together around the perimeter of the ballroom.

"You look quite lovely this evening," Annabelle began. "Your gown is beautiful. The green brings out the color of your eyes."

"Thank you," Elspeth said. They'd barely got out of hearing distance from Marianne and Mama when the smile dropped from Elspeth's face. "I have a question for you, Lady Annabelle."

The girl clearly wasn't one to waste time on pleasantries. "What's that?" Annabelle asked, trying to maintain her own smile.

"Is Lord Elmwood courting you?"

Annabelle was so taken aback that she nearly stopped walking. Never had anyone been so blunt with her about such a topic, especially not a younger unmarried woman.

"The Season has just begun," she started to say, trying to think of the best way to casually sidestep the overly familiar question.

"Everyone knows you've been the belle of the Season every year. *Until this year*," Elspeth said, a sly smile popping to her lips.

Annabelle arched a brow. "Because *you're* here now?"

Elspeth's smile widened. "Precisely."

"And you're hoping Lord Elmwood courts you?" Annabelle ventured, frowning.

Elspeth lifted her chin. "The papers are already hinting he may be the catch of the Season. If that's true, I want him."

Annabelle's nostrils flared. If she'd had any idea how calculating and cold this young woman was, she wouldn't have introduced her to David in the first place. "I hate to be the one to inform you, dear, but perhaps your mama has been remiss. Gentlemen ask the *ladies* if they are interested in courting, not the other way around. It's not a particularly fair arrangement, but's it's the way of the *ton*."

Elspeth stopped and pulled her arm away from Annabelle's. "I'm quite certain you don't miss my meaning. Lord Elmwood is the Season's catch as far as bachelors go, and I am the Season's catch of debutantes. We're clearly meant to be together."

Annabelle had to struggle to keep her face blank. The chit was mad. It was as if she was trying to claim David. As if such a thing were possible.

"Besides," Elspeth continued. "Everyone knows you've been dead set for years now on becoming a spinster. You cannot possibly mean to finally go husband-hunting this Season."

Annabelle's hands clenched into fists at her sides. Her palms tingled. She'd like nothing better than to slap the impertinent young woman—but that would be unseemly. And Annabelle was not new to the intrigues of the marriage mart, even if they weren't usually quite this egregious. No. The best way to handle a schemer like Elspeth was to make her worry.

"Perhaps the choice of gentlemen in the other Seasons wasn't to my liking," Annabelle said, ensuring a sly smile spread across *her* face this time.

"Fine." One of Elspeth's golden-brown eyebrows shot up. "Then the game is on. I do hope you're not too *old* to handle it."

This time, Annabelle couldn't help herself. Her jaw dropped momentarily and her face heated. "You should hurry back to your mother, child. She might be looking for you."

Elspeth turned to look over her shoulder at her mother and the gentlemen who were patiently waiting for her. "Yes, along with half the eligibles in London. I do hope you've enjoyed your years as the most coveted debutante, Lady Annabelle. They've come to an end."

Annabelle glanced back at her own group, which David had just rejoined. "Good night, Lady Elspeth. I'll be certain to tell Lord Elmwood you sent your regards."

Elspeth narrowed her eyes on her, while Annabelle turned on her heel and walked away.

CHAPTER FIFTEEN

David watched as Annabelle came walking back toward where he stood with Marianne and Lady Angelina. He'd just finished dancing with the last of the three ladies they'd introduced to him. Annabelle was right. All three ladies were lovely and seemed clever and well-mannered. Of course, he would need to spend more time with each before deciding if he was truly interested in courting any of them.

Lady Heloise seemed kind and guileless. Lady Titiana was more reserved, but poised and witty. Lady Elspeth had seemed particularly eager to meet him, and appeared to know the most about him. She'd asked him more than one question about Brighton. She was probably the prettiest and most talkative of the lot, though her beauty didn't compare to Annabelle's.

"Did you enjoy your dances?" Annabelle asked him the moment she returned to his side.

David bowed to her slightly. "I did indeed. Were you dancing too?"

Annabelle poked a finger in her coiffure. "No, actually. I was taking a walk around the room…with Lady Elspeth."

David's brows shot up. "Lady Elspeth? Did she happen to say anything about me?"

"Ah, ah, ah," Annabelle said as she took a flute of champagne off the tray of a passing footman. David and Marianne did the same. "A lady never discusses her private talks with other ladies."

"I see," David asked, but he couldn't help but wonder what Lady Elspeth had said to Annabelle. Had she told her he was an unredeemable mess? He supposed that news would spread like wildfire through the ballroom if so.

"David," Marianne interjected. "Do you fancy any of the ladies you've met tonight?"

David took a sip from his flute. "Fancy them? I just met them."

Marianne waved a hand in the air. "I only meant do you find any of them to be particularly attractive, either in countenance or bearing?"

David shook his head. "They were all quite lovely. But for all I know, they don't fancy me."

"Don't be difficult, David, just answer the question," Marianne replied, a smile covering her face.

"Very well." David sighed. "Lady Elspeth impressed me. She asked me about my time in the army and our lives in Brighton."

Was it his imagination or did Annabelle frown? He was about to open his mouth to praise something about Lady Heloise but a familiar-looking man with dark-blond hair in fine-cut evening attire came striding up to them.

The man bowed to Annabelle. "My lady. Good to see you again."

Annabelle made a perfect curtsy. Her face remained completely blank. "Lord Murdock."

Murdock! Of course. He looked different in his formal evening attire, but he was the same man who'd been discussing the bets on Annabelle's marriage status at White's.

"I'd hoped you had reconsidered and would do me the honor of dancing with me, Lady Annabelle," Lord Murdock said.

Reconsidered? That must mean he'd asked Annabelle to dance earlier, and she'd turned him down. That was interesting.

This time Annabelle smiled at him prettily before saying, "It would be my pleasure, my lord."

Murdock gave them all a self-satisfied smirk, while Annabelle handed her champagne flute to her mother. Lady Angelina's eyes were wide as tea saucers watching Annabelle leave their little group.

David observed them with a decided frown on his face as they made their way to the dance floor. That blowhard had bet money on whether Annabelle would marry this Season. Did he intend to be the lucky groom?

The moment the couple began the waltz that had just begun to play, Lady Angelina turned to Marianne. "That's strange. I haven't seen her accept a dance with a truly eligible gentleman in an age."

"Really?" Marianne asked, her gaze glancing from side to side. "Do you think she's finally interested?"

Lady Angelina's eyebrows shot up. "I don't know, but Lord Murdock is considered by many to be the best catch in London, especially now that Beau, Lord Worthington, and Lord Kendall are all betrothed."

"Hasn't he been after her all these years? She's shown no interest before, has she?" David interjected, suddenly feeling out of sorts. He glared at the couple on the dance floor.

"He was recently tossed over by Lady Julianna Montgomery, who is now engaged to our dear Lord Worthington," Lady Angelina added.

"Oh, yes," Marianne replied, frowning. "I remember that name now. Julianna told me he threw a fit when she jilted him. He sounded quite unpleasant."

"It was quite a scandal last autumn," Lady Angelina said, nodding. Then she lifted her light brows. "But a handsome, rich marquess is always welcome back to the marriage mart. I do hope Annabelle has changed her mind about allowing him to court her. They make a lovely pair, don't you think?"

"They do," Marianne said, a wistful tone in her voice that David didn't care for.

He scrunched up his nose and narrowed his eyes on the couple. Unfortunately, there was no doubt they made a striking pair. Was it his imagination, or did the marquess miss a step in the dance? He clearly wasn't an expert at the waltz. Annabelle deserved a better partner.

Before he had a chance to examine his motivation, David pressed his glass in his sister's hand. "Hold my drink," he said, before stomping off in the direction of Annabelle and her marquess.

ANNABELLE DIDN'T KNOW exactly what happened, but one moment she was dancing with Lord Murdock, trying to remember precisely why she'd thought he was petulant, and the next she was in David's arms.

She blinked at him several times as if her eyes were playing tricks on her. "David, what are you—?"

"I cut in," he answered, pride in his voice. "Murdock didn't seem your match for a waltz."

She stared at him as if he'd lost his senses. "Didn't seem my *what*?"

"He missed a step," David insisted, leading her perfectly in the one-two-three cadence of the waltz.

"I didn't notice," Annabelle shot back.

"He also had his hand too far down your back."

"Are you mad?" She eyed him carefully. "One doesn't just cut in on a dance floor at a ball in London."

"Yes, one does, apparently. If one is *me*." He gave her a smug smile.

Annabelle glanced around at the partygoers standing on the sidelines. There were already people whispering behind their hands. She would have to work diligently to fix this after the dance ended. "Listen to me, David. Such things are not done. I didn't mention it during our lessons because it didn't occur to me that you might do something like this, but you simply don't interrupt a couple's dance."

David's face went blank. "Perhaps that's the difference between an earl born in a cottage in Brighton versus one born in London with a silver spoon sticking out of his mouth. I do what I please."

Annabelle glanced around again. In addition to the commotion they'd caused on the sidelines, now some of the other dancers were watching their conversation become more heated. This was not good, and getting worse by the moment.

Plastering a fake smile on her face, Annabelle lowered her voice. "Very well. We'll finish this dance, for appearance's sake. But we'll need to talk about this more tomorrow morning at our next lesson."

David plastered an equally false smile on his face too. "Oh, good. I cannot wait."

Annabelle kept the fake smile on her face as she allowed herself to relax into the waltz. Just as he'd done in the salon at home, David spun her around the floor as if he'd been born to waltz. A much more fluid and confident dancer than

Lord Murdock had been, David danced as if he'd invented the steps.

She tried not to notice how good he smelled, or the feel of his muscles beneath his coat or the heat spreading through her entire body from his hand touching the small of her back. She met his gaze and their eyes remained locked. For the remainder of the dance, it was as if the entire ballroom had fallen away and they were the only two people left in the world.

When the dance finally ended, David escorted Annabelle back to their group as if nothing untoward had happened at all.

Annabelle immediately began thinking of ways to mitigate the gossip. She searched the crowd for Murdock. How had he taken the slight of having been sent packing from the dance floor? Lord Murdock was already dancing with another young woman. Thank heavens. That would surely help. If the man was pouting in a corner, the gossip would be unmanageable.

Next, Annabelle again scanned the crowd along the sidelines of the dancing. How had the mothers and chaperones felt about David's cutting in? Was he already garnering a reputation as an ill-mannered clod? She desperately hoped the *ton* would be kind, and grant him some leniency. But when had the *ton* ever been kind, or ever granted leniency? Word of this social slight would be in the papers tomorrow, no doubt.

Lady Elspeth came sliding over to David just then and declared, "Lord Elmwood, you've made cutting in all the rage this Season. I do hope you'll pay me the same regard when next I'm dancing with another gentleman."

The other ladies and gentlemen, who had followed Elspeth and were hanging on her every word, all laughed and declared the same thing. By the time a quarter hour had passed, everyone was talking about either cutting into a dance or being cut in upon.

Annabelle stared with her mouth open at the people she'd known her entire life. In the span of one evening, they'd decided that both Lady Elspeth and David were to be emulated in every particular.

Nauseating, as far as Lady Elspeth went. But welcome and wonderful when it came to David. Annabelle nodded resolutely. Fine then. She'd done her duty. She'd set him off to a fair start. Why, he might already be the most eligible bachelor of the Season, and if he wasn't, he was well on his way.

Lord Murdock was finishing his dance with the other young lady and appeared to be headed toward her again. Annabelle previously may have had a momentary lapse in judgement in which she accepted his offer to dance, but she didn't relish an awkward conversation with him now. She retrieved her champagne flute from her mother and ducked to the side. "I'm going to take some fresh air in the gardens. I'll be back soon."

WATCHING ANNABELLE GO, David whispered to Marianne. "I don't think she appreciated my cutting in."

Marianne shook her head at her brother. "Are you jesting? You've started a new trend. And your first time at a London ball, at that." Marianne lifted her champagne glass in silent salute. "I heard no less than half a dozen young ladies say they hoped you'd cut in on their next dance partner."

"I'm done with dancing for the evening," David muttered, taking a reluctant sip from his glass.

"Don't tell the young ladies that," Marianne replied in a

singsong voice. "You want to be the catch of the Season, don't you?"

David shook his head. "This *catch* is going out for some fresh air, too, but not in the gardens. Far, far, away from the gardens, actually."

"Have fun," Marianne replied, still smiling.

David made his way toward the French doors on the far opposite side of the ballroom than the ones Annabelle had left through moments earlier. The last thing he needed was more gossip about himself and Annabelle. When he'd cut in on her dance with Murdock, David had merely been trying to save her feet from an incompetent dancer. That was all. But apparently, these people turned every small gesture into gossip. Annabelle had taken him to task for it. Fine. Next time he'd allow her slippers to be stomped upon. She'd chosen to dance with Murdock, hadn't she? Even though she *claimed* she had no interest in being courted. Why did she say one thing and do another? And even more maddening, why the bloody hell did David *care*? He tossed back the final bit of his champagne before taking a fresh glass from a footman's tray and leaving the ballroom.

The chilly spring night air hit David in the face the moment he stepped outside. He breathed it in gladly. It had become stuffy in the ballroom with all the candles, the dancing, and the bodies pressed together along the sidelines.

He sauntered across the verandah, and leaning his forearms atop the stone balustrade, stared down into the darkened landscape. The evening had gone well enough so far. The three ladies Annabelle had introduced him to certainly seemed promising. But if they were so promising, why weren't any of them the one woman he was still thinking about? A vision of Annabelle in her glowing golden gown and matching gloves danced through his mind. Her laugh. The tone of her voice. The elegant arch of her neck. The way her mouth quirked up in that endearing little smile. He couldn't stop thinking about any of it. Damned inconvenient. The woman had already made it quite clear that she was singularly uninterested in being courted. And if she were, *he'd* no doubt be the last man in London she'd be interested in, given his inexperience and lack of decorum. She'd just taken him to task for cutting in, for Christ's sake. So why was he standing here wanting to court her? Was it merely that he'd always wanted what he couldn't have? Or was Annabelle special? Unlike any of the other ladies in the stuffy ballroom. A breath of air as fresh as the ones he was inhaling at the moment.

A slight noise in the bushes below caught his attention and he leaned farther to see Annabelle herself walking in the darkened gardens. She was making her way to the nearby staircase that led up to him.

David briefly considered returning to the house before she made it up the stairs. That would be the right thing to do. The intelligent thing to do. But apparently, he was neither right nor intelligent this evening, because when Annabelle stepped onto the verandah, David was standing with his back against the balustrade, his arms tightly crossed over his chest.

"Lost?" he asked, smiling at her sweetly.

Annabelle lifted her chin. "There were too many people on the other side of the house. I was…looking for more privacy."

"Sorry to keep you from it with my presence," he drawled.

"We shouldn't be seen together," Annabelle replied.

David glanced around. "No one else is here. How would we be seen?" He gave her another patient smile.

Annabelle lifted her skirts and marched past him. "I'm afraid you don't know how the *ton* works. If someone were to happen outside and see us together, there would be gossip."

David stopped her with a hand to her shoulder. "There's already gossip," he replied. "And besides, I was under the impression that we'd have to be doing something compromising to be the subject of real gossip."

~

ANNABELLE INHALED SHARPLY the moment his hand touched her. She was staring ahead into the crowded, brightly lit ballroom, struggling against the desire to lean back against him.

"That's true," she finally allowed. "I suppose as long as we remain a decent length apart and are merely talking to one another..." She moved several paces away from him along the balustrade and turned to face him.

"Very well. You stay there and I'll stay here." He motioned to the distance between them. "Did you enjoy your dance with Lord Murdock?"

"You mean *before* you cut in?" She gave him a mock-sweet smile.

David's teeth tugged at his bottom lip. "Yes."

Why did he have to look so charming and boyish when he bit his lip that way? She struggled to recall why she was annoyed with him. Oh, yes. "Why did you cut in? And don't tell me that nonsense about Lord Murdock not being a good enough waltz partner."

David leaned his right elbow on the balustrade and shrugged his left shoulder. "Why did you dance with him? I thought you said you weren't interested in being courted."

Annabelle nearly stamped her foot. "One dance is a far cry from being courted. Besides I didn't think *you* would have even noticed, what with all the dance partners *you* had this evening."

David immediately stood up straight and narrowed his eyes on her. "Oh, my God. You're jealous?"

"What? No!" Annabelle wheeled around to face out into the darkness, bracing her forearms on the balustrade. She refused to even entertain that ridiculous notion. Jealous? Her? Madness.

He stalked toward her and stopped beside her, staring at her profile. "Yes. You are. You're jealous because I didn't ask you to dance."

Still facing the darkened gardens, Annabelle lifted her nose in the air. "I wouldn't dance with you if you asked."

"Why not?" he asked softly.

She lifted her gaze to the starry night sky while David moved even closer.

"Tell me something." His voice was husky, deep. It sent a tremor through Annabelle's center. "Aside from dancing and fetching drinks, would a gentleman ever have an opportunity to, say, *kiss* a lady?"

Annabelle kept her gaze steadfastly forward, but she had to swallow a lump in her throat. "Kiss? Absolutely not." Her voice sounded stern, but it shook slightly. She was nervous. He was making her nervous.

David leaned a forearm on the balustrade next to her. He reached out with his other hand and traced the skin just above where her glove met her bare arm. "Never?"

Annabelle swallowed again and straightened her shoulders. But she did not step away from him. Her blasted, traitorous voice continued to shake. "Not unless...they were alone together."

David looked pointedly around at the empty verandah before turning and setting his glass behind him on the balustrade. Then he faced her again.

Annabelle turned to him and tipped back her head to look directly up at David. Her heart was pounding like a hare's in a trap. Why did she feel panicked and thrilled at the same time? She had to keep talking. Talking would solve this.

Talking would keep this from turning into something it shouldn't. "If a gentleman were interested in a kiss from a lady, he should most definitely *ask* first," she said in a rush, looking away. Her body was hot and cold all over and, for the second time in her life—both, coincidentally, in David's company—she felt faint. No. This wasn't truly happening. David wasn't thinking of...kissing her. Was he? That would be madness. She'd lost her mind. That's all. Her mind was gone.

She made the mistake of glancing over at him again. She shouldn't have done that, because what she saw was David's tongue flick out to dab at the corner of his mouth. All she could do was stare, her own mouth going conspicuously dry.

"Ask first?" David said, his fingertip tracing down the length of her gloved arm to linger at her wrist. "That sounds like something a fop would do."

Annabelle shook her head, trying desperately to keep her voice from shaking more. "N...n...no. It's only courteous. What if the lady doesn't welcome your advances?"

What in God's name was wrong with her? She'd never been this skittish around a man before. Through the years, she'd sent well over a score of them packing when they'd become overly familiar. What made this encounter with David any different?

"I would never force myself on a lady who didn't welcome my advances." His fingertip moved back and forth across her knuckles.

It was only her hand, her *gloved* hand, but somehow his touch was melting her. Her heart pounded so hard it hurt. Her breath came in shallow pants. "Without asking her, how could you possibly know?" She wanted to sound confident and self-assured. Instead, her voice sounded frightened and squeaky.

Stop it, Annabelle. You're making a fool of yourself.

David arched a brow at her. "I think I can tell if a lady would welcome my kiss."

"That's arrogant," she insisted, lifting her chin in the hopes that the small action would restore her control of the situation. But she knew, had known from the moment she saw him on the verandah, perhaps from the moment he'd cut in on her dance with Lord Murdock so dauntlessly...the reason this was different from the other men who'd made unwanted advances was because this was David.

And his advances weren't unwanted.

"Perhaps it is arrogant," he replied, his voice slow and husky, "but there's only one way to find out." Clutching her wrist, he pulled her expertly into his arms and his lips came crushing down on hers.

CHAPTER SIXTEEN

Annabelle *should* push David away. She *should* slap him. She *should* tell him he was not only arrogant, he was wrong. But the moment his hot mouth met hers, all thoughts flew from her head. When his lips pushed hers apart and his tongue entered her, she whimpered. No man had ever done anything so bold. And she'd never wanted it more.

In response, she pushed her arms up along his coat front and wrapped them tightly around his neck. Then she kissed him back with everything she was worth.

He pulled her closer. His hands settled on her sides at first, then one moved along the small of her back, making her a puddle, before the other cupped the back of her head, moving it so her mouth made better contact with his.

When his other hand moved slightly below the small of her back and pulled her firmly against his rock-hard body, Annabelle cried out. The sound was swallowed by his kiss.

She'd never felt anything like it. Most of the clumsy kisses she'd experienced before were wet, sloppy things that left her cold. This was nothing but heat. She didn't know where to concentrate her pleasure, on his hand that cradled her head so tenderly, or the other hand at the small of her back driving her mad. Or the feel of her entire body plastered against his. Then there were her hands that had moved to his strong shoulders, while she breathed in the heady scent of him as his tongue owned hers.

They might have been kissing for seconds or hours. Annabelle was so disoriented that when David's mouth left hers, she was nearly gasping for breath. Her nipples tingled and the intimate spot between her legs throbbed. The only thought in her head…it hadn't been enough.

"Well?" he asked, stepping back, and straightening his jacket. He looked perfectly settled, but he was slightly bereft of breath, too. Good.

"Well, what?" she managed, her chest heaving, her gloved hand braced on the balustrade for balance.

He bit his lip and tilted his head to the side. "Do I owe you an apology for that?"

She narrowed her eyes on him. She wished she could breathe normally. She wished she could think normally. None of this was normal, and she'd never responded anything like that to any man. But at the same time, no man had ever kissed her like that before, either.

It was good. Better than good. She wanted to do it again. Immediately. But she'd die before she told him that. She searched her brain for the correct words. Something adequately tutor-like and condemning. "A gentleman should never take such liberties," she forced herself to say, pressing her lips together primly, trying to pretend as if they didn't still tingle from his kisses.

A sensual half-smile tugged at his lips. "I never said I was a gentleman."

"But you're trying to be, aren't you?" Oh, no. The squeak was back. Her voice was neither clear nor confident. Perhaps talking was not the answer now. Perhaps she should shut her mouth and run inside the house. That seemed far more expedient than words at the moment.

"Not if it means missing out on a kiss like that," he answered, rubbing a finger absently against the seam of his firm lips, as if remembering.

She tried to tamp down her answering smile, but it was too late—though she recovered herself enough in time to say what she knew she must. "That was improper, David. Of both of us."

"I was merely trying to prove a point," he said, tugging at his cuff.

She turned toward the darkened gardens so he couldn't see the riot of emotions that was surely dancing across her face. "What point would that be?"

"That I'm not a complete fool. I do know when a woman welcomes my kiss."

Her fingers gripped the cold balustrade, bringing a sense of sanity back to her entire body. Why was he pushing this so far? What did he want her to say? Anger flared in her chest. She turned to face him again. "Fine. I'm not certain why you'd want to prove that to *me*, however. Shouldn't you be kissing a woman you might actually marry?"

David's chin jerked slightly as if he'd been slapped. For a moment she thought she'd seen pain flash through his eyes, but his countenance quickly turned to stone, and he squared his shoulders. "You're right, my lady," he clipped. "I should go in search of Lady Elspeth." He stalked directly past her on his way back to the ballroom, without giving her a second look.

CHAPTER SEVENTEEN

After taking a few minutes to compose herself, Annabelle had nearly made it to the French doors to re-enter the ballroom when one of them opened and Lord Murdock slid outside.

"My lord?" she said, surprise evident in her voice as she took a decided step back.

"My lady," he replied, bowing obsequiously, his smile tight.

Annabelle didn't care for the glint in his eye. "I was just about to return to my mother—" she began.

"Yes." He slipped an arm through hers and forced her to walk with him back toward the balustrade. "All in due time. First, I was hoping you'd allow me to speak with you privately for a few moments."

Annabelle glanced back at the doorway they were moving farther and farther from. A shudder traced its way up her spine. Whatever Lord Murdock wanted to say to her, it wasn't something she wanted to hear. She could sense that.

"Only for a moment," she insisted, trembling. "I really must get back."

As soon as they made it to the balustrade, Lord Murdock let his arm fall away. He stood between her and the French doors, blocking her view of the ballroom. The glint in his eye turned harder. "You don't know me very well, Lady Annabelle," the marquess began.

Annabelle nodded, her heart pounding. "No," she agreed. What was he about?

"If you did know me, you would know that I am not a man to be trifled with." His jaw was tight and for the first time, she saw anger simmering in his dark eyes.

Annabelle clutched the balustrade to steady herself. She hoped Lord Murdock couldn't tell that her entire body was shaking. "Have I done something to offend you?" she forced herself to ask in a clear, steady voice, but panic was clawing at her middle.

The marquess's dark eyes narrowed on her. "Not returning my calls, not sending thank you letters for my gifts, and allowing that buffoon from Brighton to cut in on our dance just now. I fear you've offended me many times over, *my lady*."

Annabelle sucked in her breath. She'd had no idea he'd been harboring ill will toward her, and she certainly didn't like the way the man said 'my lady.' It was as if he was claiming her for his own. "I certainly have never meant to offend you," she replied. She didn't need a powerful enemy like the Marquess of Murdock—but she refused to be berated by this man.

She made to step past him toward the ballroom. His hand shot out to grab her wrist, twisting it slightly, hurting her. She froze but refused to allow him to know she was in pain. "Have you something else to say?" she asked, her nostrils flaring. How dare this man accost her in this manner? She owed him nothing.

"Indeed, *my lady*," he ground out. "It's something important, so listen well."

Annabelle tried to wrestle her wrist from his grasp, but that only served to tighten it. She clenched her jaw and refused to look at him as he brought his mouth close to her ear. "I saw you kissing Elmwood just now," the marquess hissed. "And I can go straight back into that ballroom and tell everyone who'll listen, which will all but force you to marry him. Or…"

Fear and anger flared in Annabelle's chest. Damn this monster. He was about to blackmail her. She closed her eyes, waiting for his next words. "Or what?" she nearly spat.

"Or, you can come back inside and dance with me and *finish* the dance this time. And you can return my calls, and thank me for my presents, and allow me to take you riding in the park."

Annabelle clenched her teeth. The man was completely mad. What could he possibly think the result of this scheme would be? "I suppose next you'll demand that I marry you?" she asked in a voice that was much calmer than she felt.

"All in due time, my lady. For now, I'll thank you to stop acting as if I'm bothering you. I've spent long enough trying to do things the right way."

"What is that supposed to mean?" Annabelle asked, half-afraid to hear the answer.

"Let's just say I happen to have quite a lot of money riding on the hope that you'll finally come down off your high horse and marry this Season. Marry *me*, in fact."

Her nostrils flared. "You're insane."

"No. I'm a man who is tired of being at the beck and call of every simpering debutante who's named the catch of the Season. Lady Julianna tossed me over last year. I refuse to be humiliated again."

Annabelle wrenched her wrist from his grasp and this time he let her go. He gave her a tight smile and smoothed his coat front. "I'll see you back in the ballroom, my lady. And this time we shall dance a full dance."

CHAPTER EIGHTEEN

"What is today's lesson?" David asked the next morning as he stared out the front window of Bell's town house. He'd heard Annabelle come into the room behind him, but he hadn't turned around. If he turned around, he would see her, and if he saw her, he'd want to kiss her again, and *that* was something he couldn't allow himself to do. Not after her cold reaction last night. Well, to be fair, her reaction had been *hot* at first. So hot he'd had the passing thought that if circumstances were different, he could have taken her right there on the verandah, with her sitting atop the balustrade, her long legs straddling him, knees hugging his hips, while he slowly pumped into her. *Damn.* He shook his head. That wasn't a helpful thought.

Last night when he'd left her outside, he'd been angry, though he had no idea why. Something about the way she'd dismissed his kiss, after obviously enjoying it, had put David out of sorts. Not only had she dismissed the kiss, he'd also seen her dancing with Murdock again later that night. And she'd just told *him* a few days ago that when a couple danced more than one dance at a ball, rumors of their fondness for one another were soon to follow.

David had briefly considered asking her to dance once more with him, but he'd decided against it. No doubt she'd turn him down, and if she didn't, well, he hadn't had the heart to be charming any longer.

They'd ridden home with Marianne and Lady Angelina in nearly complete silence while poor Marianne had attempted to punctuate the silence with an opinion or two on the ball and its guests.

Now he was standing here, in Bell's town house, refusing to face Annabelle as she stood behind him.

"It's customary to bow when a lady enters the room," came her clipped voice.

Slowly, he turned to face her. She was wearing a light blue day dress and white kid slippers, with pearls at her throat and her ears. Her hair was curled into a short bob at the back of her head, and she looked as beautiful as ever, though she wore a decidedly pinched look on her face. Even so, David felt his body's reaction to her. He turned sharply to the side. "Is it? How *gauche* of me. I'm obviously in need of more lessons." He bowed. There. That had been *blasé*, hadn't it? Not at all like a man who was even now remembering their kiss so vividly it physically hurt.

She crossed her arms over her chest and glared at him. "I *would* say that today I should teach you not to take liberties with ladies on verandahs, but it's too late for that."

He winced slightly and turned away from her again, closing his eyes, grateful she couldn't see his face. "Don't worry," he ground out. "I've learned that lesson well."

"So you *didn't* kiss Lady Elspeth last night, too?" Her voice went up an octave.

David's brows snapped together. What the hell would make her think that? Gaining control over himself finally, he turned to face her once again. He put his hands on his hips and cocked his head to the side. "What do you think?"

She moved farther into the room toward the settee, not meeting his eyes. "I've no idea what you'll do one moment to the next."

"That makes two of us."

Her nostrils flared. "What is that supposed to mean?"

David shrugged. "I saw you dancing with Lord Murdock a second time. Changing your mind about marriage?"

"That's none of your affair," she shot back.

The words stung. Like arrows to the heart. But after he'd absorbed the shock, David realized immediately that she was right. "Indeed," he said, nodding once, careful to keep any inflection from his voice. He stepped forward and clicked his heels together, standing at attention, like he'd done a thousand times in the army. He wasn't here on a social call. He was here for a lesson. She'd certainly never given him any reason to believe these meetings were anything more. "My apologies. What am I learning today, my lady?"

The tension drained from Annabelle's face, and she expelled her breath slowly as if she too realized they'd had an interaction they should never repeat. She turned back toward the door of the salon and said over her shoulder, "Come with me to the dining room. I've helped the servants to set up a *faux* dinner setting. Mama should be back from the milliner any minute. We'll talk about all the different courses and silverware and the proper etiquette for dinner conversation."

"Excellent," he replied, falling in line behind her.

David followed Annabelle out of the salon, down the wide marble-floored corridor, around a corner and into an enormous dining room. It was even larger than the one in his grandfather's—no, *his*—town house. Would he ever stop thinking of everything as belong to his grandfather? The coaches, the horses, the town house, the country estate. It all felt borrowed, borrowed by the imposter in a life he was pretending to have. Spending time with Annabelle was just another part of the ruse. Normally, he'd never have had an opportunity to spend so much time with a lady as lovely and accomplished as she was. He'd had no right to kiss her last night. But she'd looked so fetching under the moonlight and she nearly dared him to, by saying that a gentleman would ask a lady for a kiss. Why, the girls he'd kissed in Brighton…he'd never had to ask first. He bloody well knew they were interested. Of course, if they hadn't been, he'd have immediately stopped. He wasn't the sort of blackguard who would force any sort of intimacy on a woman, even a mere touch, let alone a kiss. He might not be completely schooled in the ways of London Society, but he knew when a woman wanted him, and he'd seen the look in Annabelle's eyes last night when they'd danced, felt her hand tighten on his arm, seen the desire in her eyes when she'd looked up at him in the garden, and heard the tremor in her voice when he stepped near, touched her. They wanted each other. Perhaps it was wrong. It was certainly inconvenient. But they were attracted to each other, and there was something in the way that she kept denying it that made him want to test her.

Why in the bloody hell had she danced with Lord Murdock twice last night? According to her mother, it was completely out of character for her. Was Murdock such a catch or…was Annabelle trying to make David jealous?

Or was he just a fool who had imagined all of it? Damn. Perhaps he owed her an apology.

David glanced around the dining room. The table had been laid as if a large dinner party was going to be held there. The sixteen-person table was filled with a variety of dishes, plates, cups, glasses, bowls, utensils and serving ware. Not to mention napkins, tureens, platters, knives, linens, and tablecloths.

"You can't just have a simple dinner in the *Beau Monde*, can you?" he asked, shaking his head.

"No," she replied, with a short, sweet smile. She spread her hand in front of her as if presenting him the dining table. "Now, we'll begin with the basics. I'm certain you already know that guests queue up in the salon in order of rank for a dinner party."

"Yes, that much I knew."

She nodded. "You're an earl, so that means you'd only ever come after a duke, a duchess, or a marquess or marchioness."

"That's what I understand," he said with a sigh.

"If there was no female of your station at the party, you'd escort the female with the next most prestigious title into the room."

"Understood," he replied.

"I am the daughter of a marquess, so I would enter the room as if I hold that title."

"If you were to marry Murdock, you'd retain that position." The moment he said the words, David wanted to kick himself.

She nodded again, a blank look on her face. "Yes. If I were to marry Murdock, I would become a marchioness and would be even more powerful than the daughter of a marquess."

"Much better than a countess," he grumbled.

"What was that?" she asked, cupping a hand behind one ear.

"Nothing," he replied batting his eyelashes at her innocently.

She cleared her throat. "Once the couples enter the room, they are seated male, female, male, female. And depending on the type of dinner party, which is decided by your hostess, one speaks with either the people on one's left or right, or one speaks with those across the table. It's much more common to speak only with those on the left and right."

"I'm certain I've made that mistake," David said with a sigh. "In Brighton we speak to everyone at the table."

Annabelle folded her hands together primly. "That is not civilized. The conversation would quickly become unmanageable."

The sound that came out of his throat was half-snort, half-laugh. "I agree. It was often unmanageable, but always enjoyable. My parents rarely invited anyone to dinner who we didn't like."

Annabelle shook her head. "That is impossible. One must invite certain people to one's dinner parties, regardless of one's feelings."

She was speaking so formally. Quite unlike their other lessons. She was clearly trying to reiterate, after their kiss last night, that she was merely his tutor and he, her pupil. "What if one doesn't care for the company of those one must invite?" he countered.

She busied herself with straightening the already perfectly straight tableware. "Caring for their company is certainly not a pre-requisite for an invitation to a dinner party."

David rolled his eyes. "Let me guess what is…wealth, title, and status."

"Precisely. I do believe you're learning, my lord." Leaving off with the tableware, she splayed her hand toward one of the chairs. "Now, please take a seat at the head of the table. I'm going to show you how you should behave if this was a dinner party at your home."

~

NEARLY TWO HOURS LATER, Lady Angelina had yet to return from the milliner and David had learned the proper usage of every single implement on the table—and some that the servants brought up from the kitchen for show. He knew about *à la russe* and *à la francaise* dinner service, the proper usage of a finger bowl, the proper placement of a variety of confusing wine glasses, each holding a different type of wine, and how to gracefully end the dinner without a hostess. He also now knew far too much about the care and placement of napkins.

He and Annabelle had fallen into a sort of unspoken truce, where she only mentioned the lesson at hand, and he only asked questions about the same. It was far less entertaining than their previous lessons had been, but far more expedient, he supposed. He missed her laughter, her teasing him. But he supposed he couldn't blame her. He shouldn't have kissed her last night. That was all there was to it. It had only made things awkward between them. And made him want to kiss her again. Neither was good.

"Marianne should be your hostess until she is married. Then she will be the hostess here, as she will be Beau's wife," Annabelle said, interrupting his thoughts.

"And your mother will step aside?" David asked.

"Exactly," Annabelle replied. "Mama will be the dowager Marchioness of Bellingham once Beau and Marianne are married."

"Perhaps Marianne should be here too, learning all of this," David said, daring to crack a smile.

Annabelle's countenance remained completely blank and her back ramrod straight. "Lady Courtney is seeing to Marianne's lessons, and they are coming along nicely from what I can tell."

"Lady Courtney is an excellent teacher…as are you,"

David said, hoping the compliment might make her smile. Might make her seem more like the pre-kiss Annabelle.

"Thank you, my lord," she said, not even looking at him.

Damn. He did need to apologize again. Groveling was probably in order. "No, thank you, Lady Annabelle. I owe you an apology for my behavior on the verandah last night."

"I should have slapped you," she said calmly, smoothing a hand over a napkin that sat on the table in front of her.

His brows shot up. "Did you *want* to slap me?"

"No," she admitted with a slight smile. "But to do otherwise was to encourage your behavior."

David expelled his breath. Oh, she didn't have to worry about that. He was far from encouraged. "What if I promise never to do it again?"

Annabelle stood and walked to the door. "I would say you shouldn't make a promise if you're not completely certain you can keep it."

Before David had a chance to react to *that* entirely unexpected reply, Annabelle said, "I believe we've learned enough for today, my lord. I'll see you at the at the Milfords' ball tonight."

CHAPTER NINETEEN

The Milfords' ballroom was blazing with the light of a thousand candles hanging in the chandeliers high above the dance floor when David stepped in with his sister on his arm. He and Marianne had come alone tonight in his grandfather's—*his*—finest coach.

"You're taller than me, David. Do you see Annabelle or Lady Angelina?" Marianne asked soon after they'd made their way toward the dance floor.

David had already been scouring the ballroom for any sign of Annabelle. He and Marianne had come alone tonight because Lady Angelina and Lady Courtney had decided that after the previous night's incident in which David cut in on Annabelle's dance with Lord Murdock, it would be less grist for the gossip mill if they didn't arrive together again.

"I don't see what it matters," David had grumbled in the coach on the way to the party, as Marianne had been explaining it all to him. "You're going to be Lady Angelina's daughter-in-law soon and Lady Annabelle's sister-in-law. That's why we all came to the party together last night."

"Yes," Marianne had replied, "and that would have been a

perfectly lovely explanation, if you hadn't cut in on Annabelle's dance last night."

"I thought it was all the rage," David pointed out.

"So did I," Marianne replied with a sigh, "but when Lady Angelina paid me a call this morning, she explained that it still might be cause for gossip. You must remember they do things quite differently here than we're used to."

"I remember," David groaned. "Wait. Lady Angelina paid you a call? This morning?"

"Yes, why?"

"No reason other than she was supposed to be at my dinner table lesson this morning." He shook his head, dismissing the thought. David plucked two flutes of champagne from the serving tray of a passing footman while continuing to search the crowd for Annabelle and her mother.

"I don't see them," Marianne said after a few more moments of searching herself. "But I do see Lady Elspeth. She's coming this way." Marianne gave David a conspiratorial grin from behind her flute.

David barely had a chance to turn to look before Lady Elspeth and her mother were upon them. "There you are, Lord Elmwood," Lady Elspeth said. "Good to see you again this evening."

"The pleasure is mine," David replied, bowing. He couldn't help but wonder if Annabelle would be proud of him for remembering to bow. In Brighton men nodded to ladies and treated them cordially, of course, but bowing and curtsying was a more formal London requirement.

There were several moments of excruciating small talk while Marianne asked after both Lady Elspeth and her mother's health, their enjoyment of the ball so far, and some mention of the weather before Marianne not-so-subtly elbowed David in the ribs, a clear indicator that he was expected to join the conversation.

"Yes, my lady. I, too, find it unseasonably warm today," he managed, as he continued to search the crowd for any sign of Annabelle. Perhaps she'd decided not to come after all. Perhaps she'd taken ill. Why was he so worried about her whereabouts? He could act perfectly gentlemanlike without her. He'd done it before, and he would do it again. Besides, Marianne was here to keep him in line if his behavior strayed at all.

"Who are you searching for, Lord Elmwood?" came Lady Elspeth's whisper.

He glanced down to see the young woman looking up at him with adoring hazel eyes. Damn. He'd been rude to not give her his full attention. Poorly done of him. "Oh, er, no one. No one in particular." He ensured that his gaze remained fixed on Lady Elspeth while he spoke. Marianne and Elspeth's mother were engaged in their own conversation beside them.

A sly smile tugged at Lady Elspeth's lips. "You're looking for Lady Annabelle, aren't you?"

David nearly spit his champagne. "What? No. Why would you ask that?" He smoothed his hand down his shirtfront, somewhat rattled by the accusation.

Lady Elspeth rocked slowly back and forth upon her heels. She shrugged and brought her own champagne glass to her lips. "Rumor has it that you're smitten with Lady Annabelle."

He arched a brow. "Rumor, is it?" he asked, doing his best to sound nonchalant. "From what I understand, 'rumor' is filled with inaccuracies."

Lady Elspeth continued to meet his stare in a most disarming manner. "Perhaps," she allowed. "But at times rumors prove to be true."

"Lady Annabelle is soon to be my sister's new sister-in-law," David added as if that connection explained everything. "She and her mother have graciously offered to help my sister and me navigate Society."

"So you *aren't* smitten with her?" Lady Elspeth ventured.

David swallowed more champagne. This time it was nearly a gulp. "Not in the least." There. That had sounded convincing. Hadn't it? Too bad it was a damn lie.

Another sly smile spread slowly across Lady Elspeth's face. "I'm ever so pleased to hear that, my lord."

He gave her an encouraging smile. That settled it. Perhaps Lady Elspeth would tell the others and the gossip about him being smitten with Annabelle would go away. He really should spend more time with pretty Lady Elspeth. The young woman seemed interested, unlike a certain dyed-in-the-wool spinster.

"But if you *were* looking for Lady Annabelle," Elspeth added, nodding toward the dance floor, "she's just over there dancing with Lord Murdock."

CHAPTER TWENTY

Annabelle narrowed her eyes on David. He'd seemed out of sorts ever since he'd strode into the salon this morning. Last night at the Milfords' party, they'd barely spoken. He hadn't asked her to dance, and today, while she was teaching him the proper way to greet guests in a receiving line, his answers to her questions were short and clipped.

"Are you quite all right?" she finally asked.

He placed his hands on his hips and turned to face her. "Excellent. How are you?"

Annabelle crossed her arms over her chest and looked up at him. "I'm perfectly fine."

"Glad to hear it," he replied, blinking at her innocently. "Especially given the quantity of champagne you drank last night."

"I beg your pardon." She frowned at him, her mouth slightly open.

He rubbed the back of his neck. "By my count, it was at least five glasses."

She gave him a smug smile. "It was six. I had one before you arrived."

His brows shot up. "*Six* glasses of champagne? Is that seemly for a debutante?"

"I don't know, my lord, is *ten* seemly for an earl?"

He scowled. "How do you know I had ten?"

"You're not the only one who can count. And besides, the Milfords' are famous for watering down their champagne to make it last longer."

David shook his head. "Well, *that* explains quite a bit. But it doesn't explain why you danced with Lord Murdock again *twice* last night after you've told me more than once you're not interested in him."

Annabelle lifted her chin. How dare David say such a thing in an accusing voice? "I'm *not* interested in him."

"Then why were you dancing with him?" David shot back.

Annabelle plunked her fists on her hips. "What business is it of yours?" She'd spent the last two nights unable to sleep, trying to decide the best way to handle Lord Murdock's unwanted advances. She certainly didn't want the man to spread the gossip that she and David had been kissing on the Talbots' verandah, but she'd rather be ruined than marry that snake. She'd finally decided that the best course of action would be to play along with the man's demands at least until after her brother's wedding. If Murdock made good on his threats to tell everyone she'd kissed David, at least her brother and Marianne would be happily and safely married before Annabelle brought shame upon the family. It was her fault after all—she'd been the one to respond to David's kiss. If she'd slapped him and left him on the verandah, there wouldn't be much to gossip about. Instead, she'd provided that scoundrel Lord Murdock with the perfect fodder for a scandal.

David was about to open his mouth to retort when Mama walked into the room. "How's it going in here?" she asked in a sweet, happy voice.

"Excellent," they both nearly shouted simultaneously, seeming quite guilty.

Mama narrowed her eyes on them suspiciously, before turning to David. "I'm sorry I haven't had more time to devote to your lessons, Lord Elmwood. It's been a quite a job keeping up with all of Annabelle's gift deliveries." She laughed. "Though yesterday, I was delayed at the milliner's."

David refrained from pointing out that she'd also apparently paid a call on his sister, but he wasn't about to pass up the chance to say something sardonic about Annabelle's gifts. "Yes," he replied, also nodding. "But not to worry, my lady. I expect London will run out of flowers sooner or later."

Without missing a beat, Mama sighed and said, "Oh, it's a mess. They've begun sending *bon bons*, which isn't good for our waistlines. And a handful of them have begun writing poems." She turned toward Annabelle next, as she tapped her finger against her cheek. "That reminds me, darling. Lord Murdock left his card earlier when you were dressing. He brought two dozen roses and a box of sweets himself, and wanted to ensure you're still planning to go riding in the park with him this afternoon."

Annabelle's face froze and she stared at her mother without blinking. "I, er, yes, Mama. I intend to do exactly that."

"Excellent, dear," Mama said, patting Annabelle on the arm. "I'll tell the maids to prepare your clothing."

"Thank you, Mama," Annabelle replied, still refusing to meet David's eyes. She could *feel* his accusatory glare. She'd weighed the merits of telling David what Lord Murdock had said to her, but she'd decided against it. David seemed like the sort who might go beat Murdock to a pulp, and while there was a certain pleasure to be had in that thought, she didn't want to cause David any scandal. She'd promised Marianne he would be the catch of the Season, and keeping Murdock preoccupied for a bit actually served to help in that quarter as well. If Annabelle was seemingly being courted by Murdock, perhaps all the young ladies who'd had their sights set on the marquess would turn their attentions to David instead. At the end of the day, pretending to encourage Murdock seemed like a small price to pay to keep the peace until after Beau's wedding, at least.

The moment Mama left the room, David stood and turned toward Annabelle with a false smile on his face. His arms were crossed over his chest. "Going for a ride in the park with Lord Murdock later?" He batted his eyelashes at her.

Annabelle lifted her chin. "What if I am?" She hated that David thought she might actually enjoy Murdock's company, but at the same time a part of her—the defiant part—knew that it was none of David's business whom she spent time with. He had no right to be so high-handed about it. She was partially doing this to help him, after all, even though he didn't know it.

David glowered at her. "I seem to remember that a ride in the park was on the list of things you told me a gentleman asks a lady to do when they are courting."

Annabelle's nostrils flared. She wanted to stamp her foot. The man was being impossible. "It's merely a ride in the park, David. Besides, I fail to see why *you* would care what I do. You accused me of being jealous once. But it sounds as if *you're* the jealous one. I've found that men always want what they can't have. Is *that* the problem, Captain Ellsworth?" She crossed her arms over her chest this time and glared back at him. There. That should silence him on the subject.

"Certainly not," he nearly growled as he ran a hand

through his dark hair and paced away from her. "And I completely understand that a ride in the park is nothing more than a ride in the park. In fact,"—he turned back to face her—"I've asked Lady Elspeth to accompany me on just such a ride this afternoon as well."

CHAPTER TWENTY-ONE

David did his best to concentrate on the story Lady Elspeth was telling him as they rode together atop his curricle through the park that afternoon. Her mother was ensconced in the back acting as chaperone, and Lady Elspeth had just finished a story involving her younger sister and a hair ribbon they both admired. He'd never been much for pleasantries and for some reason he found himself wholly unable to concentrate on her tale. Hopefully, she wouldn't ask him any questions. What bothered him the most, however, wasn't the story or even the chill in the air and the gray sky that hung over the city like a dirty handkerchief. No. What was bothering him this afternoon was his lesson with Annabelle this morning and his ridiculous behavior during it.

He'd acted like a complete arse and had no excuse for it. What in the bloody hell was wrong with him? Why did he care if she went riding in the park with Lord Murdock? Why did he care if she'd danced with Murdock *twice* the night before? What did he care that Murdock had apparently hand-delivered two dozen roses and some sweets to her house that morning? Why did he care about any of it?

David had tried to tell himself that those things bothered him only because Annabelle had been so adamant about not wanting to be courted by anyone. She was being hypocritical. But the more he thought about it, the more he realized that reasoning made no sense. It wasn't up to him to monitor her actions and compare them to her words. Perhaps she'd changed her mind. That was none of his business, exactly as she'd told him. Even if she couldn't or wouldn't admit that she was allowing Lord Murdock to court her, what business was it of David's? She was his sister's future sister-in-law. She was his tutor in the ways of Society. Perhaps she was his friend, but she didn't owe him anything, including explanations for her actions or their lack of continuity. She was a grown woman who had handled her own affairs all these years. She certainly didn't need David to stroll into town and begin taking her to task for her decisions.

So, why had he behaved like such an unmitigated arse? Why was he acting as if she owed him an explanation? *Why did he care what she did when she wasn't with him?* And why in the bloody hell had he gone and kissed her of all things? All it had done was make their interactions tense and uncomfortable. These questions had rolled around and around in his brain, making him half-mad all day.

Fine. He was smitten with Annabelle. He wasn't proud of it, and he wasn't particularly pleased to know it. It made him predictable, didn't it? Now he was just one of the *many* gentlemen in London who fancied Annabelle Bellham. What, was he going to begin sending her flowers, too? Asking her to go for rides in the park? There was no way she would agree to such liberties. The lady had made it quite clear she wasn't interested in marriage. And now here he was, smitten with her. Another one in a long line of sad sops who could claim the same fate: wanting a woman they couldn't have.

She'd accused him of being jealous and he'd denied it. But now he realized she was right. He was jealous. Blindly, unreasonably jealous of Murdock, of all blasted people. What could she possibly see in that man? He was a pompous prick.

She'd also accused David of only being interested in her because men wanted what they couldn't have. Could that possibly be true? Hadn't Annabelle herself explained to him that all the men who were trying to court her only wanted her because she was the equivalent of prize hog to be won? Was David that predictable and ignoble? Was he truly that obvious and insipid? No. He wasn't, and he hated that she'd lumped him in with the rest of the foolish men of the *ton*. The type of men who placed bets on women's marriage prospects. He wasn't one of them, and he never would be.

But he mustn't allow his baser instincts, specifically his inconvenient jealously, to cost him a friendship with Annabelle. And that is exactly what would happen if he were to be idiotic enough to tell her he was smitten with her, or to attempt to court her or win her in any way. Annabelle was clever. She would detect his game immediately. She would consider him to be in the same exact group as all the other fools who sent her flowers and or wrote her poems. Not that he was a poem writer. Certainly not. But flowers were bad enough, and he'd actually contemplated sending some!

Flowers would be a catastrophe. He would *not* send flowers. He would not ask her to go riding in the park. And he certainly wouldn't attempt to kiss her again. And if she wanted to go driving around with Lord Murdock and accept his two dozen roses (the amount was pretentious if you asked David) then that was her affair and none of his. The woman had introduced him to other young ladies, for God's sake. If there was a clearer sign that *she* wasn't interested in him, what could it possibly be? No. He needed to push any thoughts about Annabelle's sweet lips, her silken hair, her soft skin... Damn it. He needed to focus his attention back on a woman who actually might be interested in his suit. Specifically, Lady Elspeth, who was even now prattling on in the seat next to him.

"It's really too bad about the weather today," he heard her say when he began listening again.

Thank heavens. Weather. Something he could respond to. He forced a smile to his lips. Lady Elspeth deserved better from him. She'd gamely agreed to go riding in the park when he'd suddenly arrived at her home earlier this afternoon and asked. Of course, he'd lied to Annabelle about having already made the plans. He didn't want to seem like a complete horse's arse. He shook his head and concentrated on what Lady Elspeth had said. "Yes, it is too bad. Hopefully, the rain will stay off until we return home."

"I hope so too," Lady Elspeth replied. "Oh, you know where we should go next? Down to the trail near the duck pond. That's where most couples go to be seen together in the park."

Normally, David wouldn't give a toss where most couples went to be *seen together*, but his next thought was: if most couples went there, it stood to reason that Annabelle and Murdock might be there. And although David was steadfast in his commitment to not attempt to court her, he had to admit he was somewhat curious about her ride with Murdock. Would she be happy and laughing or would she be silent and frowning, wishing the ride was over? Was she enjoying herself, or miserable?

There was only one way to find out.

"Then by all means," he said, lifting the reins and giving Lady Elspeth a wide smile. "Let's be seen."

He shook out the reins and called to the horses to step lively.

Despite the wind that was picking up when the curricle pulled up to the trail near the duck pond, there were at least a dozen other small conveyances there. He'd followed Elspeth's expert directions and they'd made it there in only a few minutes' time.

Elspeth's gaze was already taking in every couple in the area. "Look." She pointed. "Over there. I do believe that's Lord Murdock's carriage."

David couldn't have been more pleased with her random observation if he'd asked her himself. "Really?" He tried to sound nonchalant. "The one with the two lions on the door?"

"Yes, that's the one. We'll have to greet them when they come around. Drive in the circle. We'll pass them eventually."

"Very well," David replied, still trying to sound nonchalant. Had he mentioned to Lady Elspeth that Annabelle was riding with Lord Murdock today? Or did she guess? He supposed it didn't matter.

David let his two matched black stallions prance over toward the line of carriages. Once the curricle fell into step with the other conveyances, they proceeded quite slowly. The long line of vehicles moved at the pace of an injured, recalcitrant donkey around a trail that was shaped like a large oblong. It was arranged so that at some point each coach would pass the others as they made the rounds. Some of the carriages would stop the progression to speak to the occupants of the carriage they were passing. The arrangement made the whole affair that much more excruciatingly slow.

David kept his eye on Murdock's black coach. It was nearly a halfway away from them. Given the current angle, David couldn't see either Murdock or Annabelle. While Lady

Elspeth and her mother called out greetings to the occupants of the other coaches as they moved along the trail, David did his best to smile cordially and tip his hat to each person who passed by.

"So, this is where everyone comes to be seen? Why is that?" he finally asked.

Lady Elspeth warmed to the topic immediately, clasping her gloved hands together in her lap and smiling widely. "Rotten Row is *the* place to be seen, of course, but this is also a popular path."

"To be seen by whom?" David asked.

She blinked at him, a confused look on her face as if she didn't understand the question. "Everyone," she finally ventured. "Those that are here, at least."

"And why would one want to be seen?" he prodded.

This time she cocked her head to the side and frowned. It was as if he'd asked the question in a different language. "What do you mean?" she asked, the smile momentarily slipping from her lips.

"Never mind," David said, shaking his head. That was clearly a question for Annabelle to answer. Not one for poor Lady Elspeth.

After their failed attempt at communication, David and Lady Elspeth sat in silence for several moments only smiling and nodding to the others who passed by. Finally, after what seemed to be an agonizing wait, they approached Murdock's carriage.

Annabelle was sitting next to the marquess atop the seat, her back perfectly straight. Her cheeks flushed from the cool spring air. Her light-blue pelisse buttoned up and her bonnet with a matching blue ribbon tied expertly beneath her chin at a jaunty, fetching angle. Her gloved hands sat in her lap and her face was completely devoid of any emotion. Wasn't that just like her? To be out on a ride in the park with a man and display neither enjoyment nor misery? Members of the *ton*, David had learned, were taught from birth to give nothing away with their facial expressions. It seemed far too much work, as far as he was concerned.

As Murdock's coach passed by, Lady Elspeth was the one to begin the conversation. "Good afternoon, my lord," she called over to Lord Murdock.

Murdock and David were both forced out of politeness to bring their respective conveyances to a halt. David eyed Murdock's carriage. Expensive. Well-tailored. His horses looked good. The man himself was handsome, David supposed, if one didn't mind eyes that were set too closely together. But Murdock was certainly well-dressed and appeared wealthy. Apparently, one could not tell from mere looks if one was prone to throwing fits.

"Elmwood," Murdock intoned after returning Lady Elspeth's greeting. "We were just talking about you." The marquess turned to Annabelle whose cheeks became even more pink.

"Were you?" David drawled. "What, pray tell, were you saying? Something good, I hope."

An unctuous smile spread across Murdock's face. "Lady Annabelle was asking me if I'll be attending your sister's wedding next week."

"Yes, you know it's also the wedding of Lord *Worthington*, and Lord Kendall," David was quick to point out.

"Oh, yes. Yes, of course," Murdock replied, waving a hand in the air as if the name Worthington held no significance to him.

"Well." David forced himself to keep a smile plastered to his face. "What did you answer, Murdock? Are you coming to the wedding?"

Murdock's smile grew even more obsequious if that were possible. "Why, I wouldn't miss it. Things may not have worked out the way I'd hoped between Lady Julianna and myself, but I wish her nothing but the best." There. Murdock had ground out that last bit through clenched teeth. He wasn't as unaffected as he pretended to be.

Was it David's imagination or did Annabelle bite her lip at that pronouncement?

"So, you *were* invited?" David asked. Behind Murdock, Annabelle's eyes widened, and she gave David a look that clearly indicated he should not have asked such a thing.

The marquess's eyes narrowed. "My invitation was no doubt lost in the post," he clipped. "But no matter, Lady Annabelle here has agreed to allow me to escort her to the wedding. I will come as her guest." Murdock finished that pronouncement with a thin smile.

Annabelle's gaze quickly dropped to her boots.

"Is that so?" David clarified.

"Excellent," came Lady Elspeth's bright voice from beside him. "Mother and I have been invited as well. Haven't we, Mother?" Lady Elspeth glanced back toward her mother, who gave her a nod and a doting look. "We'll see you both there," Lady Elspeth finished, turning her attention back to Lord Murdock.

David didn't quite like how she referred to the two of them as 'we,' but he was hardly in a position to correct her when apparently Annabelle had invited Murdock, of all people, to the weddings.

Annabelle cleared her throat. "Yes, well, we should be going." She placed a gloved hand on Murdock's coat sleeve.

"Of course, my lady," Murdock replied, nodding and shaking the reins. He tipped his hat to David and Lady Elspeth.

As the carriage line started up again, David didn't hear a

word Lady Elspeth was saying. The sight of Annabelle's gloved hand touching Murdock's sleeve was burned into David's brain, making him want to punch something.

Damn. If there had ever been any doubt, there was none now. He was definitely jealous of Murdock.

CHAPTER TWENTY-TWO

David strode into the salon at Bell's town house the next morning, completely resolute. Today would be his last lesson. He didn't care how much more he needed to learn. Spending more time with Annabelle was a bad idea for several reasons.

If he *was* smitten with her, it certainly wouldn't help things to continue to spend more time with her. And if he *wasn't* smitten with her... Well, all signs currently pointed to his being smitten and he certainly didn't want to make more of an arse out of himself than he already had.

Additionally, after yesterday's meeting in the park, David couldn't bear to listen to her deny the fact that she was allowing Murdock to court her. It was none of David's business, true, but he also didn't need to continue to expose himself to the harsh reality that if Annabelle was interested in being courted, it was clearly by the Marquess of Murdock and not him.

Regardless, the less time David spent with Annabelle in future, the better. Starting with an end to the lessons.

Besides, Annabelle had said a few things recently that

made him think the lessons were already coming to an end soon. They'd planned to finish before the weddings, and the weddings were in only a few days' time. Whatever else he needed to learn, perhaps she could include in this last day's lesson. Speed things up. Regardless, he'd rather take his chances on being uneducated in Society than to spend another excruciating day in Annabelle's company, wanting to kiss her again but knowing he could not.

He stepped into the salon and stopped short. Marianne was there, pacing in front of the fireplace. She had a worried look on her face.

"David," came Annabelle's startled voice. His gaze swung toward the window where Annabelle was sitting on the settee, fidgeting with a handkerchief.

He frowned. "My apologies for interrupting, ladies. Were you not expecting me?"

"Oh, er, yes, of course," Annabelle hastened to say, standing. "It's just that…I didn't realize it was already ten."

Marianne turned toward David and he could read the worry in her bright blue eyes. "How do *you* think I should handle it, David?"

David frowned. "Handle what?" He had no earthly idea what they were talking about.

Annabelle stood and made her way over to Marianne. She wrapped an arm across Marianne's shoulders. "I'm certain your brother isn't interested in such inane details."

"Inane?" Marianne replied, clearly still upset. "But I have no idea how I'm going to tell Julianna that you've invited Lord Murdock to her wedding. She won't be pleased."

David frowned. "Lady Julianna and Lord Murdock breaking off their wedding was done so with animosity, I take it."

"Yes," Marianne replied. "Awful animosity. I remembered Julianna telling me at Christmastide that Lord Murdock hadn't taken it well, but to be honest, I'd forgotten the details. When I spoke to Julianna yesterday, thinking our dear Annabelle here might be developing an affection for Lord Murdock, Julianna reminded me of all the awful things—"

"Now, now, Marianne," Annabelle said, patting Marianne on the back and ushering her toward the salon door. "I told you. *I'll* handle it. In fact, I'll pay a call to Lady Julianna this afternoon and explain everything. If you'll excuse us, your brother and I must begin our lesson. Mama will be here any moment. I'll walk you to the front door."

David's brows shot up, but he watched in fascinated silence as Annabelle ushered his sister out of the salon. Clearly Annabelle didn't want him to hear any more of Marianne's concerns. *That* was curious.

Marianne nodded and dutifully made her way to the door. David waved to his sister, and she waved back, but the look of apprehension remained on her face as she and Annabelle slipped into the foyer.

Several minutes later, Annabelle came hurrying back into the room. She seemed slightly flustered but cleared her throat and smoothed a hand down her bright yellow skirts.

"Marianne seemed upset," David offered, wondering how much Annabelle would give away.

"No, no. She's fine. It will be fine," Annabelle replied, in a voice that was too loud and too bright. "I'll speak to Lady Julianna myself. Nothing to worry about. Now, shall we begin?" She glanced around as if looking for something.

David arched a brow and leaned back against the nearby wall, crossing his arms over his chest. "Why do I have the distinct impression you don't want to discuss this subject with me?"

Annabelle pushed a lock of blond hair behind her ear. She did not meet his gaze. "I'm glad to hear your impression is distinct, because that's precisely the case. I *don't* want to discuss the subject with you."

David had to smile. He shook his head. "Very well. What you do and whom you bring to the wedding is your affair. But I want you to know that I think it's best if today is our last lesson."

Annabelle's head snapped to face him. Surprise flashed through her eyes. "Last lesson?"

"Yes," David replied with a firm nod. "I think it's for the best. Besides, I believe you said there was not much more to learn."

Annabelle appeared to contemplate the matter for a moment. "There are endless things to learn, but I suppose we can make this the last lesson. If that's what you prefer," she finished softly.

"I do," he said, nodding. It took everything in him to stop himself from asking if it were true that she was developing an 'affection' for Murdock as Marianne said, but instead, he expelled his breath and simply said, "Now, what are we studying today?"

Annabelle straightened her shoulders and seemed to shake off whatever fluster was left from her conversation with Marianne. "Mama suggested we discuss correct behavior while traveling."

David bit the inside of his cheek and nodded. "Ah, because I'll be traveling to the wedding next week."

"Precisely." Annabelle glanced toward the door. "I cannot think what could be keeping Mama this morning. She told me at breakfast she'd be here on the spot of ten."

"Would you like me to ask after her?" David offered, starting toward the door.

"No. No. Most likely it's nothing and she'll be here momentarily. Let's go ahead and get started."

David nodded and made his way over to the settee where

they normally sat for such lessons. Annabelle came over and sat too, but David couldn't help but notice she was perched as far from him as possible. She was nearly sitting on the arm of the thing.

He cursed himself again for having kissed her and turning all their interactions awkward.

Annabelle cleared her throat. "*Ahem.* The first thing to know about travel is that you must always send word ahead of your arrival."

David nodded. "Simple enough."

"In this case, of course, it's known that everyone is coming for the wedding, as invitations were sent and replies were received, but otherwise, it must be quite clear in a series of correspondence that one is arriving at a friend's house."

"Understood." He glanced away from her. The light was coming through the large bay window in front of them at an angle that made her look like an angel come down from heaven. Not helpful. Not helpful in the least. "What else?" The words came out more gruff than he'd meant them to.

She plucked at her skirts. "As you may imagine, a lady never arrives at a gentleman's house alone."

"Yes," he replied. He'd fixed his gaze on a spot on the wall behind her. Much safer that way.

"Let's see," she continued. "In a carriage, a man always sits facing backward. And he should never sit next to a lady when he is alone with her in a carriage unless he is her direct relation."

David frowned. "I sat next to you on the way to the Talbots'. Are you saying that was incorrect?"

"Yes," she replied. "But Mama sat with Marianne facing backward, so you had no choice other than to take the seat that you did. That was quite curious. I'm still not certain why Mama sat there."

David cracked a smile. "So, the rule is only a rule until

another more esteemed member of the company changes the rule. Is that correct?"

That endearing little smile popped to Annabelle's lips. "Yes. That sums it up perfectly."

David chuckled and shook his head. At least they were speaking to each other again as they once had, like friends. Perhaps they could end these lessons cordially and go about their respective lives in the *ton* as pleasant acquaintances, instead of uneasy former friends.

"Of course, guests may stay for many weeks. Erm, how long do you plan to stay at Lord Worthington's house?" she asked.

"Just until the day after the wedding," David assured her. "You?"

"Mama and I will be headed back to town the morning after the wedding, to give Beau and Marianne privacy. They're going to Bellingham Hall."

The door to the salon flew open and Lady Angelina came bursting through with Bell at her side. "My apologies for being unpunctual," she said. "But I was fetching Beau. I've brought him here to relate to Lord Elmwood all the things required of a gentleman at a house party, like drinking port and playing cards, hunting and the like. I daresay Beau will be a better tutor than we are for such things, darling."

Annabelle's gaze flew to her mother and brother, and she shot to her feet.

David followed suit.

Beau chuckled. "I never pictured myself a tutor, but if you'd like to hear the basics, Elmwood, I propose we take our lesson to my study where you at least may have a drink while we discuss it."

"It's not yet half past ten, Beau," Lady Angelina pointed out.

"It's never too early to retire to the study, Mother," Beau said, leaning down and kissing his mother on the cheek.

"Mama," Annabelle said, wringing her hands ever so slightly. "Lord Elmwood has asked that today's lesson be his last."

"What?" Lady Angelina frowned.

"I fear there's not much more that will stick in this wooden brain of mine, my lady," David said, bowing to the marchioness.

"Oh, nonsense, Elmwood." Lady Angelina waved a hand in the air. "I daresay you're one of the most intelligent young men I've come across in this town, next to Beau and his set. But I can take a hint that our fussing and prodding has worn out your patience. I'm pleased you've made it this long, honestly."

"I'm grateful for your assistance, madame." He turned toward Annabelle. "And for yours, Lady Annabelle."

Annabelle nodded and quickly averted her gaze.

"I suppose I'll just go see about the bon bons," Lady Angelina said, waving her hand again. "We must take them below stairs before they melt. Good day, Lord Elmwood." The woman breezed out of the door.

Bell had already made his way back toward the door to the salon and was holding it open. "Coming, Elmwood?"

"Yes," David called, without taking his gaze from Annabelle. He took a step toward her and spoke under his breath where Bell could not hear. "I suppose this is it?" Why did it suddenly feel as if the air had been sucked from the room?

"Yes, I suppose so." Annabelle folded her hands together in front of her and didn't quite meet his eyes. "I should say 'best of luck.'"

David chuckled. "Thank you. I'm certain to need it. And

truly, thank you again for your help. I owe you a debt, my lady."

"You owe me nothing, David," her voice was small and low. He loved that she still called him David.

"On the contrary. I'm certain to have made an even larger fool of myself if you hadn't shown me all that you have." He stepped past her toward the door.

"Will you be…?" Her voice stopped him, and he turned to look at her once more. She cleared her throat and began again. "Are you planning to attend all of the wedding festivities next week?"

The plan was for a three-day house party with all the guests leading up to the wedding on Thursday morning and a wedding feast and ball on Thursday evening at Lord Worthington's country estate. She was asking him if he would be attending the house party.

"Yes," David replied. "I'll be escorting Marianne to Worthington Manor on Sunday."

Annabelle nodded and turned away. "Very well, then. I suppose if nothing else, I shall see you in the country."

CHAPTER TWENTY-THREE

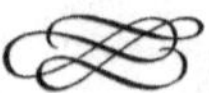

Annabelle couldn't sleep. She slipped out of bed, pulled on a dressing gown, and hurried over to the window where she stared down into the darkened gardens behind the town house.

It was unseasonably warm—she told herself—that's why she couldn't sleep. But she knew it was a lie. She couldn't sleep because every time she closed her eyes, memories of David's kiss hurtled through her mind. She'd been like this for days, ever since he'd kissed her. It was all she could think about, all she could remember. She'd practically been a ghost walking through the paces of her life these last few days.

Why couldn't she stop thinking about it? Why couldn't she stop remembering it? Imagining it? And why, oh why, had she allowed Lord Murdock to blackmail her into inviting him to the house party? He'd threatened her again, of course, while they'd been on their ride in the park. He'd threatened her and thrown in a new threat against Beau and Marianne, claiming he'd ruin her brother's wedding if Annabelle didn't see to it that he was allowed in as a guest.

She'd done a bad job of explaining it to Marianne this

morning. Annabelle had decided that it would be less upsetting to her future sister-in-law if she simply claimed to have invited the man because of her interest in him as a suitor. But Marianne had apparently already spoken to Julianna and had learned from that lady that Lord Murdock was a complete snake. Annabelle had been forced to pay poor Julianna a visit this afternoon. The betrothed woman took the news of her former *fiancé*'s invitation to her wedding better than Annabelle had expected, given Marianne's worry earlier in the day. Annabelle decided to tell Julianna the truth. Without revealing the details, she essentially imparted the news that the man had forced her to provide him with an invitation. Julianna, having seen firsthand the atrocious behavior Lord Murdock was capable of, had no problem believing Annabelle's story. In fact, Julianna had ultimately decided it was better to keep her enemy close than wonder what sort of schemes Lord Murdock would get up to while she was marrying Lord Worthington if the man wasn't invited.

Julianna's father and Murdock had apparently agreed to keep everything cordial for Society's sake, but Lady Julianna told Annabelle about some truly outrageous behavior Lord Murdock had displayed when she'd called off their wedding. It reminded Annabelle why she'd never cared much for Lord Murdock in the first place. Even before the blackguard had threatened her.

She'd only ever agreed to dance with the marquess at the Talbots' ball that first time to show silly Lady Elspeth that she wasn't too old to garner the attention of one of the most sought-after bachelors of the Season. That, and, if she were being honest, she'd done it to possibly make David the slightest bit jealous after his dance with Lady Heloise. Which was petty and stupid and wrong, in retrospect. But if Annabelle had had any idea the marquess would have taken their one dance as an invitation to follow her and an opening to blackmail her, she would have happily remained on the sidelines alone the entire evening. Oh, this was why she never wanted to marry to begin with. Men were manipulative, self-serving asses, and Murdock reminded her of her father. A man who'd left nothing but sadness and destruction in his path, and only cared about his own needs and wants.

And spending time with him these last few days had only confirmed Murdock was as self-obsessed a bore as ever. He'd proved that on their second dance at the Milfords' house. He'd reminded her what a catch he was and even went so far as to tell her that even if the Earl of Elmwood became popular, the title of earl wasn't as prestigious as the title of marquess and never would be. As if she cared about that.

She would have to find a way out of her predicament, of course. But there would be time enough after Beau's wedding to figure out how to handle Lord Murdock. He was a blowhard but even he wouldn't be crass enough to ask her to marry him at her brother's wedding. No. He'd wait until they returned to London for that ridiculousness. And there was no possible way she'd say yes.

In the meantime, she'd be forced to spend more time with him at the wedding. God help her. Julianna had agreed to allow him to come and had promised to convince Lord Worthington to allow it as well. At least that was settled. All Annabelle needed to do now was get through the four days of the house party and weddings and get out of there. Then she would work out how to remove the odious Lord Murdock from her company forever, with or without causing a scandal.

Expelling her breath, Annabelle traced the letter A on the window the same way she'd done when she was a little girl and wanted to calm herself. Why was her heart beating so fast now? In the middle of the night? Alone in her room?

Because even now, she was remembering her kiss with David.

David.

Today David had asked to end his lessons. Annabelle could guess why. Because ever since their kiss, she'd treated him as if he shouldn't come within twenty paces of her. She'd acted formally in front of him, erasing all the comradery they'd shared during their first lessons. She'd been as skittish as an untrained foal about to bolt every time she'd seen him. Today she'd even nearly toppled off the side of the settee trying to sit as far from him as possible. And why? Because she felt something for him. Something she could not allow herself to feel. And she was truly frightened. Because if any man was, David was marriage material.

It was for the best that he'd ended the lessons, however. Despite her many attempts at acting normal in the man's presence since their kiss, she clearly couldn't manage it. And what better way to announce the fact that she wasn't normal than acting as ridiculously in his presence as she had these past few days?

David was right to stop the lessons, and she was nothing but thankful for it. She would attend a few of the Season's parties and dinners before Sunday, and leave for Worthington Manor with Mama and Beau that morning. Then she would devote herself to keeping Lord Murdock preoccupied and away from Lady Julianna and Lord Worthington during the wedding. Nothing in the country needed to be awkward. She would see David, acknowledge him, perhaps even share a few moments of normal conversation with him, and then they'd be back to their own affairs, their own companions.

Lady Elspeth was coming to the wedding, wasn't she? No doubt the chit would do all she could to keep David occupied. Annabelle had nothing to worry about, and if Lady

Elspeth wanted to stake a claim on David, so be it. It was none of Annabelle's affair if David chose to court and marry Elspeth. She might have seemed cold and calculating when Annabelle spoke to her at the Talbots' ball. But couldn't all the ladies of the *ton* be calculating when it came to making a match? Besides, Annabelle had no say in David's choice of wife, and if Elspeth truly was a bad choice, no doubt Marianne would see the truth and warn her brother. Yes. Perfect. Annabelle wouldn't worry about it again. That was that.

She wandered back to her bed and tossed the dressing gown along the bottom of it. Then she climbed beneath the covers again and willed herself to sleep. But as her eyes drifted closed, the memory of David's scent and the feel of his hot body pressed tightly against hers filled her mind, making her moan.

She balled her hands into fists and pressed them against her closed eyes, willing the thoughts away. This wedding party was certain to be the longest four nights of her life.

CHAPTER TWENTY-FOUR

The ride to Worthington's country estate took the better part of the day. Marianne had packed all her things and said good-bye to Lady Courtney, who would be attending the wedding but traveling separately. David knew he was tasked with fulfilling the role his parents would normally play in the wedding festivities. Beyond Marianne's dowry, Bell had insisted that no money change hands. Apparently, the marquess had won a large bet last year, beating out his friends Kendall and Worthington, and had promised to spend the earnings on the wedding three of the couples would share.

David hadn't seen Annabelle in three days. Not since the morning of their final lesson. He'd done his damnedest not to wonder what she'd been doing since then. Was Annabelle riding in the park with Murdock? Was she dancing with the marquess at balls? David had no idea because he'd steadfastly steered clear of all Society events specifically so he wouldn't see her. He didn't want to see her. No good could come of it. Especially if she were with Murdock.

David had spent the last three days doing a variety of

things. He'd visited the club with Bell. He'd gone riding in the park with an old friend from Brighton, though he'd been certain to go nowhere near the places where couples 'went to be seen.' David had even had dinner with Lady Courtney and Marianne, who both asked him why he wasn't attending more of the events of the Season. He'd given them some weak excuse about how the Season was already overwhelming him. Marianne had reminded him that when he escorted her to Lord Worthington's estate for the wedding, he would be forced to be on his best Society-worthy behavior. He'd assured her that he would do exactly that. In fact, he had every intention of playing the rules-obsessed earl giving his only sister away in marriage. Marianne deserved no less. He would not embarrass her.

He also refused to inquire about Annabelle. He managed to make it through the entire dinner without mentioning her once. He didn't need to know anything about Annabelle. She would be just another guest at his sister's wedding. He would no doubt see her and greet her, but that would be the end to it. There was no need to make their relationship into something it wasn't. It was all quite simple, really.

David spent the coach ride to Worthington Manor reading a new book. He made it through nearly the entire journey before he cracked. Slapping his book closed he asked, "So, did Lady Annabelle convince Lady Julianna to allow Murdock to attend the wedding?" The question had been lingering on his tongue for hours. It had finally broken loose, and it felt like a weight had lifted from his chest.

Marianne had been engrossed in reading a book of her own, but she immediately shut it and leaned toward him. "It turned out it wasn't Lady Julianna who needed the convincing—it was Lord Worthington. The duke was adamant that Murdock wouldn't step foot in his home. But Julianna apparently calmed Worthington and talked him into it. According to Annabelle, Julianna convinced Worthington that it would be bad form if he were to deny the man entrance to his home and attendance at his wedding after stealing his *fiancée*. She said it was the least Worthington could do to be the bigger man."

David snorted. "I suppose that's *one* way to look at it."

Marianne sighed. "If I'm being honest, I think it was too kind of Julianna. You know the man tried to kick her dog?" Marianne shuddered and shook her head.

David's jaw dropped. "What? Murdock kicked Lady Julianna's dog?"

Marianne shook her head. "No. He *tried* to kick her dog. He missed. Thank heavens."

David's brows were furrowed. "Why in God's name would he try to kick her dog? Or any dog for that matter?"

Marianne sighed and shook her head. "As I said, Julianna reminded me of all the hideous things he'd done. Apparently, Lord Murdock took the news of Julianna tossing him over quite poorly. He broke items in her father's drawing room and called both Julianna and her parents terrible names."

This time David arched a brow and sat back against his seat, shaking his head. "Good God. I don't blame Worthington. I wouldn't let that scoundrel in the house."

"Neither would I," Marianne replied.

David waited a few seconds before narrowing his eyes and asking, "Did you happen to tell Lady Annabelle the bit about the dog-kicking?"

Marianne nodded. "Yes, we spoke about it at length."

David nearly growled. "And she still wants the man to escort her to the wedding?"

Marianne waved her hand in the air and shrugged. "You know how these Society people are. They have such different rules for everything. Being a marquess gives you the right to be insane, I suppose."

"Not in my book," David replied, scowling again.

"Or mine either," Marianne replied. "I can tell you Beau wasn't pleased to hear that his sister is being escorted to the wedding by Lord Murdock."

David tossed a hand in the air. "Finally, someone who sees reason."

Marianne nodded. "Yes, but his mother talked him out of discussing it with Annabelle. Apparently, Lady Angelina was quite firm with him. Lord Murdock is the first man in all these years Annabelle has shown the slightest interest in, and his mother told Beau that if he interferes with their courtship, he'll have to answer to her."

David's frown deepened. "That's ridiculous. Bell is the man of the house. He should know who is right for his sister."

"Yes, well, Beau isn't pleased. But he agreed to leave it alone for the duration of the wedding at least. Now, enough about Lord Murdock. How is it going with Lady Elspeth? I'm ensuring that you're seated together at dinner, you know."

David tried to conjure some excitement for that news. "Very well," was all he could muster.

"'Very well'?" Marianne narrowed her eyes on him. "That doesn't sound particularly fervent. I thought you liked Lady Elspeth."

"She's perfectly fine," David replied, suddenly wishing the conversation were over.

Marianne arched a red brow. "If you want me to seat you next to someone else, David, do let me know."

"No. Lady Elspeth will be a fine dinner companion," David grumbled.

Marianne gave him a sidewise stare before returning her attention to her book. David sat in silence for the remainder of the journey, stewing over what Marianne had told him. Lady Angelina and her daughter couldn't possibly be so enamored with the title of marquess that they'd overlook Murdock's obvious faults, would they? If so, they were ludicrous, and Annabelle would deserve to be paired with a dog-kicker.

No, that was an awful thing to think. But why was Annabelle spending so much time with Lord Murdock? Was it possible that she actually fancied him? Was she planning to marry finally? Even a lady as steadfastly against marriage as Annabelle was would need to marry *eventually*, wouldn't she?

"You know, if you're having any doubts about this wedding, we can turn around and be in Brighton by nightfall," David offered, with a smile.

Marianne glanced at him, before smiling too and shaking your head. "No doubts whatsoever. You know what Mama always used to say…marry for love and you'll never regret it."

David nodded. "She did say that, didn't she?" He stared at his sister who'd already begun reading her book again. Marianne was someone who'd fallen in love. Real love, apparently. Perhaps she knew something that could help him sort out his true feelings. Although he wasn't about to admit to his sister that he was likely smitten with a woman who didn't want him.

"Marianne," he ventured, leaning forward and clasping his hands together between his knees.

His sister looked up from her book again. She wrapped a red curl around her finger. "Yes?"

"How did you know that Bell was right for you? The right man, I mean. How did you know it for certain?"

Marianne smiled and continued to play with her hair. "The truth is, at first I could barely countenance him. And I thought he was a valet named Nicholas Baxter, but that's beside the point." She wrapped the curl around her finger in silence before she added, "I suppose I knew for certain when

I got a funny feeling in the pit of my stomach every time he was in the same room with me."

David frowned. "A funny feeling? Like what?"

Marianne released the curl and it sprung away from her finger. "I'm not entirely certain how to describe it. But it made me feel excited and a bit ill at the same time. Like I was about to ride a wild horse or go on an adventure or something."

"So, you felt funny every time he was in the room?" David asked to be certain he had it correctly.

"Yes," Marianne nodded, and a sly smile popped to her lips, "and when he wasn't in the room, I began to miss that feeling. That's when I knew."

CHAPTER TWENTY-FIVE

After arriving at Worthington's estate, David managed to keep busy the remainder of the day. He found Bell and the other gentlemen in Worthington's study, and they all went for a ride across the duke's vast property. David returned in time to clean up, change clothing, and make his way downstairs to the dinner party in the large dining room. Both the room and the table were enormous, but he spotted Annabelle sitting next to Murdock on the far end of the space. David refrained from shaking his head.

David was seated next to Lady Elspeth, his sister's planning obviously at work. Lady Elspeth was her usual talkative self, and for once, he was glad for the distraction. He answered her questions and inquired after her sisters and mother and generally kept his attention fixed upon the young woman. He refused to look toward Annabelle.

David made it nearly halfway through dinner before he could no longer stand the small talk. He had to get some fresh air. A cigar wouldn't be unwelcomed, either.

Excusing himself from the table, he made his way out of

the dining room, down the corridor, and into the huge foyer. He glanced around the marble-filled space realizing he had no idea how to make it to the gardens. He tracked down a footman and asked how he might get outside.

The footman provided him directions to a patio off the library and David made his way there posthaste. He peered through the French doors to ensure the space was empty before stepping out into the cool breeze. He breathed it in and closed his eyes. It felt good to be alone and in complete silence for a few moments. The pleasantries in the dining room were wearing on him. Would he ever get used to exchanging such inane banter with people he barely knew?

He strode over to the edge of the stone patio near a hedgerow and pulled a cigar from his inside coat pocket. He *would* quit smoking. He would. For Marianne's sake. But at the moment, he needed something familiar. He pulled a flint from his pocket and lit the cigar. Then he pulled it into his mouth and inhaled deeply, closing his eyes and letting the comfortable feeling wash over him. If he stayed like this for a few moments, he might be able to believe he was back on the Continent, standing near his tent, his compatriots sleeping on mats around him. He might feel as if he had turned back time. Only, the scent of flowers instead of a dirty battlefield was on the air tonight. An unmistakable difference.

David had taken several more drags when a quiet sound behind him caught his attention. He turned to see Annabelle step onto the patio. The soft evening wind blew the curls at her cheeks. The skirts of the light-green gown she was wearing fluttered in the breeze. She looked so beautiful, he felt it in his gut.

"There you are, David." His name came from her lips like a whisper.

He furrowed his brow. "Come to tell me it was rude of me to leave the dining table? Believe me, I'd already guessed."

"I left, too." She pointed out. "May I?" She stepped toward him and gestured to the cigar.

David arched a brow. "By all means." He handed it to her.

She took a deep pull and blew the smoke in the opposite direction. "This reminds me of the night we met."

The hint of a smile touched his lips. "Yes, but this time you followed *me* outside."

"Guilty," she breathed, taking another pull.

David scratched the back of his neck. "Why did you come?"

She handed him the cigar again. "I wanted to see if you were all right."

David bowed his head and kicked at the stones beneath his boots. "I needed some fresh air. Some quiet."

She nodded. "I understand. I'll go–"

"No." He reached for her but let his hand drop before he touched her. "Stay, please."

Annabelle turned back and studied his face. "Are you certain?"

"Yes. I'm certain." He blew out the smoke he'd inhaled and returned the cigar to her.

"Very well." Annabelle took another long drag. "So. Where have you been? I haven't seen you in days. You weren't at the Merriweathers' dinner party three nights ago and I haven't seen you riding in the park."

"I've been staying at home." He pulled the cigar from her fingers and took another drag.

"Yes, well. I suppose the last thing I said to you was that I'd see you at the wedding, and here we are."

"I find I don't like attending many of the social affairs of the Season," David replied.

"But the social affairs were the reason I gave you lessons. Aren't you looking for a wife?"

David paced away from her and scrubbed a hand through his hair. "I should be. Are you looking for a husband?"

"I should be." Her voice was small.

"I have something for you, Annabelle." He turned back and moved toward her again.

A puzzled expression played across her face. "Something...for me?"

"Yes, something to say 'thank you' for all the help you've given me." Handing her the cigar, he pulled open his coat and took out a small parcel wrapped in brown paper and tied with a string. He handed it to her, taking back the cigar.

Annabelle accepted the parcel and turned it over in her hands. "What is it?"

He nodded toward the package. "Open it."

She pulled off the string and unwrapped it. "It's..." She glanced up at him. Tears shimmered in her ice-blue eyes. "A book."

"Not just *any* book," he said, biting his bottom lip and closely watching her face for her reaction.

Her hand gently caressed the book's cover. "It's *Pride and Prejudice*, the one I said I wanted. Where did you find it?"

David tipped his head to the side. "I went to a bookstore in London just before coming here."

"Thank you," she breathed, hugging the book to her chest. "No one has ever given me something so thoughtful." She tilted back her head to meet his gaze.

He hadn't been mistaken about the tears. She was even now blinking them away.

"Better than flowers or bon bons?" he prompted.

A smile touched her lips. She nodded. "So much better."

He reached out and tapped the top of the book. "Curious that the book you wanted is about a young lady who has no intent to marry until the right man comes along."

Her eyes were wide, and her mouth formed an O. "You read it?"

"Indeed, I did. Quite enjoyable," he replied. "Lizzie reminded me of you."

"She did?" Annabelle breathed.

"Certainly. Clever, determined, refuses to be told what to do," he replied, handing her the cigar once more. "Magnificent. Just like you," he said, and with that, he turned on his heel and strode back through the French doors.

On the way back to the dining room, David smiled to himself. He'd surprised her with the book and the fact that he'd read it. The look on her face had been pure wonder. That had been lovely. But a frown quickly took the place of his smile, because he realized he was in a great deal of trouble. There had been a funny feeling in his middle the entire time he'd been in Annabelle's presence. And now he missed it.

CHAPTER TWENTY-SIX

The next night, Annabelle stood along the sidelines of the dancing, catching her breath. She'd just finished her second dance with that ass, Lord Murdock, and was doing her best not to look around to see if David was dancing with Lady Elspeth again.

Tonight, the wedding festivities consisted of a country dance out in one of Worthington's barns, which had been transformed into a lovely spot for a party, with flowers and candles and pastel-colored ribbons wrapped around the rough wooden posts.

Annabelle was wearing a simple white gown with scalloped sleeves that had tiny daisies embroidered around the hem, the empire waist, and the neckline. She wore soft white kid slippers and had daisies woven through her hair. She looked and felt young tonight. As if she were a first-Season debutante. The two glasses of punch that one of the bridegrooms (almost certainly not Beau) had obviously laced with alcohol had served to put a glow in her cheeks.

Her smile faded, however, as the memory of seeing David last night on the patio swept through her mind. Talking to him again had been even more excruciating than she'd expected. She still couldn't stop replaying their kiss at the Talbots' ball in her mind. She'd since gone to dinner parties, attended other balls, and been riding in the park with Lord Murdock, participating in each event with a smile pasted on her face. But all she could think about was David. And it made no sense. She'd only known David for a short time. He was an outsider. Nearly a stranger. How could she miss him? Why did she miss him?

But the feeling had been there, night after night, as she attended the normal events of the Season. The same events she'd attended for the last five years. What made this Season any different? She craned her neck in every crowd looking for him. She closely watched Lady Elspeth, in case David appeared at her side. Annabelle even went so far as to ask Marianne where her brother had got off to. But Marianne had offered little help in explaining David's absence.

Annabelle had told herself again and again to stop. It didn't matter where David was. They'd finished their lessons and he'd gone his own way. They had no ties to each other, and he certainly hadn't promised to see her again. Why would he? Why should he? She'd made it clear time and again that she wasn't interested in being courted. Not that David had ever indicated he wanted to court her, but something about their interaction on the patio last night had been excruciating. *Did* he want to court her? Was that why he asked if she was looking for a husband?

When she'd seen him leave the table last night, she'd been compelled to follow him. She had no reason for it. It was almost as if her body had moved on its own volition, without input from her mind.

The musicians in the corner of the barn struck up another song and Annabelle glanced up in time to see David pull away from the crowd and disappear down a shadowy corridor. Where was he going now? Perhaps to have another cigar? She should *not* follow him. She didn't want to be courted. She didn't want a husband. But that kiss had made her hot and cold and achy. That kiss had made her feel things she'd never felt before. It was the first time in her life she'd truly desired a man. She was attracted to David. She'd never felt that way before. It scared her senseless.

And then there was the book he'd given her. For heaven's sake, why did the man have to be so different from all other men? Why did he listen when she spoke, and why did he care about what she said? Why did he make her feel things she didn't want to feel, and make her want things she didn't want to want?

She could not marry, *would not* marry. Marriage was a trap for a woman. She refused to belong to any man. She would not allow herself and any children to be abused. David needed a wife. He was an earl, after all, and would be expected to marry and produce an heir. He was nothing but a distraction leading her in the wrong direction from her well-ordered life. But even as she had that thought, she glanced quickly toward Lord Murdock to ensure he wasn't watching, then slipped away to follow David into the shadowy darkness on the far end of the enormous barn…as if she had no choice.

Still mentally arguing with herself, Annabelle kicked at the bits of hay that lay strewn along the path she was following between the horse stalls. The barn was clean and smelled like fresh bales of hay. Occasionally, a horse would neigh when she passed.

She was drawn toward a flicker of candlelight glowing in the darkness. She found David sitting on a bale of hay in one of the empty stalls. In addition to the bale, hay covered the entire floor of the stall, at least three paces high. David's knees were drawn up onto the bale and his wrists rested atop them. He was wearing buff-colored breeches, a white shirt open at the top, and black boots. His short, dark hair was mussed as if he'd been running his fingers through it. She'd already learned that he did that whenever he was frustrated.

Annabelle stepped into the round pattern of light cast from the lantern he'd lit. "What are you doing here?"

He shrugged. "I could ask you the same thing."

She took another step closer and stood directly in front of him. "Very well. Ask me."

He reached out and gently captured her wrist. "What if I told you I came here hoping you'd follow me?"

Heat suffused her body. "Wh…why?" she managed to ask through dry lips.

He stood and moved slowly forward while she moved back until her shoulders were pressed against the stall door. He braced both palms against the wood directly over her shoulders and leaned down. His lips were mere inches from hers. When he spoke, his breath caressed her cheek. "What if I told you I want to kiss you again? That I want to touch you?"

She swallowed hard. Her breath coming out in short pants. "Is that true?"

"If it was, what would you say?" He reached out and gently stroked her hair.

Her eyes met his and sparks leaped between them. She lifted up on her tiptoes and wrapped her arms around his neck. "I'd tell you I followed you for the same reason. Touch me, David."

CHAPTER TWENTY-SEVEN

The moment Annabelle's lips touched his, David pulled her against him, hard. Their bodies pressed together, their tongues tangled. He turned and fell backward onto the soft hay, taking her with him. She was atop him, and his hands couldn't touch her enough. They moved up her sides, down her thighs, to her breasts, to her backside, pulling her tight against his rock-hard cock.

"David," she breathed against his lips.

Hearing his name on her lips made him ache. "Kiss me, Annabelle," he demanded.

Annabelle kissed him. She kissed his cheek and his lips and his neck and even darted her tongue into the curve of his ear, making his entire body buck beneath her. Every touch of her lips made him harder. One of his hands cupped her arse, and he pressed her tight against his erection. She moaned in the back of her throat. It was the most erotic sound he'd ever heard.

He swiftly flipped them over so that she was cushioned in the fluffy hay, and he was atop her. He ground his hips against the softness between her legs. She moaned again.

Summoning his will, he sat her up, reached behind her, and undid the buttons of her gown before pulling the sash to release the bow at her back. Her gown fell away from her shoulders, and she lifted up and shimmied it down her body to pool around her waist.

His mouth traced a hot path down her neck to the top of her shift, which he quickly pulled down to expose one perfect breast.

Panting, his lips moved down to her swollen nipple, and he sucked it, then flicked his tongue back and forth across the hardened nub. Her hands in his hair, Annabelle gasped and David smiled against her tender skin.

He moved to her other breast, sucking the nipple, and lavishing it with the same attention until her head fell back and she cried out.

He slowly moved his hand down to the hem of her skirts and dragged them up to her thighs. His hand caressed the silken flesh of her legs, while his knee slipped between them to slightly spread them. His hand moved inexorably to the intimate spot that he hoped was throbbing as hard as he was.

When he stroked one finger across her nub of pleasure, her body bucked. He couldn't help his proud smile. He kissed her deeply again and then moved his mouth to her ear. "Do you like that?" He rubbed her with the tip of his finger.

"David," she breathed, clutching at his shoulders. "Don't stop."

David didn't need to hear another word. Her wish was his command. He rubbed her in tiny circles, pressing the intimate flesh while she writhed beneath him. Her legs tried to gain purchase in the hay, but they slipped out from under her each time she tried to move closer to his hand. She grabbed his wrist, holding it tight against her as if frightened that he might end her exquisite torture.

"I won't stop," he whispered in her ear. "I'm going to make you fly."

ANNABELLE'S BREATH came in tight, short pants. She had no idea how David knew precisely where to touch her, but she wasn't about to allow him to stop. Her entire body felt as if it was stretched tight on a rack, and the longer he rubbed her, the wetter the spot between her legs, and the more she wanted to cry out. Her jaw was clenched tight. Her legs were locked beneath his, and she clutched at his wrist as if it were the last line off a sinking ship.

"Please, David," she moaned, not certain what she was asking for. But she wanted it. Her entire body wanted it. Badly.

"Hold on, Annabelle," David ordered roughly into her ear. "You're almost there."

Annabelle's head tipped back, her jaw fell open, and her entire body tensed seconds before stars shot across the backs of her closed eyes. Her hips jerked and her knees clamped together against David's forearm.

It was several moments before her breathing slowed to anything like a normal rhythm. She lifted her head and opened her eyes to see David, with his mouth quirked up, looking quite proud of himself. She expelled a long breath. The man *should* be proud after what he'd just done to her.

He leaned down and nuzzled her neck. Annabelle let her head fall to the side to give him better access. Every touch made her feel as if her body was going up in smoke. That's what this man did to her.

DAVID KISSED Annabelle on the lips one last time before helping her stand and pull her shift and gown back up. He moved behind her to redo the buttons at the back of her gown, and he tied her sash, however inexpertly.

He'd tried to stay away from her. Tried to tell himself that no good could come from seeing her again. Last night after he'd given her the book and walked away, he'd told himself he would leave her be for the remainder of the house party. But then he'd recognized that funny feeling in his middle, the one Marianne had told him about. He didn't want to risk never feeling it again. That's when he realized that he'd never actually tried to tell her he wanted her. He'd never actually said the words out loud. If he was going to give her up, let her go forever, he had to try at least.

He'd tossed and turned all night last night, trying to decide how best tell her. In the wee hours of the morning, the perfect solution finally occurred to him. He would give *her* the power. Let *her* make the decision. If she came to him, if she followed him out of the dance tonight, the same way she'd followed him outside last night, she'd be making her choice. And he would tell her how he truly felt. It was time to learn the truth.

If her body's reaction to him just now wasn't the truth, he didn't know what was. He pulled her into his arms again and kissed her deeply. Then he pulled his lips away and pressed his forehead against hers. They were both panting. Her hands were resting on his shoulders, and she slowly moved them down his arms before placing them back at her sides. Her eyes remained closed and her breathing, erratic.

David took both of her hands in his and laced their fingers together. He opened his eyes and pulled his forehead away to see her face. "Let me court you, Annabelle. I want you to be my wife."

Pain flashed across her pretty face. Pain, and something

else he couldn't quite define, perhaps *regret*. She opened her eyes too. "No," she breathed. "I can't."

"No?" Pulling his hands away from hers, he shook his head and searched her face. "Why not? I don't understand."

"I cannot marry anyone, David." She wrapped her arms around her middle as if she were cold.

His jaw turned to stone. "Cannot, or *will not?*"

She jerked her head to the side. "Does it matter?"

"It matters to me," he nearly growled.

"Fine, then I *will not*," she replied through clenched teeth, the pained expression still on her face.

"If you don't want me, say it," he demanded.

"I *do* want you, David," she murmured, "more than you know."

He scrubbed both hands frantically through his hair. "You're speaking in riddles. It makes no sense."

She bowed her head. "I'm sorry, David. I don't want to hurt you."

David pulled a piece of hay from his hair and flung it to the ground. "No, I'm the sorry one, Annabelle." He pushed open the stable door and stalked away into the darkness.

ANNABELLE WATCHED him go with a lump in her throat. She spent the next several minutes combing hay from her hair with her fingers and smoothing her skirts. There was no way she could return to the dance now. She would have to sneak back to the house and have Cara help her right her clothing first.

Annabelle let out a long groan. Should she even return at all? She clearly wasn't making the best choices tonight. Why had she followed David here? Why had she kissed him? Why had she allowed him to touch her that way?

But she already knew why. The answer to all those questions was the same…she couldn't stop herself. Her mind told her to stay far away from him, but her body traipsed after him, wanting more. And she did want more. Even now. She wanted him badly. The release she'd just experienced had done nothing to slake her desire for him. If she'd been unable to forget his kiss, she would *never* forget the way he'd touched her tonight. She never *wanted* to forget. And she wanted to touch him too. Make him feel the same way.

At least she had her answer. He *did* want to court her. She'd suspected that, of course. Though they were already well beyond courting. They should be talking about marriage after what they'd just done. She'd handled her reaction poorly. Instead of simply saying she would not marry, she should have told him that if she ever considered marrying *any* man it would be him. But what did that matter? That wouldn't satisfy him. She wanted him, but she couldn't marry him. So she'd rejected him.

A desperate idea flashed through her mind. Could she spend the night with him, and have the strength to leave him afterward? Was she that brave?

CHAPTER TWENTY-EIGHT

David spent the next day torn between misery every time he thought about how much he wanted Annabelle, and anger at allowing himself to become embroiled in this situation. Why had he thought it was a good idea to spend time in the company of the most notoriously unattainable spinster in London? Oh, yes. Earl Lessons.

He didn't *want* to want Annabelle. He didn't *want* to love her. But with each passing moment he was more certain it was too late.

There was one thing he was clear on, however. He wanted Annabelle for *Annabelle*, not because she was a prize to be won. Spending time with her, talking to her, he'd learned that she wasn't the vain princess he'd first thought her to be: Lady Presumptuous. Instead, she was funny and witty and wise. She was bold and passionate. She truly cared about others and loved her family deeply. She was someone who would do a large favor for a near stranger. And she was kind. She'd readily accepted Marianne in her family, hadn't she? Annabelle just wanted to be seen and heard. She wanted someone to look past her beauty and realize what a treasure of a person she was. And he had. He *had*. But for some reason that she would not discuss, she refused to marry.

He had no one to blame but himself for his misery. Annabelle had made it clear from the moment they'd begun their lessons that she wasn't looking for a husband. And David had been the idiot who'd gone and…fallen in love with her.

The partygoers were having a quiet, light supper this evening in expectation of the large wedding feast and ball that would be held tomorrow night after the morning wedding, but David had sent down his regrets to the dinner table tonight. He simply hadn't been able to stand being in the same room with Annabelle, especially if she was at the side of that horse's arse, Murdock. David wanted to kick the man (in defense of the dog) every time he saw him.

Now, David was in his bed, tossing and turning, completely unable to sleep. A slight knock on his bedchamber door caught his attention. Shirtless and bare-foot, wearing only his breeches, he threw back the covers and strode to the door. Who could it be? Hopefully not his sister having second thoughts about marrying into such an illustrious family. He'd never seen a couple more in love than Marianne and Beau, and his sister was more than good enough to be a marchioness. He was hardly able to recount all the reasons why Marianne would make an excellent marchioness. He only hoped she knew it because David was still having difficulty thinking of himself as an earl. There were still days he wanted to grab his sister's hand and take the first mail coach back to Brighton, renouncing the title the same way their father had.

But when the door swung open, it wasn't Marianne, it was Annabelle. She stood there with a glass of champagne in her hand, an inscrutable expression on her face. She was wearing a lavender gown with a gauze overskirt and a white sash around her middle. Her hair was swept up in a chignon and diamonds dangled from her ears. His mouth went dry just looking at her. But why was she here? After she'd rejected him soundly last night, he was determined not to see her again, and this time he meant it.

"Annabelle," he muttered, knowing what a useless thing to say that was. If anyone saw her standing outside his bedchamber door, she'd be ruined.

"May I come in?" she asked in a sultry voice, arching a blond brow.

He bit his bottom lip. "You know, we never precisely covered this in our lessons, but I don't think it's proper for a lady to come alone to a man's bedchamber in the middle of the night."

"Oh, I'm well aware. There's nothing *proper* about this visit."

David gulped. He stuck his head out of the door to quickly look both ways to ensure no one was watching before standing back to allow her entrance to his room. The moment she stepped in, he closed the door behind her.

David lit a candle on the table next to the bed, then turned back to face her.

"Your shirt is off," she said.

He couldn't help but smile at that. Good. At least he wasn't the only one saying obvious things tonight.

"I don't sleep with it on," he informed her. "Too many nights in camp when it was wet and too cold to wear."

Her gaze traced his naked chest. "I, *ahem*." She tucked an errant strand of hair behind her ear. "I can't say it's an unwelcome sight."

He laughed outright at that. "I'm certainly glad to hear it. Would it make you more comfortable if I put on a shirt?"

"No!" she nearly shouted, before clearing her throat and saying. "I mean, if you like. Whatever you prefer."

He grinned at her and remained shirtless.

Annabelle held up her champagne glass, studying the bubbly liquid inside. "Do you know my brother doesn't drink? Ever. Not even on the eve of his wedding."

"I do know that," David replied, nodding. He'd never seen so much as a sip of alcohol pass Bell's lips. Had she truly come to his room in the middle of the night, risking ruination, to inform him that her brother didn't drink? "But you do drink, I see."

"Yes." She nodded. "I do. Do you know why?"

David shook his head, still bemused as to where the conversation was headed. "No, why?"

"Because I can control myself when I drink."

David frowned. "Are you saying Bell can't?"

Annabelle shrugged. "To my knowledge, he's never tried. But there's every reason to believe he might not be able to control himself."

David continued to frown. "What does that mean?"

She slowly walked toward the canopied bed and stared down at the mattress as if it were a foreign object. "Why weren't you at dinner?"

The conversation had taken another turn. It took everything in him to keep from asking her why she cared, why she'd come, but instead he rubbed the back of his neck and said, "I didn't feel up to it tonight."

She traced a finger along the top of the bedspread. "Up to what?"

David blew out a deep breath. When he'd first seen her at the door, he'd been concerned that she was foxed, but she wasn't. Now that he'd spoken to her, he could tell that she was perfectly sober. Then why had she risked scandal to come to his door? And how would he ever get her back to her own room without her being seen? But first he had something to say. He'd been wanting to apologize to her all day. But apologizing to someone you had no intention of coming within fifty paces of was difficult. Now that she was in his bedchamber, he might as well take advantage of the opportunity. However unexpected.

"Look, Lady Annabelle," he began, putting his hands on his hips.

"Lady Annabelle?" she echoed. "So formal? I thought we were long past titles, David."

She wasn't making this easy for him. He cleared his throat. "You're right. Fine, then. Annabelle. I want to apologize for my behavior last night."

"Which behavior?" she asked, blinking at him in an adorable manner.

He couldn't think clearly when she was standing that close to his bed. Images of their naked bodies intertwined atop it kept scorching through his mind. What had she just said? Oh, yes. He supposed he deserved that last question. "I shouldn't have questioned your decision not to marry. It's none of my concern. I'm sorry." There. He'd apologized. Now he could truly move on with his life. He wanted her more than he'd ever wanted any woman, but he'd gone about it all wrong. He'd ham-handed his attempted courtship and been nothing but an ass about it. He'd told her she was speaking in riddles, that she made no sense.

"David, I owe you an explanation…"

"You owe me nothing," he continued, shaking his head. "Least of all an explanation of why you're not interested in me."

A short burst of laughter escaped her lips. "I'm *not* interested in *you*? Why, that's news to me."

His brows shot up at *that* pronouncement, but he was determined to set things straight and leave them there. This was his last chance. "Whatever your reasons for not wanting to be courted or to marry, they are your own, and I had no right to demand an explanation from you."

"Do you want to know something?" she asked, leaning a hip against the mattress.

He eyed her warily, not wanting the conversation to take yet *another* turn. "What?"

"I don't even like Lord Murdock." She lifted her nose in the air.

"Really?" David arched a brow. This time he couldn't help himself. "Then why are you spending so much time with him? The man kicks dogs, for Christ's sake."

She drained the champagne glass and set it on the bedside table and stared out the window. "I could ask you the same question. Why have you been spending so much time with Lady Elspeth?"

"To my knowledge, she's never kicked a dog," he shot back, hand on his hips again.

"I'm not defending Lord Murdock," Annabelle retorted.

"Fine, but you still didn't answer me. Why are you spending so much time with him if you don't even like him?" Why was he continuing this argument? He'd said what he needed to say. It was over. He should be escorting her to the door and praying the corridor was still empty.

Annabelle wrapped her arms around her middle. "Because...because...he's an ass."

"What?"

"Oh, it's all become so complicated—but none of that matters. I suppose I danced with him that first night at the Talbots' because...I wanted *you* to care." Her voice was broken.

"What?" His voice was hoarse now, shaking slightly. The question was completely different than the same word he'd just uttered moments before. He stalked toward her and spun her around to face him. Clutching her upper arms, he stared deeply into her ice-blue eyes. "Damn it, Annabelle. You already know I care. I can't stop thinking about you. I can't stop wondering what you're going to do next. I think about you every minute. I want you every second. I can't stop."

Annabelle's eyes were wide as moons as she stared up at him. "What did you say?" came her nearly silent whisper.

"I said I can't stop," he repeated.

She froze, tears pooled in her eyes. "Before that?" she whispered brokenly.

He pulled her into his arms. "I want you every second," he repeated, his lips inches from hers. "But I can't keep doing this, Annabelle. You've made it clear you don't want me."

"But I *do* want you, David. That's why I came here tonight." She reached up and wound her arms around his neck. "Make me yours."

CHAPTER TWENTY-NINE

Hope and lust flared in David's chest. "Are you certain, Annabelle?" He searched her face. She needed to be sure beyond any doubt.

"I've never been more certain about anything. There's only one thing I ask…" She bit her lip.

"What's that, love?" He pushed a lock of her hair behind her ear and traced his finger along the line of her cheek.

"I cannot get with child."

He leaned down and kissed her gently on the lips. "I'll make sure." It stood to reason that she would ask such a thing. Their wedding might not be for months, and a scandal would ensue if a baby came too soon.

She nodded, relief washing over her features.

That was enough. David allowed the lust to win. He was going to make love with Annabelle. First, he reached behind her and unbuttoned her gown. Then he slowly untied the sash. Next, he helped her pull the gown over her head, so she was standing in front of him with only a chemise and stockings. She'd already kicked off her slippers.

He let his gaze roam over her. "You're gorgeous, Annabelle. Do you know that?"

"So are you," she said with the hint of a smile on her face. She reached up and placed a hand on his rough cheek.

He leaned down and gently kissed her lips, but Annabelle clearly didn't want things to be gentle. She pulled his head down to hers and kissed him with abandon. David reached down to pull her chemise over her head. She helped him and the garment was soon discarded on the floor.

David sucked in his breath. The sight of Annabelle clad only in her stockings would be burned in his memory forever. Her body was lithe and slender. Her legs long. Her breasts, supple and perfectly rounded. She looked like Venus having just emerged from the seashell.

Annabelle pulled the pins from her coiffure and placed them on the table beside the bed. Then she shook out her long blond hair so that fell in thick waves over her shoulders. He watched, in awe of her beauty.

"Take off your breeches," she ordered after allowing his gaze to roam over her thoroughly.

"With pleasure, my lady." He unbuttoned the fall of the garment, and pulled them down to his ankles, where he kicked them off.

It was Annabelle's turn to look at him. "*You're* gorgeous, David," she breathed. Stepping forward, she placed her hand on his chest and moved it along the muscles of his flat abdomen where the skin jumped in reflex to her touch.

He closed his eyes briefly, allowing her to caress him. Her hand slipped down between his legs, and she closed her fist over his cock. David sucked in his breath. He clutched the canopy post, bracing himself against the unholy surge of desire that nearly brought him to his knees.

He had to control his breathing and his body's reaction to her or he'd embarrass himself tonight, and all he wanted to do was make it special for her. So special. He allowed her to squeeze him inexpertly at first, but learning fast. Too fast. He plucked her hand away. He lifted her in his arms and laid her gingerly on the bed. Then he climbed in after her and lowered himself atop her. They kissed and rolled until they were in the center of the mattress.

"Please tell me I can take these stockings off of you," he growled, his cock so hard it ached.

"Please do." She pushed herself up, bracing against her wrists, giving him a seductive look from beneath her lashes.

David intended to enjoy every moment of this. He moved his hands down the soft plane of her belly, skimming over her womanhood, before caressing the outsides of her thighs. He started at the scalloped edge of the stocking, licking his lips, before reaching out and rolling it down her thigh, inch by silken inch.

Annabelle pulled up her knee to give him better access, but David took his time, moving the stocking down her leg, trailing his hot fingertips along with it.

ANNABELLE LET her head fall back, her hair skimming the mattress behind her. She stared at the canopy and just allowed herself to feel David's strong hands on her quivering thighs. He was going so slowly it was driving her mad. When he finally pulled the first stocking off her foot, she lifted her head and met his dark-blue gaze. His eyes had turned into deep pools. His jaw was hard, and his cheekbones pronounced in the soft candlelight.

She watched him this time as he went about removing the second stocking with the same excruciating slowness. "Are you *trying* to torture me?" she asked, panting a little in anticipation.

"How did you guess?" he replied, his tongue flicking out to lick his bottom lip.

She groaned in the back of her throat.

When the second stocking was off, he balled them both together and tossed them high over his shoulder. Annabelle couldn't help but laugh when one of them landed on the edge of the canopy, hanging from it.

They were both completely nude now and stared at each other in awe, their gazes skimming each other's bodies to take in every inch.

"Can I touch you, David?"

"God, yes."

Annabelle reached up and caressed his chest, moving her hand down along his abdomen again. David closed his eyes.

"What does it feel like when I touch you?" she asked breathlessly.

"Torture," he replied, opening his eyes again. "Can I touch you now, please?" The side of his mouth quirked up. "With my tongue?"

Her eyes flared. What precisely did he mean by that? She wasn't entirely certain, but she desperately wanted to find out.

"Yes," she breathed.

David pushed her gently down on the mattress and covered her with his body. Then he kissed her lips, her cheeks, her ear, her neck. He nuzzled down to her collarbone and hefted each breast in his hand, sucking the nubs and gently biting them. Annabelle's back arched off the mattress. She pulled at his shoulders, wanting more.

He lavished first one nipple then the next with his rough tongue, sucking just enough to make her core ache. Her legs moved fitfully against the sheets. Her hands tangled in his hair. When he began to move lower, kissing her belly, her breath caught in her throat.

"What are you doing?" Her voice was hoarse.

"Kissing you…everywhere."

She gulped, her breaths coming so hard it hurt.

His head moved lower, and he wrapped his arms around her thighs, pulling them apart gently. Annabelle forgot to breathe.

David's tongue nudged between the folds of her sex, finding the same nub of pleasure he'd found last night. Only this time, he *licked* it. He sucked it into his mouth and nibbled it ever-so-lightly with his teeth. Then he brushed his tongue over it again.

Annabelle was mindless. Her legs turned to water, and she clutched at his dark head. She glanced down to see his mouth working between her legs and whimpered. If she'd thought last night had been unforgettable, tonight was going to break her.

David's tongue settled into a pattern of stroking her in tiny circles again and again all while his strong arms kept her thighs locked in place. His tongue flicked out again and again to torture her and she arched her back again, bracing against her wrists once more.

Her eyes rolled back, and her breathing hitched as he kept up the gentle assault with his tongue until her thighs tensed and her knees quivered and she cried out, clutching at his head, wanting him to come up and kiss her, while spasms rocked her body.

David licked her until her tremors subsided before obliging her by moving up her body and kissing her deeply.

She moaned into his mouth, tasting herself on his tongue.

He parted her legs and moved his hand down between her thighs. "Do you know how wet you are?"

She nodded.

"Wet and ready for me."

Her eyes went wide but she nodded again. "Take me, David."

~

DAVID POSITIONED himself between her legs and nudged gently into her wet warmth. It was unholy torture moving so slowly, but he remained determined to make this good for her. He slid into her an inch and stopped. "Tell me if I'm hurting you."

"You're not." Her arms were locked around his neck.

He nodded, sweat beading on his brow. He nudged in another inch, this time using the expression on her face to gauge whether she was enjoying it.

He inched in again. "You're all right?"

"Yes," she breathed. "Take me."

David's resistance broke. He pushed into her all the way, expelling his breath in a rush, then groaning. She felt so damn good, hot, and wet, and so tight she clutched his cock like a vise.

Her eyes flew wide, but a smile soon appeared on her face and she wrapped her arms around his neck harder.

"I want you, Annabelle," he groaned. "I want you so damn bad."

She lifted her knees to press against his hips. He pulled out and plunged back in, his hips pumping into her. "I want you. So. Damn. Bad." Each word was another thrust and each time he thrust she moaned, the sound like music to his ears.

David thrust into her again and again, the feeling so raw and intense he had to bite the inside of his cheek to stop himself from coming. He'd promised her that there would be no child, and he would keep that promise.

He allowed himself a few more strokes, just a few more moments to experience the unholy perfection of being inside of her. Then, he pulled out and flung himself back on the pillows beside her, breathing so heavily, he thought his heart might burst from his chest.

Annabelle's eyes flew wide, and she leaned up on one arm to look at him. "Was that…? Did you…?"

David took her other hand and placed it over his heart. "Do you see what you've done to me?"

A frown wrinkled her brow. "But did you…? Feel the same way I did?"

She was asking him if he'd had an orgasm, and going about it in the most adorable fashion. "Annabelle," he breathed. "There are many ways to make love. That is only one of them."

"But you didn't…" Her voice trailed off and her cheeks turned pink. She buried her head against her shoulder.

He cleared his throat. "If I had…*ahem*…finished, it's possible you would end up with child."

Annabelle peeked out one eye. "Oh. I suppose I didn't hear that part when I was listening at the door as Lady Courtney was telling Marianne about it."

David's eyes flew wide. "What?"

She kept her nose pressed to his shoulder. "I wanted to know how it worked, so I listened at the door."

"And you learned what exactly?" he asked tentatively.

"Enough to know that it was a lot like the horses at Bellingham Hall, but clearly not enough to know how a baby is created."

Despite his still-labored breathing, David chuckled. He leaned up on his arm and kissed her forehead. "Promise me you won't ever change, my darling."

Annabelle frowned at that. "But David, you still need to…"

David had flopped back onto the mattress. He eyed her from the corners of his eyes.

"You said there are many ways to make love." Her cheeks were pink again, but she held his gaze.

"So I did." He glanced down at his cock, still standing at attention, more than ready.

"Show me," she said, leaning over him and kissing his lips. "Tell me what to do."

David stared up at the canopy for a few moments. Was it the proper thing to do to teach one's future wife what he had in mind? Probably not, but in this case, he was the tutor, and she was the pupil. What a *heavenly* turn of events.

"Are you certain?" he asked, praying she said yes, but perfectly willing to stop if she had any doubts.

"Yes." She nodded.

He said a brief prayer of thankfulness before he let his hands drop on either side of his hips atop the sheets. "Very well." Nearly panting in anticipation, he tried to control his voice. "There are at least two other things we can do that would produce the same result without creating a child."

She leaned toward him, eyes wide, clearly interested in the topic. Thank Christ.

"What things?" she asked.

He closed his eyes and expelled his breath. "The first is… you can…touch me."

"Touch you?" she repeated.

"Yes. Take me in your hand, the same way you did when I first took off my breeches."

"Ooh!" Her eyes became even wider. Then a sly smile covered her face, and she moved her hand down his bare abdomen until she wrapped her fist around his length.

David swallowed and opened his eyes again. He was slowly breathing in and out, trying not to lose his mind.

"Like this?" she asked.

"Yes," he groaned. "*Exactly* like that."

"Now what? Should I squeeze it?"

"No." He shook his head. "Str...stroke it."

When Annabelle began slowly moving her hand up and down his cock, David stopped breathing. He fisted his hands in the sheets near his hips and clenched his jaw.

"Am I doing it correctly?" she asked, her voice a tentative whisper.

"So correctly," he whispered back on a groan.

She stroked him again and again while David's hips were captive to her hand. He thrust up into her clenched fist, while she watched in obvious awe. She stroked him again and again and again, while he bit the inside of his cheek, praying that he didn't spill his seed in her hand.

"You said there was another thing to do," she whispered in his ear. "What is it?" Her voice held a wicked note of debauchery.

If propriety was his goal, he was *positive* he shouldn't tell her the next thing. But the overwhelming desire to see Annabelle's full pink lips covering his cock was more than he could bear.

She stopped stroking him, waiting for his next lesson. Her hand remained wrapped around him.

"Tell me, David," she prompted. "What else can I do?"

David briefly said another prayer before meeting her gaze and saying in hoarse whisper, "You can suck me."

Unmistakable desire flared in her eyes as she moved to straddle him. Her knees on either side of his hips, she leaned down and kissed his mouth, then her lips moved to his cheek, his ear, his neck. Oh, God. She was doing to him exactly what he'd done to her. She ran her tongue down his chest, lightly scraping her fingernails against his nipples, before lapping at his abdomen and then going even lower.

The breath caught in David's dry throat when her mouth hovered over his cock. He bent his neck to look down at her.

It was an even more erotic sight than he'd guessed it would be. He throbbed.

She wrapped her thumb and forefinger around him before leaning down and licking just the tip. His hips nearly came off the bed. "Damn it, Annabelle. Don't tease me."

Her smile was sly. "Isn't that what you did to me?"

His breath was coming in short pants. He couldn't nod, couldn't speak, all he could do was watch as her lips lowered over him, and she took the head of his cock fully into her mouth.

He gripped the sheets in both hands again and prayed for mercy. But when Annabelle's mouth began moving up and down his length, every thought flew from his mind. An unrecognizable sound came from the back of his throat. It was half groan, half growl. A plea.

She stroked him with her mouth, the same way she'd done with her tongue, and David was mindless. He tried to keep his hips from moving, but they undulated on their own accord. When she began to stroke him with her hand and suck him, he reached down to pull her away. She was too fast of a learner. There was no way he wouldn't finish if she kept at it.

Annabelle squirmed away from his arms, resisting his attempt to stop her. She lifted her lips off him and said, "I want to keep doing this until it happens."

He eyed her warily. How much did she know? "Until what happens?"

Her mouth quirked up. "The same thing that would happen when you were inside me."

He expelled his breath and rubbed both hands roughly through his hair. Jesus Christ. How would he ever explain this?

"Annabelle, you don't understand. If you keep doing that, I'll—"

"You'll expel your seed," she said, matter-of-factly.

David swallowed. Oh, God. He couldn't laugh. Not now. Perhaps he should have explained all this before they began. Regardless, there was no going back now. "Yes," he replied simply. But he wanted to be certain she understood. "In your *mouth*."

"I know," she replied, just before lowering her lips over him again.

"Holy Christ," David breathed.

She was already sucking him again, and stroking him, too. Damn. Such. A. Quick. Learner. His bollocks tightened. His jaw locked. God. He hoped she wouldn't regret this afterward. But when she pulled her wet lips off him and sucked his tip, before stroking down the *entire* length of him again, David knew it was too late. He moved one hand to the back of her head and gently grabbed a handful of her luxurious hair.

"Damn it, Annabelle," he growled, grinding his teeth together as she slid down on him once more. "It's too good." He pumped himself into her mouth for the final time, his back arching, a tremendous groan ripped from his chest.

In the aftermath, he laid there, stunned. In his entire life he'd never had a climax grip him so hard. He'd wanted this woman for so long, and now that he'd had her, he only wanted more. And she was going to be his wife.

He waited for his breathing to set back to rights, while Annabelle snuggled against his chest with a grin on her face. He glanced at her twice. She didn't look appalled. She looked…proud.

He pulled her toward him in the crook of his arm and kissed the top of her head. "That was…amazing."

"Funny. That is the same word I would use to describe what you did to me," she agreed. "I hope I wasn't talking too much."

He cracked a grin. "Love, when you touch me like that, you can talk as much as you want."

She pushed herself up on one arm and leaned down to kiss his lips once, hard.

"I'm glad we did that," she said, already sliding off the bed. "I'll remember it forever."

Warning bells sounded in the back of David's skull as Annabelle pulled on her chemise.

He pushed himself off the bed, pulling the sheet with him to cover his hips. "The next time will be even better," he said, watching her face carefully.

Her head snapped to face him. "Oh, no. David. This can never happen again, and of course, you mustn't tell anyone." She turned to stare at the bed. "Which reminds me. We should probably do something with the sheets, so the maids don't—"

Dread poured through David's veins like ice water. "I'll take care of the sheets, Annabelle." He couldn't keep the desperation from his tone. "What do you mean 'it can't happen again'? You asked me to make you mine."

"Yes, and it was…" She sighed and stretched her arms far above her head. "*Lovely*. But I think you'd agree that if we continue as lovers, it would only end in pain."

He cocked his head to the side and stared at her as if she didn't understand what she was saying. "'Lovers'? 'End'? I thought you'd changed your mind. I thought you wanted to marry me."

Annabelle's mouth snapped shut and horror doused her features. "Oh, no, David." She shook her head so vigorously her hair flew over her shoulders. "I thought I was clear last night. I'll never marry."

"You only wanted me for one night?" he ground out, narrowing his eyes on her. "That's what you meant when you said, 'make me yours'?"

Annabelle reached out to cup his cheek, regret etched on her face. "Anything more would be too much of a risk."

Letting the blasted bedsheet drop to the carpet, David grabbed his breeches from the floor, and pulled them on. Then he stalked over to the sideboard and poured a brandy. He downed nearly half the glass, guzzling it, before turning back to face her. "No, Annabelle. This time it's not so simple. You're not leaving here without telling me *why*. Why won't you allow yourself to try?"

"You're drinking?" she intoned, staring at the glass in his hand as if it were a poisonous snake.

David was so incensed by her sudden change of attitude he barely registered her words. She was trying to change the subject again and he had no intention of allowing it. He raised his voice. "*Why* are you so unwilling to commit to a man? Why are you *so afraid of marriage?*"

Annabelle's face turned to stone. Her nostrils flared. "Just because I don't fall at the feet of the first man who comes courting doesn't mean I'm *afraid*." Her eyes flashed ice-blue fire.

He tossed a hand in the air, and the rest of the drink down his throat. He set the glass back on the sideboard with a thud. "Oh, that's right, you won't fall at the feet of *any* man who comes courting! You just want to collect them all around your skirts."

The moment the words passed his lips, he regretted them. But it was too late, and he was too angry to take them back.

"How dare you!" She leaned over and scooped her gown from the floor, pulling it over her head.

David came around the bed and towered over her. He was still incensed, but he didn't want her to leave her like this, and there was still the issue of her getting back to her own bedchamber without being seen. He had to put aside his anger and help her dress at least. "Damn it, Annabelle," he ground out as he flung up his arm to retrieve her errant stocking from the canopy.

A small cry issued from her throat and Annabelle ducked and crouched into a low ball on the floor.

David's eyes went wide. He lowered his arm and stared down at her in disbelief. "Oh, God, Annabelle. You didn't think—" He quickly crouched beside her, studying her face. "Please tell me you didn't think I was going to strike you."

"No." Her voice shook. She wouldn't meet his gaze. "No, of course not." She pushed herself to her feet again and took the stocking from him. He watched helplessly as she pulled on the rest of her clothing the best she could. The last few seconds played over and over in his mind. She'd denied it, but it was too late. He'd seen the look of terror in her eyes when she'd ducked. She *had* thought he was going to strike her. He was certain of it. He was horrified.

"Annabelle." He reached for her, but she quickly moved away from him toward the door. "I'm sorry. I didn't mean to frighten you." She couldn't leave like this. He'd never be able to live with himself. He'd scared her. He'd truly scared her. He'd seen the fear in her eyes.

Her clothes were askew. Her hair was a mess. Her gown wasn't buttoned, and her sash wasn't tied. But apparently, she intended to sneak back to her own room that way.

She opened the door a crack and peeked out.

"Annabelle, wait—" David called, in a last desperate attempt to get her to talk to him.

"Good-bye," she whispered, before slipping out the door.

CHAPTER THIRTY

The weddings were lovely. Three brides. Three grooms. Three sets of vows and three couples promising to love each other for all eternity. As the bishop performed the ceremony the next morning, David couldn't help but glance toward Annabelle. He'd glanced at her a hundred times already and she'd never once been glancing back.

Annabelle sat between her mother and Lord Murdock, who wore an obviously false grin on his face, especially during the parts of the ceremony when Lady Julianna declared her love for Lord Worthington. Annabelle's countenance didn't change, however, as she watched the couples declare themselves. She sat ramrod straight in her chair and stared directly ahead with a perfectly proper look on her face.

When it was Beau and Marianne's turn to recite their vows, David was convinced he'd got something in his eye. He was beyond happy for his sister, who looked gorgeous on her special day. Marianne wore a lacy white gown, a white veil, and she carried a bouquet of lilies. She'd never looked lovelier. If their parents and Frederick were still alive, they would all be as proud as David was.

After the ceremony, a large breakfast was served in the great hall. After that, most of the guests retired to their rooms to rest and prepare for the night's grand wedding ball.

David didn't even attempt to rest. Instead, he took a walk through the nearby woods, picking up sticks and evaluating them on their merits for whittling projects. But he had no interest in keeping any of them. Instead, he tossed them each back onto the ground with a curse.

Last night had been both the best and the worst night of his life. Making love to Annabelle had been perfect. He'd loved every moment of it. But afterward, the dream had turned into a nightmare.

David scrubbed a hand through his hair and flung another stick away. Why? Why was Annabelle so set on remaining a spinster? There *had* to be a reason. Did she want to retain control of her life? He had no intention of telling her what to do. Was she frightened of childbirth? It was true that many women died while giving birth, but her own mother had had two successful births. There was every reason to believe Annabelle could, too.

It certainly wasn't that she was unattracted to men. He knew that for certain. She hadn't mentioned any grand desire to study a subject, or travel the world. *What* was it that made her intent upon remaining a spinster?

The image of her crouching beside the bed last night haunted him. He winced every time he thought about it. Annabelle had been frightened. Of him. She'd truly thought he was going to strike her. But why? He certainly had never done so before—to any woman—or given her any reason to believe he might.

Damn it. There were no answers. Only more questions.

He grudgingly made his way back to the house. He had a book to study.

~

THE GRAND BALLROOM of Worthington Manor was filled with flowers, candles, and over five hundred wedding guests all celebrating the marriages of three of the most handsome and eligible bachelors of the *ton*, to three of the most beautiful and accomplished ladies.

David made the rounds as Marianne's only living family member. He greeted people, spoke to them, asked after their health, and even made plans to meet some of them again in London. He downed glass after glass of champagne to stave off his nerves, but he forced himself to speak to most the ballroom's occupants. He'd spent the afternoon studying that damned *Debrett's* so he wouldn't embarrass himself or Marianne on this night.

He danced with Lady Julianna and Lady Frances, wishing them well on their nuptials, and finally, he escorted his sister to the floor.

"You look beautiful, Marianne," he said as they twirled around in a waltz. "Mama, Papa, and Frederick would be proud."

Tears glistened in Marianne's bright blue eyes. "Oh, I hope so, David. I'm so thankful that *you're* here. I nearly lost you, too. There's nothing more comforting to me than knowing you are no longer in harm's way. I'm not certain I could live without my *entire* family."

David's breath caught in his throat. All this time he'd been wanting to return to the army, to the battlefield, to the place he knew best, where life made sense to him, but that would be selfish. If he put himself in harm's way, Marianne might end up completely alone. She would have Bell, of course, but her family, the family who'd raised her, would be entirely gone. Marianne had saved his life once…with a book. He would never purposely cause his beloved sister that sort of pain.

He twirled her around and around in three-step count, as a wide smile spread across his face. "For the first time, I can honestly say, I'm glad I'm here, too, Marianne."

His sister returned the smile. "Good, because while I may have been quite preoccupied today, I didn't fail to notice you've looked as if something has been troubling you."

He sighed. "Nothing I don't deserve."

"I doubt that," Marianne replied. "But after this, do ask Lady Elspeth to dance. She's been watching you like a dog watches its meal all evening."

David chuckled. "I will."

When the dance with Marianne came to an end, David did exactly that. He didn't have far to look to find Lady Elspeth, who was only too pleased to accept his invitation to dance.

He escorted her to the floor as the musicians struck up another waltz. She began to prattle about the details of the wedding and David did his best to follow along until Murdock and Annabelle twirled past them on the dance floor.

He immediately fell silent, and Lady Elspeth did not fail to notice.

"Are you quite all right, my lord?" she asked, tipping her head to the side to look at him.

"Yes. Yes, of course." But he couldn't even manage a fake smile. It drove him mad that Annabelle was dancing with Murdock. She'd told him last night she didn't even *like* the man. She'd called him an ass. What was her game now? The woman was maddening.

"It's Lady Annabelle, isn't it, my lord?" Lady Elspeth asked next in a resigned voice.

David expelled his breath. It was time to admit the truth. Lady Elspeth deserved better than a man who was in love with another woman. He had no hope of winning Annabelle any longer, but he had no intention of courting Lady Elspeth, either, and he needed to be honest with the young woman. "Yes, Lady Elspeth. It *is* Lady Annabelle."

"You fancy her?" Lady Elspeth said, a resigned though disappointed look on her face.

"I'm sorry, Lady Elspeth. I don't want to give you false hope."

Lady Elspeth lifted her chin and stared past his shoulder. "I see," was all she said, her face a mask.

When the music stopped, David escorted Lady Elspeth back to her mother. He thanked her for the dance, and she curtsied to him prettily, while he executed his most formal bow. Then he took his leave, a feeling of relief rushing through him. At least he'd managed to do one thing right at this house party. Set Lady Elspeth free. It was the right thing to do when all he could seem to think about was Annabelle. Inconvenient and fruitless as it was.

Two hours and five more glasses of champagne later, David was propped against a wall in the ballroom standing next to a potted palm. The palm was some of the best company he'd enjoyed all evening. It didn't speak and it didn't seem to mind that he didn't either. He'd made the rounds earlier for Marianne's sake, but he was quickly wishing he could sneak off to his bedchamber and fall into a blissful, forgetful slumber.

Downing the last bit of champagne in his glass, he pushed away from the wall, intent on doing exactly that.

CHAPTER THIRTY-ONE

Annabelle couldn't sleep. She was slumped against the pillows in her bed at Worthington Manor staring into the darkness. She'd watched the most beautiful weddings today. All three couples had declared their undying love for one another. The gowns had been gorgeous. The flowers had been lovely. The grooms had been handsome. The meal had been splendid, and the ball divine. Weddings themselves were always beautiful. It's what came after that was ugly.

Lord Murdock had sat at her side, his knuckles turning white as he clenched the arms of his chair when Lady Julianna declared herself to Lord Worthington. Lord Murdock obviously didn't care for Lady Julianna herself. He was simply unhappy because he'd lost her to Worthington. He couldn't stand to be defeated in the biggest game of the Season. And now Annabelle was his new prey. He didn't give a whit about her, either. It was obvious in the way he never asked her about herself. All his comments were about himself, his title, his money, and his social standing. None of which impressed Annabelle one whit. And they never would.

She probably shouldn't have gone to bed with David last night, but she couldn't quite bring herself to regret it. The man was incredibly handsome, and she'd wanted him fiercely. Only at the end, she'd remembered why men were much safer at arm's distance. He hadn't tried to strike her, but for one panic-filled moment, she'd somehow been convinced he was about to. He'd been drinking and he was angry. She hadn't been able to stop her body's instinctive response when he'd flung up his arm so near her.

Of course he didn't understand why she'd been so frightened. She didn't understand it herself. How could she possibly explain it to *him*?

She regretted that he'd misunderstood what she'd wanted from him last night. She certainly hadn't meant to mislead him. She'd assumed he'd be nothing but pleased with the arrangement. No promises made. No future implied. What man wouldn't be interested in such a convenient proposal? But apparently, she'd grossly underestimated David. She had felt bad about it, of course. Only, the regret was short lived after he'd accused her of being afraid. Her regret had been instantly replaced with white-hot anger.

And now that she'd had all day to think about it, she knew why his comment had bothered her so much.

Because she *was* afraid.

She was a coward, and always had been. She'd never been able to muster the courage to stand up to her father the way Beau had. And now not only did she not have the courage to take a husband, she didn't even have the courage to tell the man *why*. David deserved better than that. He deserved a woman he could love and who would love him back. Precisely as he'd said during their first lesson. Annabelle had no right to take such happiness away from him.

The rap at her bedchamber door made her sit up straight. Was she imagining it or had someone truly just knocked? She scrambled out of bed and wrapped her dressing gown around her before hurrying to the door and opening it a crack.

David was standing there looking so handsome she wanted to sigh. Tall, dark, fashionable. He was still wearing the fine black evening attire he'd worn to the ball tonight. He'd looked so dashing, she had barely been able to keep her eyes off him. When he didn't know she was looking, of course. Now his hair was slightly mussed, and he had a drink in his hand.

"May I come in, my lady?" he asked, bowing to her in an overblown fashion. "I swear I come bearing apologies."

Was he in his cups? "You don't owe me any apology, David."

"Yes, I do!" He announced loudly, bowing to her once again. Annabelle quickly decided it would behoove her to let him in before he caused such a commotion in the corridor that other guests began peeking out to see what was the matter. It would not do for them to be seen together like this.

She darted her head into the corridor to ensure no one was watching before she grabbed his wrist and tugged him inside.

She closed the door behind him. "Shh," she admonished.

He bowed again, and lowered his voice. "Would you care for a drink?"

"No." She shook her head.

"Neither would I." A grin spread across his face.

She had to smile. He'd clearly had a drink too many, but he was being entertaining, slightly silly, not angry. That was…different.

"First, I would like to apologize for frightening you last night," he said, bowing a third time.

She nodded. "David, you don't—"

"Second, I want to ask you a question," he said, interrupting her and pointing his finger in the air again.

She eyed him warily. A question. That sounded ominous. She didn't want this to end in another argument. "What question?"

"Has…my apologies, my lady, but there's no easy way to say this. Has anyone ever struck you before?"

The blood drained from Annabelle's face. Her heart pounded so hard it hurt. How did he know? Did David know the terror she'd lived in as a child? Was it obvious? Or had he simply guessed because of her reaction last night?

"I don't know what you mean," she insisted, shaking her head, and glancing down at her bare feet. She needed to get him out of her bedchamber as quickly as possible.

He narrowed his eyes on her. "I think you do. I'm asking if anyone has ever struck you. A man, I mean."

Swallowing the huge lump in her throat, she shook her head but couldn't quite meet his eyes. "No. No one." But even *she* didn't believe herself. Her voice had cracked. Oh, God. She was the worst kind of coward. She couldn't even tell the truth when faced with someone who'd guessed her past.

David turned away from her and cursed under his breath. His voice was low, nearly a whisper. "You *still* won't open up to me. After all this time."

"I don't know what you want me to say," she breathed. She had to get him out of here. He might not be violent or angry, but the drinking was making him far too honest. He was asking too many questions she had no intention of answering.

Reminding herself that it was better for David if she sent him away, she made her way to the door and opened it a crack. "Please leave," she said, pointing into the corridor.

David's jaw went rock hard. "Why?"

"Because I don't want to talk about this." She clenched her jaw and stared at the wall, still unable to meet his gaze.

"Is it the reason why you won't marry?" he asked. Sadness and regret sounded in his tone.

Annabelle expelled her breath and hung her head. She couldn't take this. She couldn't take his pity and she couldn't answer his questions. She *wouldn't* answer them. She wrenched the door open wide. "Please leave." But this time it was more of a plea.

Hurt and rejection flickered across his drawn face as David strode past her directly into the corridor.

"Oh, dear," a lady's voice sounded.

Fear gripped Annabelle tightly as her gaze swung into the hall to see Lady Elspeth and her mother standing not two paces from David. He'd obviously nearly run into them.

Lady Elspeth's mother's eyes were wide as carriage wheels when she saw Annabelle standing in the doorway in her night rail.

"Oh, my goodness!" Lady Elspeth cried, glancing back and forth between David and Annabelle, just before she swooned into a dead faint.

CHAPTER THIRTY-TWO

David was sitting in a chair next to the fireplace in his room the next morning, nursing both a sick head and a memory full of regrets. The previous night had ended after Lady Elspeth's scream had brought half the occupants of the floor running toward Annabelle's bedchamber—including Beau and Marianne.

They'd all eventually gone back to their rooms, but not before the damage had been done. Half of the *ton* had seen David standing outside Annabelle's bedchamber while Annabelle was undressed, and the other half of the *ton* seemed to have heard about it by morning. Lady Elspeth and her mother wasted no time spreading the news that David had come directly out of Annabelle's room in the middle of the night.

There was no use denying it. The truth was the truth, and he'd be nothing but a scoundrel if he called Lady Elspeth and her mother liars. But that didn't make the fallout any better. He'd made his share of bad decisions in his time, but none of them compared to his getting jug-bitten at his sister's wedding and going to Annabelle's bedchamber last night. He and Annabelle had managed to be together the night before without any consequences. Chance wasn't that forgiving. He'd been a complete fool to have attempted it a second time.

David read the same sentence for a fourth time before closing the book he'd been pretending to read, and tossing it onto his bed. He wasn't precisely hiding in his bedchamber, but he wasn't anxious to leave it either, not until he'd had a chance to speak to his sister and assess the damage. He'd already met with Lady Angelina and Beau last night. It was amazing how quickly one could become sober when one was faced with a scandal. He'd promised Annabelle's mother and brother he'd do the right thing by marrying her. He'd further promised to agree to any marriage contract terms they deemed fit. He would not ruin her reputation and walk away.

His assurances and willingness to extend his hand appeased both Beau and Lady Angelina, but it wasn't their opinions David was worried about. It was Annabelle's. Hers was truly all that mattered.

He wasn't about to go traipsing back to Annabelle's room to ask to speak with her, however. For all he knew, she'd take a pistol to him. He needed someone else to tell him how she was acting. To that end, he'd sent a note to his sister requesting a visit.

A few moments later, a soft knock sounded at the door and Marianne opened it and slipped inside. "There you are," she breathed, looking relieved.

David couldn't muster a smile. "Where else would I be?"

Marianne came sauntering up to him, her arms crossed over her chest. "I don't know, out playing pall mall on the lawn with the ladies and their mothers, perhaps."

"You are terribly amusing," he grumbled, crossing his arms over his chest, too, and slumping down in his chair. He pushed his booted feet out in front of him.

"I am, aren't I?" Marianne replied, smiling brightly.

David took a deep breath. This was not the time for jests. He needed to take responsibility for his poor choices and his reckless actions. "I'm sorry for ruining your wedding, Marianne."

Marianne's red brows shot up. "Nonsense. The wedding was over, and besides, everyone will be talking about it for years to come. I'd say it was a rousing success. The *ton* adores gossip, you know. Frances is thrilled, by the by. She thinks this may replace her father's arrest at the top of the list of recent scandals."

David shook his head and then grabbed it. He shouldn't have done that. He'd had far too much to drink last night for head-shaking this morning. "I'm glad *you* can see the humor in this situation," he continued, "but I feel it necessary to point out that I doubt this will end well for either our family or Bell's. Scandals aren't good. I know enough to know that."

Marianne stepped closer and put a hand on his shoulder. "I don't care what the *ton* thinks. I care how my brother is feeling about a marriage he's going to be forced into."

David frowned. "Forced into? Lady Annabelle would make anyone a fine wife."

Marianne searched his face. "But do you *love* her, David?"

Not meeting his sister's eyes, he rubbed his jaw that was rough with day-old stubble. "I've been around the *Beau Monde* long enough to know that love isn't necessary for marriage."

Marianne crossed her arms over her chest again and stared down at him. "Papa obviously thought it was. He gave up everything he knew for love, including his title."

David nodded. "Indeed, he did." Why did she have to remind him about their *father* at a time like this?

"And I love Beau with all my heart, and I know Julianna and Rhys, and Frances and Lucas love each other, too," Marianne continued.

David nodded again. "Yes, but Annabelle has made it clear to me time and time again that she is wholly uninterested in marriage."

"Forgive me, but at this point in the conversation, I feel compelled to ask. What were you doing in her bedchamber, David?"

David scrubbed a hand through his hair. "Would you believe me if I told you I was being a drunken idiot?"

Marianne arched a brow and shrugged. "I suppose I must."

"Fine. Then I was being a drunken idiot. Absolutely nothing untoward happened last night." There. That was true at least.

"That may be," Marianne replied, "but the *ton* doesn't care about the truth. They care about the salacious details, and unfortunately, Lady Elspeth and her mother seem all too eager to share those details."

"How is Lady Elspeth?" David asked.

"The poor girl needed a half a bottle of smelling salts last night. Thank heavens you caught her before she hit her head on the floor."

David winced. "Is she suffering any lingering ill-effects?"

Marianne shrugged. "She seemed right as rain when she was leaving this morning. In fact, she seemed pleased with the turn of events."

"Pleased?" David frowned. Was Lady Elspeth such a gossip that she was pleased to have stumbled upon a scandal?

Marianne nodded. "Yes, she was nearly giddy when she told Lord Murdock what she'd seen."

David groaned.

"Speaking of Lord Murdock," Marianne continued, "at least you saved Annabelle from that awful man. He left here ranting about how unstable women are. Until Lady Elspeth calmed him down."

"I'm not sure Annabelle would characterize what I did as 'saving' her," he replied.

"Honestly, I love you both, and I don't want to see either one of you do something you'll regret." Marianne leaned over and squeezed David's shoulder. "Just please promise me you'll remember what Mama said."

"Marry for love and you'll never regret it," David breathed. Why did she have to remind him about their *mother* at a time like this? He scratched his chin again and contemplated the words. Love? He loved Annabelle. He knew it. That was the funny feeling that spread through his middle every time she was near. He certainly was missing it now. But it didn't matter that he loved her. The problem was, she didn't love *him*.

"I'm not certain Mama's words are true any longer," David added with a sigh.

"Whyever not?" Marianne asked, scrunching her brow.

David couldn't bring himself to tell his sister that he'd ruined Annabelle's life. That she'd never intended to marry anyone. That wasn't his secret to tell.

After Marianne left, David leaned back in his chair and expelled a deep breath. He'd really gone and done it this time, hadn't he? He was entirely to blame for last night. He'd arrived at Annabelle's doorstep foxed and demanding answers from her again, like the arse he was. He never should have gone to her bedchamber last night and now he was about to ruin her life with his ill-mannered, cloddish behavior. The truth was, he didn't deserve a woman as fine as Annabelle and he wouldn't blame her if she hated him forever.

CHAPTER THIRTY-THREE

Apparently, one of the advantages of being a nobleman was the ability to procure a special marriage license from the archbishop of Canterbury. In fact, Worthington sent for it immediately and it arrived not a day later by special messenger. An excruciating day in which David remained in his bedchamber while the rest of the wedding guests (save for Lady Angelina and Annabelle) packed up and left, all with the story of how Lady Annabelle Bellham was finally brought to the altar by gossip, of all sordid things.

According to Marianne, Lord Murdock had left in a raging fit, Lady Angelina was beside herself with glee, and Annabelle was holed up in her own bedchamber not speaking to anyone.

David couldn't stand it any longer. He refused to marry Annabelle without at least speaking to her first. The many notes he'd sent to her room via footmen went unanswered until he finally marched over and knocked on her door. The damage was already done. It wasn't as if he could ruin her reputation *again*.

Lady Angelina answered the door on the first knock. When she saw the look on David's face, she turned to Annabelle and said, "I think I'll just go for a walk around Lord Worthington's gardens."

"No, Mama. Wait!" Annabelle called.

But it was too late. The older lady took off down the corridor before Annabelle had a chance to say another word.

David watched her go, surprised by her speed. He shook his head and stepped into Annabelle's room. He was thankful for the privacy, but careful to leave the door open for propriety's sake...not that it mattered any longer.

Annabelle was standing near the fireplace, wearing a pink gown. Her clothing and her hair looked simple and sweet, but her face wore a thunderous expression.

"You didn't answer any of my notes," he said, immediately wanting to kick himself for saying something so obvious. Why did he always say obvious things in front of her?

"I didn't want to speak with you," she clipped.

He had to smile. *That* was obvious too. "I'm certain your mother has told you, but Lord Worthington has procured a special license for us to marry. The vicar is coming in the morning."

"Yes, Mama told me." Her voice was devoid of emotion.

"And?" he prompted.

"And what?" She flashed him an inscrutable look.

"Do you intend to go through with it? Do you intend to marry me?" Anxiety tinged his voice.

Annabelle laughed a humorless laugh. "You ask as if I have a choice in the matter."

"You do, Annabelle. Of course you do. I would never force you into a marriage you don't want, no matter the circumstances."

Another humorless laugh. She stepped toward him, her arms tightly crossed over her chest. "Spoken just like a man.

You have a choice. You could leave me and my reputation in tatters. I've seen what scandals like this do to women. I'd be an outcast. Mama and Beau would be treated like vermin. I have no choice."

David hung his head. "I'm sorry it has to be like this."

Annabelle's voice was filled with anger. "I suppose next you'll tell me if this had happened in Brighton, it would be different. Brighton doesn't have the strict rules of the *ton*. Go on. Tell me."

David shook his head. "I've nothing to say. The truth is, if I'd been discovered in your bedchamber in Brighton, we'd be planning a wedding right now also. Only the archbishop wouldn't be involved and there'd be longer to wait."

Annabelle turned away from him and moved toward the window. Her voice was low and came through clenched teeth. "I want to make something quite clear. We shall be married in name only. You will *not* own my body and you will *not* own me!"

THE DOOR SHUT BEHIND DAVID, and Annabelle turned to the empty room with tears welling in her eyes. Her entire body was shaking. She wrapped her arms around her middle. He hadn't said a word. She had just told him they'd be married in name only, and he hadn't said a word. Hadn't argued with her, hadn't asked her why. Was that because he had no intention of living that way, or was he so filled with guilt he didn't want to argue with her at the moment? She had no way of knowing, but she did know one thing...he would not harm her. She would not allow it. And if he didn't touch her, if they weren't intimate, she would not give him children whom he could ever hurt, either.

Annabelle walked to her bed on legs that felt like water

and nearly collapsed atop it. The situation they were in was not entirely David's fault. She knew that. She shouldn't have played such a dangerous game with her body and her emotions, let alone his. But ever since she'd heard Lady Elspeth's shriek in the corridor, Annabelle had been racked with soul-numbing fear. It had invaded her entire body, leaving her numb and shaky. First, she'd been fearful that a scandal would ensue. Then, when everyone had come running, that fear had been replaced by the prospect of being an outcast from the only Society she'd known. Later, when she'd been huddled in bed with Mama stroking her head and telling her everything would be all right, Annabelle had been afraid there was no way out of getting married. And late this morning, after she'd nearly turned into a puddle going through almost every possible emotion, she'd been afraid that she might actually *want* to marry David. And that was the most frightening thought of them all.

But when David had come to the door this afternoon and demanded to see her, the overwhelming fear that had been coursing through her for hours and hours had turned immediately into white-hot anger. He didn't even necessarily deserve her anger, but she hadn't been able to control it. All the fears she'd pushed aside since childhood had turned to rage and come roiling through her body and out her mouth, demanding that David agree to a marriage in name only so she wouldn't have to be petrified of the future.

Sobs racked her body, and she buried her face in the mattress. She was weak. As all cowards were. Instead of telling him she felt something for him—instead of telling him she just might love him, even—she'd lashed out at him and blamed him for their predicament. Oh, she was the worst sort of coward. She wasn't even brave enough to tell the truth.

CHAPTER THIRTY-FOUR

"I wouldn't blame you if you call me out, Bell," David said later that afternoon as he sat in a large leather chair in the study. David was nursing a brandy and spinning the glass around on the desktop in front of him. He'd asked the other men to give them their privacy. This conversation between himself and Bell was overdue. "Though I must say in Brighton, a solid beating is much more expedient," David continued. "We don't do this 'calling out' nonsense. Far too formal. If you want to meet me out on the lawn for fisticuffs, however, I'll gladly—"

"Call you out? For what?" Bell was drinking a cup of tea as if they were at afternoon garden party, for Christ's sake, instead of in the middle of a bloody catastrophe.

David widened his eyes and stared at the marquess as if he'd lost his mind. "Ruining your sister? Remember?"

Bell threw back his head and laughed. "You didn't ruin her. You're marrying her. Mother is thrilled, by the by."

David tossed back the remainder of the contents in his glass and stood to walk over to the sideboard and pour himself another. "Well, that makes one person in your family who's thrilled. Annabelle certainly isn't."

Bell frowned. "What gives you that idea? I assumed she was partial to you, or she wouldn't have been, *ahem*, doing whatever you two were doing that necessitates the wedding."

David shook his head. "Partial, perhaps. But wanting to marry, never."

Bell shook his head. "I don't understand."

"Frankly, neither do I. Have you ever wondered why your sister has refused all offers of marriage?" David replied.

"I've wondered, but according to Annabelle, she simply hadn't met the chap she wanted to spend the rest of her life with."

"I'm not certain that chap exists," David replied.

Bell frowned again. "What do you mean?"

"Your sister has told me time and again that she's singularly uninterested in marriage. She wasn't planning to marry Murdock, and she isn't at all happy about having to marry me. She's opposed to the institution itself."

Bell plucked at his lower lip. "Did she tell you that?"

"In nearly as many words." David left his glass on the desktop and turned to face his friend. It hadn't occurred to him until this moment, but Bell might be able to answer the question Annabelle wouldn't. "The other night, when I was alone with Annabelle, I raised my hand sharply while standing next to her. I meant her no harm, of course, but she fell to the floor and curled into a ball." David took a deep breath and met his friend's eyes. "Why would she do that, Bell? Has a man ever struck her?"

David had never seen the Marquess of Bellingham at a loss for words. Nor had he ever seen the confident spy turn pale, and he'd certainly never heard all the breath rush from his lungs. But when all three things happened simultaneously, it caused the hair on the back of David's neck to prickle.

Panic clutched at David's middle. "Please tell me 'no,'" he breathed, still carefully watching Bell's face.

"No," Bell finally uttered, but his face remained colorless, and he turned his head to stare straight ahead at the wall, shaken, as if he'd seen a ghost. "At least, not that I ever witnessed, but…"

David sat up straighter in his chair. He leaned toward Bell. "But what? What is it? Why is she so afraid of men?"

Bell braced an elbow atop the desk and let his head drop into his palm. He took a long, deep breath. "God, Elmwood. How could I have been so bloody stupid all these years?"

"What? Tell me." David's voice was rough, demanding.

"Our father," Bell continued. He lifted his head to stare at the wall again. His jaw was tight. "The blackguard drank to excess and became abusive when he did so. He beat Mother, and…at times…he beat me."

David swallowed the lump in his throat that had been forming ever since he'd seen the look of pure anguish on Bell's face. "And Annabelle witnessed it?"

Bell nodded slowly. A pulse ticked in his jaw. "I'm ashamed to say she did. The bastard never struck her that I'm aware of. But she saw things. On more occasions than I care to recall."

David pressed his lips together and briefly closed his eyes. What did he say to his strong, proud friend, who was admitting something that had to be beyond difficult? David didn't trust himself not to speak in anger.

The pulse continued to throb in Bell's jaw and a look of pure hatred shone in his ice-blue eyes. "Of course, that was when I was a child. When it wasn't a fair fight. The moment I became old enough, big enough to hit back and do damage, the bastard stopped. Annabelle was still quite young then. I…

I mistakenly believed she hadn't been affected, perhaps didn't even remember it." Bell shook his head. "I've been a fool."

Another lump formed in David's throat. He could only imagine what it had cost his friend to stand up to his own father that way. No wonder Bell was so strong.

"Annabelle thinks a man striking his wife is normal behavior," David finally breathed, his mind racing. "Which would explain her fear. She also told me she didn't want any children." David's chest was tight. It all made sense now. So much sense. Awful sense, but it explained all of Annabelle's reticence.

Bell nodded gravely. "It makes me ill to think that, but it stands to reason. I've heard her mention things through the years about not wanting to 'belong' to a man."

So many things made sense now. David nodded toward Bell's teacup. "It's why you don't drink, isn't it?"

"Yes," Bell said, lifting his cup in the semblance of a salute. "Though for years, I've lived with the regret of not coming to my father's bedside when he was dying. The man was a bastard most of his life, and I never could forgive him. But apparently he was regretful in the end."

David reached out and clapped a hand on his friend's shoulder. "I don't blame you. And if you ask me, you should have no regrets. Any man who beats a woman or child isn't worthy of any title, especially that of 'father'."

Bell nodded, once.

"As for drinking, you must know you're nothing like him," David continued.

The marquess stared unseeing at the wall again. "Perhaps, but I never trusted that I wouldn't turn into him if I drank. That is a fear I've never been able to conquer."

"That sort of violence isn't in you, Bell," David assured him, pulling his hand away.

"I hope not, Elmwood. But I don't intend to ever find out." Bell stood and walked toward the door.

"Where are you going?" David asked, turning in his seat to face him.

"To have a long overdue talk with my sister."

CHAPTER THIRTY-FIVE

Annabelle was in Lord Worthington's splendid conservatory as dusk approached. The magnificent space was filled with all sorts of flowers, including orchids, of all lovely things. Annabelle had always adored orchids. So unique and beautiful. None of her silly suitors in London had ever thought to send her any. None of them had ever asked what she preferred. She was sitting on a stone bench near the delicate flowers when her brother came hiking through the mulch toward her.

Without saying a word, Beau sat beside her and expelled his breath. He stared straight ahead, not looking at her, his forearms resting on his knees.

Annabelle waited for him to say something. Beau was never at a loss for words, but when several interminable minutes passed without so much as a greeting, she decided to be the one to speak.

"Yes?" she prodded. She knew her brother well enough to know he hadn't just happened by. When Beau came looking for you, it was because he had something to say, usually something one would do well to listen to. "Why have you come?"

"To speak with you," he replied simply, as he stared directly ahead at the orchids.

"And yet you do not speak." She tried to smile at the jest, but Beau turned to look at her just then and their gazes met. Were those tears in her brother's eyes? Oh, no. She couldn't stand it if Beau cried. Beau was the strongest, bravest person she knew. What was wrong? Why did he have tears in his eyes? Tears filled her eyes too.

"The problem is," Beau finally said softly, "for once in my life, I'm not entirely certain what to say."

Annabelle swallowed a lump in her throat. "Do you want to say something about my impending marriage, perhaps?" she offered. That had to be why he was here. She'd embarrassed her brother by being caught in a scandal at his wedding, of all events. Was Beau ashamed of her? She couldn't bear it if he was ashamed of her.

"It has to do with your impending marriage, in a way," Beau replied.

Annabelle's hands were beginning to perspire. Worry was quickly spreading through her veins. "You're frightening me, Beau. Please say it. It cannot be worse than what I'm imagining."

Beau took another deep breath. He hung his head and stared at the mulch beneath his boots. "Annabelle," he began. Her chest ached to hear her brother's voice so vulnerable and raw. "Do you think I would ever strike Marianne?"

Annabelle gasped. What did he say? Unthinkable. "No, of course not." She shook her head vigorously.

Beau nodded slowly before asking, "Do you think I would ever strike you? Or Mother?"

"Never," she breathed, but the lump she'd swallowed was back and so large she could barely breathe. And the tears in her eyes had welled to a point where she couldn't even see. The conservatory was a mostly green blur.

Beau nodded again, his head still bowed. "In the same way that I would never strike you, or Mother, or Marianne, there are other men who would never do such things either. Our father just wasn't one of them."

The tears slipped down Annabelle's cheeks. They hadn't spoken about these things in years. Never spoken about them as adults, certainly. The scars of their childhood had healed over without any discussion. That was the way of their set, wasn't it? Stiff upper lip and all that. Now her brother was ripping open those long-forgotten wounds with a few simple words. "What are you saying, Beau?" she managed to ask, though her throat ached terribly.

Beau pushed himself back on the bench and met her gaze again. Ever the gentleman, he pulled a snowy white handkerchief from his inside coat pocket and handed it to her. "I'm saying I believe Elmwood is a good man. The type of man who would never raise a hand to you. I've seen him in his cups. He's more of a jester than a fighter when he's foxed."

Annabelle wiped at her eyes with the handkerchief. "I suppose I'm a fool, but I've lived all these years never even considering the fact that *you* would never strike anyone. Of course that means there must be other men who were honorable as well."

"You're not a fool, Annabelle. You're a young woman who was exposed to things at a very young age you never should have had to see. I'm the fool who should have realized why you never wished to marry."

"You're not a fool, Beau." Her voice cracked. "You were a boy who endured things he never should have had to endure."

"I didn't let that stop me from finding love, however," Beau pointed out. "I was afraid of opening up too, believe me. I was married to my work until I met Marianne. But the right person only comes along once, Annabelle, and I'd hate to see you lose him because of your fear of the past."

Annabelle sucked in her breath. Her brother, her wise, thoughtful, older brother, was telling her precisely what she needed to hear at precisely the moment she needed to hear it. Just like he always did with all his friends and loved ones. All she could do was nod.

"Have you ever wondered why all these years I haven't insisted you marry?" Beau asked next.

Annabelle dabbed at her eyes again. "I...I thought it was because I told you I hadn't yet picked a suitor I wished to marry."

Beau nodded. "Partially, but I was under no delusion that you intended to pick anyone anytime soon."

She laughed, though the tears continued to drip from her eyes. "I should have known I wasn't fooling you."

"Or Mother, either," Beau continued. "The truth is we knew you weren't ready to marry, and we didn't want to force you."

"You've always been the best older brother, Beau." She reached over and placed her small hand atop his large one. "I hardly deserve you."

The side of Beau's mouth quirked up in a grin. "I don't know about that. But more than anything, I want you to be happy, Annabelle. Whether that's with or without a husband. I've always felt that way."

She nodded, pressing the handkerchief to her eyes to dry what she hoped would be the last of the tears. "Thank you, Beau."

"I won't force you to marry now, either, but I have to ask. Do you think you could love Elmwood, if you weren't so afraid of the past?"

Annabelle took a deep breath. She wrapped her arms

around her middle. "I'm frightened, Beau. I've never been as strong or as brave as you are." She hung her head. "I'm a coward."

"I beg your pardon," Beau sat up straight, a completely affronted look on his face. "You're a Bellham, sister dear. You're no coward, and you never have been."

She shook her head dejectedly and let her hands drop into her lap again. "I never stood up to Father. I never fought him like you did."

Beau reached over and squeezed her hands. "Think what you're saying, Annabelle. You were a *child*. A *little girl*. Much younger than me. You were never a match for an adult man. And you never would be. Just like Mother was unable to win against him. It was never a fair fight. And as for you being cowardly, that's nonsense. You had to run—with *blood on your clothing*—through the house at all hours of the night to find your governess and ask for help. How many little girls are brave enough to do that? You were frightened of the dark, Annabelle. Yet you still went. Think if *you* had a little daughter. Would you want her to stand up to a grown man who was swinging a weapon, as Father often was?"

Annabelle felt as if the air had been knocked from her chest. Beau was right. She would never expect a child to fight a grown man. Why hadn't she been able to think of it that way all these years? She *had* been brave. She'd gone to fetch Mary time and again in the terrifying darkness.

She took a deep breath, met her brother's gaze, and nodded. "You're right, Beau. You're always right, of course." She managed a smile.

"Now, I'm going to ask you again. Do you think you could love Elmwood?"

Considering her brother's words for a few moments, Annabelle took a shaky breath and then blew it out. When she spoke, her voice shook too. "I think I already do."

Beau knocked his shoulder against hers. "Good, because I mentioned to Elmwood that our father was an abusive drunk and I think he loves you more now than he did before."

Annabelle smiled through her tears. "I don't know that he loves me, but I intend to find out."

Beau regarded her from the sides of his eyes. "It takes courage to lead a full and happy life, you know."

She nodded, taking another shaky breath. "Yes."

"And you've *never* been a coward, Annabelle."

She nodded again before standing and lifting her chin. "I certainly don't intend to be one now." Raising her skirts, she rushed away.

CHAPTER THIRTY-SIX

David was sitting on a long leather sofa in Worthington's library. He'd come into the room to look for a copy of *Debrett's* again. He needed to do better, to be better at all the things pertaining to Society. If he were going to be married to Annabelle, he would die before embarrassing her and her family any more than he already had.

The door to the grand room opened and David glanced up to see Annabelle step inside, a tentative smile on her face. Had she spoken to Bell? How had *that* gone?

"What are you doing?" she asked, coming to stand next to him.

"Reading *Debrett's*," he offered, watching her carefully. Was she still angry? She didn't *look* angry. She didn't *sound* angry. But he couldn't be certain.

"Are you serious?" she asked, a smile on her face.

All right. He was fairly certain she *wasn't* angry. But why? What had Bell said to change her mood? "Yes, I'm serious," he replied. "I need to learn everyone's titles and family histories."

"No, you don't." She laughed.

He narrowed his eyes on her. "Why not?"

She lowered herself to the sofa beside him. "May I tell you a secret?"

"Please do."

"I don't know everyone's titles and family histories."

David gave her a skeptical glance. "I don't believe you."

She laughed again. "It's true. I paid some attention in finishing school, but I don't have it all memorized."

He lifted both brows. "You don't?"

"No. In fact, I've learned you can usually tell a person's title based on how the person closest to them is behaving. And if that doesn't work, just smile and nod until someone mentions it."

He blinked at her. "You must be jesting."

"Not at all. It works. Try it."

"So, there are people who meet me and have no idea I'm an earl?" he said with a laugh.

"Of course. Like when I met you."

David nodded. "That's true. I had nearly forgotten about that."

She leaned over and whispered in a conspiratorial tone, "May I tell you something else?"

He leaned toward her too. Their lips were inches apart. "Of course."

"I haven't prayed since I was a little girl, but I came here directly from the conservatory and I prayed the entire way."

He furrowed his brow. He had no idea how this conversation was about to unfold, but he was profoundly curious. She seemed almost playful, completely different from the last time he'd seen her only a few hours earlier. "Why were you praying?" he ventured.

"I was praying it wasn't too late." Tears sparkled in her eyes.

"Too late for what?"

"To apologize."

He sucked in his breath.

"David, I'm sorry." Her voice was low. Contrition was written across her features.

"Sorry? For what?" He searched her face.

"For taking this long to tell you that I *do* want to marry you. If you'll still have me, of course."

"Annabelle, are you certain? I don't want to force you into it."

"No. I'm here of my own free will, and I would have come to the realization that I love you much sooner if—"

"What was that?" He felt the blood drain from his face.

She bit her lip and peered at him. "I love you. There. I can say that now. I think I've loved you since the moment you were rude to me in the Harrisons' gardens."

He chuckled. "Why would you love me for that?"

She shrugged. "I'd never met anyone like you before. I was used to the gentlemen of the *ton* falling at my feet. I'd never met a man who didn't give a fig who I was."

"I didn't know who you were."

"Precisely. I suppose I found it irresistible when you told me I was the last lady in London you'd ever court."

He laughed. "I forgot I said that. I was a fool."

"No, you weren't. It was no more than I deserved." She cleared her throat. "Now, are you going to tell me you love me, too, or must I wait even longer?" Her face was so pretty, so pretty and so vulnerable.

David scrambled off the sofa so quickly he nearly fell off. He got down on one knee in front of her and grabbed both of her hands. "I love you, Annabelle. I didn't want you to think I only *thought* I loved you because you were a prize to be won. That's not it. I love it when your mouth quirks up in that adorable way of yours. I have a funny feeling in my middle whenever you're here and I miss it when you're gone."

"What?" She furrowed her brows.

"It doesn't matter. What matters is that I do a proper job of asking you to marry me." David took a deep breath and met her eyes. He squeezed her hands in his. "Annabelle Bellham, will you do me the honor of becoming my wife?"

More tears pooled in her ice-blue eyes. "Yes, David Ellsworth. I will."

He leaned up to kiss her and pulled her into his arms. "I'm going to learn how to be the best earl in the country. Believe me. I'll make you proud."

When they'd both settled back into their seats, still holding hands, Annabelle said to him, "Don't you understand, David? You don't need to be the best earl in the country. You're already the best Earl of Elmwood and that's all you need to be."

"How am I the best Earl of Elmwood? I know nothing about the title."

"You don't have to know anything. That's just it. It was clearly in the Elmwood bloodline for your father to abandon the title and it's in you to take it back up. For all you know, our son will want to escape to Brighton and marry a commoner."

David's jaw dropped. "Our son? But I thought you said—?"

"I know what I said." She shook her head. "And I was wrong. I've been afraid of the demons in my past for far too long. I know you'd never raise a hand to me, or our children, David."

David met her gaze with a tentative stare. "Bell told me…"

"I know. He's a good brother, Beau Bellham. I love him very much. It was shortsighted of me to think that you weren't as good a man as Beau is. I know for certain Beau would never hurt me, or Marianne, or anyone, for that matter."

"That's true," David said with a nod. "I promise I will never raise a hand to you, Annabelle. And if you'd like me to give up drinking, I will."

Annabelle shook her head. "No. You don't have to do that. Beau has made the choice to do that, but I don't want to be a prisoner to my father's poor decisions. I want to be free, David. Free from the monsters in my memory. I told you once that a great deal of the correct behavior in the *ton* involves pretending. The truth is, I've been pretending for years. Pretending I was aloof, instead of admitting I was frightened. Pretending I didn't care, when I really just wanted someone to love me for myself. I didn't think that was possible until I met you. I don't want to pretend anymore, David."

"Neither do I. And you're right. I may not be like the other noblemen. But I'm the only Earl of Elmwood there is. I'll be the most unconventional earl in London if I must. I refuse to be anyone other than who I truly am. And if I bungle a title or use the wrong fork at dinner, so be it."

"That's the spirit, Lord Elmwood!" she said, clapping a hand on his knee.

David pulled her into his arms and kissed her again. "I cannot wait to take you to Brighton and show you the cottage where Marianne and I grew up. It's the only thing I own that wasn't my grandfather's. It's mine. It's my home, and I want to share it with you."

"It sounds like the perfect place for a honeymoon," Annabelle replied with a laugh. "We can smoke cigars and do as we please."

"I like how you think." He kissed her deeply again.

A few moments later, a knock at the library door interrupted them. They broke off their kiss just before the door swung wide and Bell and Marianne, Worthington and Julianna, Kendall and Frances, and Lady Angelina all came traipsing into the room one after the other.

Worthington took in the sight of David and Annabelle smiling and holding hands and said, "So, does this mean there will be a fourth happy wedding here tomorrow morning?"

Annabelle nodded. "It does, indeed, Your Grace. I cannot wait to be Lady Elmwood."

"I'm just glad you didn't accept Lord Murdock's suit," said Julianna with a sigh. "I was quite worried for you."

"Oh, that reminds me," Frances said. "I went poking around this morning before all the guests left, and you'll never believe what I learned from one of my friends."

"What?" Annabelle asked.

"It turns out Elspeth planned the entire episode. She wanted Lord Murdock for herself," Frances replied.

"You must be jesting," Marianne interjected.

"No. I have it on good authority that Lady Elspeth told anyone who would listen that she was behind the entire affair," Frances replied. "She spied on Lord Elmwood last night and followed him to Annabelle's bedchamber. Then she went to fetch her mother to have a witness when he left."

"Good God," Worthington said. "A young lady with a mission in the marriage mart is a formidable foe, indeed."

"Apparently, she'd set her sights on Lord Murdock before the Season began, and she refused to be thwarted," Frances added. "She was convinced that Lord Murdock was about to ask Annabelle to marry him."

David shook his head and chuckled. "And here I thought Lady Elspeth was after *me*."

"She was spending time with you, Elmwood, to make Annabelle jealous so she'd leave off with Murdock," Frances explained.

"What? That's madness," Annabelle said, shaking her head. "Elspeth is a scheming liar. She told me at the Talbots' ball that she meant to have David because she was the most sought-after *debutante* and he was the most sought-after bachelor. She was lying the entire time."

"If she *was* after Lord Murdock all along, she can have him. If you ask me, those two deserve each other," Marianne said, shaking her head.

"I couldn't agree with you more," Julianna replied, nodding.

"Yes, well. I suppose I *could* have been a marchioness, but I heard Lord Murdock is a dog kicker," Annabelle said with a sigh, winking at David.

David squeezed her hand and gave her a kiss on the cheek. "You'll just have to make do with a husband who is a lowly earl, and become a lowly countess."

"I take offense to that," Lord Kendall said, his grin belying his words.

"As do I," Frances said, also smiling.

"Well, we cannot all be dukes and duchesses like Worthington and Julianna here," Bell replied with a grin.

"Or marquesses and marchionesses," Marianne added with a laugh, before her face turned serious. "Oh, Annabelle. I just realized. When you marry David, you will be my sister twice over. I cannot wait."

She leaned down and hugged Annabelle, who returned both her hug and her smile.

"I, for one, couldn't be happier," Lady Angelina declared. "You were about to turn the last of my hairs gray, Annabelle. Especially when we weren't entirely certain our match-making efforts were working."

Annabelle narrowed her eyes on her mother. "Match-making efforts?"

"Yes," Lady Angelina replied. "The lot of us. We were all in on it, attempting to get you and Lord Elmwood together from the start. Why else do you think we suggested he take lessons from you?"

"Mama!" Annabelle's mouth fell open and she braced both fists on her hips.

"And you've no idea how difficult it was coming up with excuses day after day to leave you two alone together," Lady Angelina continued, waggling her eyebrows.

"Mama!" Annabelle repeated. "I cannot believe you."

"Believe it," Beau declared. "It was all of us. The earl lessons bit was Marianne's idea."

Marianne had a sly smile on her face. "Ingenious, if you ask me."

"What?" David blinked incredulously at his sister. "I thought you were trying to pair me with Lady Elspeth this whole time."

"Oh, David, that's far too obvious. I was only trying to make you *think* I was trying to pair you with Elspeth so you wouldn't know I was actually trying to pair you with Annabelle."

"That's what I get for spending time with spies, I suppose," David replied, shaking his head at his sister, but his smile belied the content of his words.

"Oh, and the disgust I had to swallow to allow that hideous Lord Murdock near you, Annabelle. It certainly seemed to make David jealous, but it wasn't my first choice," Lady Angelina added.

"Yes, well, what none of you know is that Lord Murdock had blackmailed me." Annabelle announced.

"What?" half of the room asked in unison.

Annabelle nodded, but directed her words to David, who looked as though he might sprint from the room immediately to find Murdock and beat him soundly. "At the Talbots' ball, he found me on the balcony and threatened to tell everyone in the ballroom he'd seen me kissing you if I didn't dance with him again and allow him to court me."

"That piece of rubbish!" Julianna declared, scowling.

"I had a much worse word for him," Annabelle replied, with a smile, "but I'll keep that to myself."

"I'll kill him," David intoned, a pulse ticking in his jaw.

"No, darling," Annabelle said, rubbing David's shoulder. "Let him go. He has a much worse fate ahead of him, marrying Lady Elspeth. And apparently, he's about to lose a fortune on his bet."

David relaxed and cracked a grin. "I suppose he does deserve to listen to her prattling the rest of his days. And he deserves to lose a fortune, too." David turned to the room at large. "Now, if you're all quite through with your confessions, I'd like to say that regardless of your reasons or your methods, I'm quite happy with the outcome, so I forgive you. And, now, if you'll excuse us, I'd like to have a few more moments alone with my future wife."

The occupants of the room scrambled to leave, and within moments, David and Annabelle were alone together in the library once more.

"That was quite impressive," Annabelle said, wrapping her arms around David's neck. "You sent them all packing with only a few words."

"Yes. Well, that was the tone of voice I used in the army. My commands were never disobeyed."

Annabelle snuggled closer to him. "Oh, really. You'll have to demonstrate…in bed tonight."

"Tonight?" David's brows shot up. "But we're not getting married until tomorrow morning."

"I won't tell if you won't," Annabelle replied, nipping his ear.

"I like that way you think, Future Lady Elmwood."

"And," she replied with a sigh, "we may be done with your lessons, but we're just starting with mine."

David pulled her onto his lap and kissed her soundly. "I have *so* many things to teach you."

FIND out what happens when Annabelle and David escape to Brighton for their honeymoon—and the new Countess of Elmwood asks her former army captain to give her a few very improper orders. CLICK HERE to read the steamy bonus epilogue and join my newsletter or type https://dl.bookfunnel.com/bpibntk9p9 into your browser.

Thank you for reading *Earl Lessons*. The next book in the Lords in Disguise series is *The Duke is Back*. Find out what happens when Phillip Grayson returns to Society to claim both his title and the woman he loved. CLICK HERE TO READ *The Duke is Back* now.

ALSO BY VALERIE BOWMAN

The Wallflowers' Revolt

The Wallflower's Great Escape (Book 1)

The Wallflower's Secret War (Book 2)

The Wallflower Takes All (Book 3)

Love's a Game

The Duchess Hunt (Book 1)

The Duke Dare (Book 2)

The Marquess Match (Book 3)

The Whitmorelands

The Duke Deal (Book 1)

The Marquess Move (Book 2)

The Debutante Dilemma (Book 3)

The Wallflower Win (Book 4)

Lords in Disguise

The Footman is an Earl (Book 1)

Duke Looks Like a Groomsman (Book 2)

The Marquess Who Loved Me (Book 3)

Save a Horse, Ride a Viscount (Book 4)

Earl Lessons (Book 5)

The Duke is Back (Book 6)

Playful Brides

The Unexpected Duchess (Book 1)

The Accidental Countess (Book 2)

The Unlikely Lady (Book 3)

The Irresistible Rogue (Book 4)

The Unforgettable Hero (Book 4.5)

The Untamed Earl (Book 5)

The Legendary Lord (Book 6)

Never Trust a Pirate (Book 7)

The Right Kind of Rogue (Book 8)

A Duke Like No Other (Book 9)

Kiss Me At Christmas (Book 10)

Mr. Hunt, I Presume (Book 10.5)

No Other Duke But You (Book 11)

Secret Brides

Secrets of a Wedding Night (Book 1)

A Secret Proposal (Book 1.5)

Secrets of a Runaway Bride (Book 2)

A Secret Affair (Book 2.5)

Secrets of a Scandalous Marriage (Book 3)

It Happened Under the Mistletoe (Book 3.5)

Thank you for reading *Earl Lessons.* David and Annabelle and their smoking antics were really fun to write about.

I'd love to keep in touch.

- Visit my website for information about upcoming books, excerpts, and to sign up for my email newsletter: www.ValerieBowmanBooks.com or at www.ValerieBowmanBooks.com/subscribe.
- Join me on Facebook: http://Facebook.com/ValerieBowmanAuthor.
- Join me on Instagram: http://www.instagram.com/valeriegbowman/
- Reviews help other readers find books. I appreciate all reviews. Thank you so much for considering it!

Want to read the other Lords in Disguise books?

- The Footman is an Earl
- Duke Looks Like a Groomsman
- The Marquess Who Loved Me
- Save a Horse, Ride a Viscount
- The Duke is Back

ABOUT THE AUTHOR

Valerie Bowman grew up in Illinois with six sisters (she's number seven) and a huge supply of romance novels.

After a cold and snowy stint earning a degree in English with a minor in history at Smith College, she moved to Florida the first chance she got.

Valerie now lives in Jacksonville with her family including her two rascally dogs. When she's not writing, she keeps busy reading, traveling, or vacillating between watching crazy reality TV and PBS.

Valerie loves to hear from readers. Find her on the web at www.ValerieBowmanBooks.com.

facebook.com/ValerieBowmanAuthor

instagram.com/valeriegbowman

goodreads.com/Valerie_Bowman

bookbub.com/authors/valerie-bowman

amazon.com/author/valeriebowman